FAKES AND LIES

FAKES AND LIES

A Naomi Blake Novel

Jane A. Adams

Severn House Large Print
London & New York

This first large print edition published 2019
in Great Britain and the USA by
SEVERN HOUSE PUBLISHERS LTD of
Eardley House, 4 Uxbridge Street, London W8 7SY.
First world regular print edition published 2018 by
Severn House Publishers Ltd.

British Library Cataloguing in Publication Data
A CIP catalogue record for this title is available from the British Library.

ISBN-13: 9780727829436

Severn House Publishers support the Forest Stewardship Council™
[FSC™], the leading international forest certification organisation. All
our titles that are printed on FSC certified paper carry the FSC logo.

MIX
Paper from
responsible sources
FSC
www.fsc.org   FSC® C013056

Typeset by Palimpsest Book Production Ltd.,
Falkirk, Stirlingshire, Scotland.
Printed and bound in Great Britain by
T J International, Padstow, Cornwall.

Prologue

The gallery was halfway up the hill on the High Pavement heading out of the city of Mallingham. It was double fronted, with two deep bay windows that curved either side of the Victorian tiled entrance way. The entrance itself was recessed, the heavy wooden door only partly glazed. It was not on the main thoroughfares and it was a good ten minute walk from the city centre; the inference was that if you went there, it was with the intent to buy and with full knowledge of what the place might have in stock. It was not a location frequented by the dilettante or the time waster and it had in part built its reputation on discovering new talent, building and encouraging that talent and then profiting from the increased prices when those artists became well known. Its client base, both the sellers and the buyers, were known to be loyal.

Today Antonia Scott was expecting a visitor, a new artist her brother had dealt with and who was due to bring work for Antonia to see, hoping for her final approval. Matthew Scott might be the more astute business partner but Antonia was very much their father's daughter in terms of her artistic knowledge and ability to predict which of their potential clients might bring the most money into the business in future. Scotts had survived for almost seventy years, grandfather,

1

father and now twin siblings curating and agenting and dealing, and on that Wednesday morning the future looked very healthy.

Antonia, arriving to open the gallery a half hour before her scheduled meeting, was not surprised to see the young woman standing outside holding a portfolio. She had a carrier for canvases at her feet and looked nervous and harassed, the wind blowing her blond hair across her face. The artist she was expecting was not actually due yet but in Antonia's experience new artists were always early.

'Good morning,' Antonia said. 'You must be Jenny. Come along inside out of the wind. I think we might get some snow. Spring is taking its time this year.'

She bent and unlocked the metal grille and pushed it up over her head, then trotted forward between the deep bay windows to the big black door and unlocked that. The young woman hoisted her portfolio and carrier and followed her.

'Matthew's told me so much about you. He is very excited and I'm sure I will be too. You understand that the final decision always rests with me? But I don't anticipate any problems. From what I've seen of your work so far I'm very impressed, so I'm sure this will just be a formality.'

She swung the door wide and invited the younger woman to step through first. The shop alarm had begun to beep a warning and Antonia turned her attention to that. 'The light switch is on your side, that's it on the wall just beside the door.' The light

2

came on and Antonia began to input the code to shut off the alarm. 'Now,' she said, 'I'm sure we'd both like a nice cup of tea.'

Fifteen minutes later, when Jennifer Colombi *actually* arrived, she found the door open. She stepped inside and called out, 'Miss Scott, I'm sorry I'm a little early, but I just . . .'

The words died. Antonia Scott lay on the floor just a few feet inside the shop. Blood had flowed out from beneath her and when Jennifer knelt and touched her hand she was sure that the fingers flexed and that Antonia was still alive. Several things went through Jennifer's mind at that point. That she needed to get help, that the person who attacked Antonia Scott might still be there, and finally that she was utterly terrified.

To her credit, Jennifer managed to make the phone call to the ambulance and the police before finally breaking down, and when the paramedics arrived they found her crying and trembling on the pavement and very much in need of treatment for shock. Since Antonia Scott was by then very, very dead they were able to give Jennifer their full attention, so that by the time the police arrived the young artist was least coherent. Not that she could tell them very much.

She had arrived for an appointment about fifteen minutes early and had found the woman she was supposed to meet lying on the floor. No, she had gone no further into the shop and yes, she had touched Antonia on the hand and called her name. At that point, Jennifer confirmed, she was sure that the woman had

3

still been alive. She was sure that her fingers had twitched and she had been equally sure that there was nothing she could do and that more experienced and expert help was required.

'So I ran outside and called the police and the ambulance,' she told the officer. 'I kept watching the shop just in case anyone else came out. I was terrified in case the killer was still in there.'

'And you heard no one else inside the shop?'

Jennifer shook her head and then said, 'But I wasn't really listening. I wasn't really taking anything in apart from the body lying on the floor. There was so much blood. I wanted to know if she was still alive, if I could help. I thought . . . I thought she might still be alive but I didn't know what to do.'

'You did the right thing,' the officer told her. 'You got yourself out and you called us and called the ambulance.'

The DI left her sitting in the back of the ambulance. The paramedics wanted to take Jennifer to hospital to get checked over, but already the colour had returned to her cheeks and she was pretty sure that the girl would be OK when she got over the shock. She wondered if Jennifer would remember anything else. One of the paramedics followed the DI and asked if they could take the girl away. Inspector Morgan glanced back once at the young woman and then nodded her head. 'You may as well. I'll get someone to come and chat to her later but I doubt she can tell us much.'

DI Karen Morgan went back to stand in the shop doorway, watching the CSIs as they went

4

about the task of examining the body and the scene. The crime scene manager glanced up.

'What can you tell me?' Karen said.

'That she was facing her killer, that there seem to be no defensive wounds and that the death blow was a single stab wound, up through the diaphragm and into the rib cage, probably nicked the liver too. There'll be more blood inside the body cavity than there is on the floor. Whoever did it knew what they were about.'

'Any signs of theft?'

'Nothing obvious, and a shop like this is sure to have a detailed inventory. You know about Scotts, do you?'

'Know about it in what way?' Karen asked.

'Oh, nothing criminal. But their reputation for finding new artists, for predicting the next big thing.' The crime scene manager shrugged. 'My youngest is at art college; her ambition is to be hung here, in this gallery. Sees it as the first step towards London and places . . . well, wherever artists want to be these days. It's family run – Antonia Scott and her brother. I think the grandfather is still around but I'm pretty sure the father died a few years ago.'

Karen nodded. It was good to have some local knowledge. 'The brother's on his way, I believe.' She wandered back out again. There was very little she could do until the CSIs had finished. The ambulance had already gone. A small knot of onlookers had gathered across the street and Karen recognized a couple of local journalists chatting to one of the constables. She smiled grimly, knowing they'd get nothing out of PC

5

Elwood; he was rumoured to be so tight-lipped he didn't even talk to his own wife.

It must be theft, Karen Morgan thought. Why else would you attack a gallery owner? Though if the crime scene manager was right, the accuracy of the stab wound was something to be considered. Most opportunist thieves (and for that matter those who were stealing to order) would be more likely to bash someone over the head, take what they wanted and run away rather than face a murder charge if they were caught. It seemed excessive and also, if the woman was facing her assailant, then it was someone she did not feel threatened by. Or didn't have the time to feel threatened by. It could have happened very fast. Either way, a stab wound like that meant getting in close and personal.

A month later, and Karen Morgan was still puzzling over the killing of Antonia Scott. By early March the case had definitely gone cold; not that it had ever warmed up. Karen Morgan glared at the folder on her desk and then moved on to more pressing things. The inventory of the shop had indeed been detailed, and according to Antonia's brother only one thing seemed to be missing, a small portfolio containing a series of drawings and oil sketches from the estate of a man called Frederick Albert Jones, who had died a couple of weeks before Antonia Scott had been murdered. Freddie Jones was an artist they had represented; he was also a known forger.

One

Patrick was alone in the studio when the doorbell rang. The owners of the house, Bob Taylor, in whose studio he was working, and Bob's wife, Annie Raven, were both out. Patrick was used to fielding phone calls and dealing with emails but it was quite unusual for anyone to come ringing the doorbell. Even more unusually, he hadn't heard a car pull up and Bob Taylor's house was almost a mile down a long track. It was not somewhere you got to by accident.

Patrick went back through the house and opened the front door. A young girl stood there, looking very nervous. He judged her to be about nineteen, somewhere around his own age. She looked upset.

'Are you lost?' Patrick asked. Then, realizing that perhaps this was not the most useful question, he began again. 'Hello, who're you looking for?'

'Um, this is Bob Taylor's house? I wanted to see Bob.'

Patrick frowned. This was unexpected and he wasn't good at dealing with the unexpected. 'Does he know you're coming?'

'No, no he doesn't. Is he here?'

Patrick fervently wished he was. He shook his head. 'Don't know when he'll be back; maybe you could wait in your car.' He looked around

7

wondering where the car was. She must have come in a vehicle.

She shook her head impatiently. 'I left it back down the main road, didn't realize it was this far up. It's only a little car, not very good with the mud and the ruts. Can I come in?'

'I don't even know who you are. I can't just let you in.'

'I don't even know who *you* are,' she retaliated. She held out her hand. 'I'm Beatrix Jones,' she said. 'Though people usually call me Bee, or Trixie, or just about anything apart from Beatrix.'

Patrick laughed. 'We've got the same last name,' he said. 'I'm Patrick Jones.'

She nodded. 'I thought you might be. Bob said he'd got a new studio assistant. You might have heard of my dad. His name was Frederick, Freddie. He was an artist. Bob was a friend of his. He died a little while ago and that's why I want to talk to Bob.'

Patrick looked at her properly for the first time. 'I didn't know Freddie Jones had a daughter,' he said. He studied her carefully. She was actually very pretty, he thought. Mixed heritage, he guessed, with caramel skin and slightly crinkly hair that was a rich golden brown. She had startlingly green eyes and he realized also that she looked cold, shivering in just a thin corduroy jacket with her hands thrust into the pockets.

'You better come in,' Patrick decided. 'You look frozen and I know Annie wouldn't want me to leave you on the doorstep in the cold.' He realized he was making a big hash of this but

8

meeting strangers wasn't really his thing and he often *did* make a big hash of it.

He stood aside and then led her through to the kitchen. He'd just finished making coffee when Annie arrived back, much to Patrick's relief, and to his even greater relief Annie seemed to know the girl slightly.

Annie fussed over Bee for a while and reassured Patrick that he'd been right to make their guest feel welcome.

'I'd best get on,' Patrick said. 'Bob left me jobs to do I've not finished yet.'

Annie waved him back into his seat. 'Those can wait,' she said gently but firmly. Patrick sat down again, feeling a little puzzled. Bee smiled at him; she still looked cold despite Annie having wrapped a blanket around her shoulders. She was holding a mug of warm coffee between her hands and Patrick suddenly realized that this was more than just chill, that Annie had already recognized something frozen within the girl. Something that needed defrosting – urgently.

'I'm not sure what time Bob will be back,' Annie told her, 'but if we can be any help . . .?'

Patrick blinked and looked doubtfully at Annie, wondering what on earth *he* was supposed to do, then he nodded. Annie and Bob had helped *him* when he'd really needed it so he would definitely do what he could for this girl because that was just the way it was in Bob and Annie's house.

'Your dad painted the Madonna that Bob's got here, didn't he? It's absolutely gorgeous.' The painting in question had been attributed to a sixteenth-century master but Bob Taylor was pretty sure that it was the work of Freddie Jones. He'd been asked to look into the attribution about a month before, just a few days after Freddie had died.

She nodded. 'Yeah, that was probably one of Dad's. I'm never quite sure. I'd go into the studio and there'd be all these things and some of them would be his and some would be genuine and . . . sometimes he could remember what was what. Sometimes he'd be asked about stuff that he might have done twenty years ago and it would be all, "Well, yeah, I might have done it, but I don't remember any more", and he probably didn't. He was getting a bit, like, absent, if you know what I mean.'

'Bob was really sorry to hear about his death,' Annie said. 'I know he regarded Freddie as a good friend. I believe he was Bob's mentor a long time ago.'

Patrick looked at her in surprise. Bob was certainly *his* mentor now but he found it odd to think that Bob had needed support himself when he first started out.

'I didn't even know that Freddie was my dad, not until about five years ago. I pestered Mum for ages to tell me and she finally did. It came out in an argument. I think she was just so angry with me for going on about it all the time. But she settled down and she even phoned him for me, said I wanted to see him. No strings – they decided that years ago. He put money in a bank account for me, but my mum didn't like to use that. She said it should stay there until I decided what I wanted to do about university. Thankfully, she didn't really need his money so . . . We were really lucky like that.'

'And so you went to meet him. That must have been interesting?' Annie smiled gently. 'He was quite a character.'

'I thought he was nuts,' Bee said frankly. 'I couldn't believe my mum had ever been in love with him. I mean, he was so old.' She smiled. 'He seemed really old anyway, until I got to know him. Then I realized he was just a two-year-old pretending to be an adult.'

Annie nodded. 'From what little I knew of him,' she said, 'that sounds about right. He was never very good at the responsibility thing.'

'No, my mum always said it was fun while it lasted but there was never any future in it. When she fell pregnant it was a shock to both of them, but she wanted to keep me. Freddie apparently said that he'd make a terrible father but promised to help out financially as much as he could, and that's what they agreed. Then Mum died a year ago, and Freddie was all I had. I even took his last name, did the deed poll and everything. Mum's idea.' She shrugged almost apologetically. 'She thought it would be better if I looked like I belonged somewhere, said it would make life less complicated, but I think she just wanted to let me know it was all right to be with my dad. That we had her blessing, you know? And then *he* went.'

Annie reached out across the table and took Bee's hand. 'I'm so sorry,' she said. 'I was in my early teens when I lost both of my parents. I remember how it felt.'

They were all silent for a moment and then Annie asked, 'So what brings you here to Bob? What can we do for you?'

Bee took a deep breath and looked from Annie to Patrick as if what she was going to say next would be very difficult and she wasn't sure what she hoped their reaction would be. 'You're both going to think I'm crazy, or upset, or in shock because I've lost both my mum and my dad within a year, but really I'm not. You see I think my dad was murdered.'

Patrick knew he looked shocked but Annie's only reaction was a slight critical raise of one eyebrow.

'What makes you think that?' he asked. 'I thought your dad had a heart attack. Bob said he drank and smoked even though the doctors had told him not to.'

'And that's all true,' Bee agreed, 'but, you see, he told me . . . he told me his life was in danger. He told me there were people out to get him. The next thing I know he's dead. The police don't believe me of course, nobody does. In fact *I'd* stopped believing me too. I thought what they told me was true, that I was just upset and imagining things, and friends of Freddie's – of Dad's – always told me that he was a bit, well, imaginative. You know, like making things up.'

'But something's happened to make you think there's more to it?' Annie asked.

The girl nodded slowly. From out of the pocket of her jacket she took a folded piece of newspaper and smoothed it out on the table top. 'It was this,' she said. 'This happened.'

12

Annie turned the paper around so that she and Patrick could both see. 'It's about Antonia Scott's murder,' she said. 'That was a terrible tragedy, an awful thing to happen. Antonia was such a lovely woman. I heard the police thought it was a theft gone wrong.'

'Something was stolen,' Bee said. 'But I bet you don't know what it was.'

'No, I have no idea. The murder was on the news, of course, and Bob phoned Antonia's brother to give his condolences and see if there was anything we could do to help, but that's all we know. So what was taken?'

'It was a portfolio,' Bee told her. 'Dad dropped it off at the gallery a few days before he died. It was a portfolio of Freddie's work.'

Two

Bob Taylor arrived about half an hour after his wife. He recognized Bee immediately and expressed condolence for her father's death. 'He was a good friend,' Bob said. 'I'd known him for years, of course. I knew your mother too.'

Bob helped himself to coffee and then came and sat at the table. Bee repeated the story that she'd already told Annie and Patrick. Patrick could see Bob considering carefully and wondering how to respond to her. Eventually he said, 'I agree it is something of a coincidence, Antonia's murder and the theft of the portfolio, though from

13

what I've heard the police are still treating it as a robbery. Other things might have been taken, you know.'

'Coincidences do happen,' Annie said gently. 'Just because something bad happens to two people in the same time period doesn't necessarily mean those two events are connected.'

Patrick blinked. It felt as though Annie was being unusually restrained and unsympathetic, after her first efforts to comfort this near stranger who had come so unexpectedly to her door. Tears began to well in the girl's eyes and Patrick looked to Annie to see what she would do but Annie was leaning back in her chair, as though keeping her distance. She sipped her coffee, her expression neutral. Annie caught Patrick's look and shook her head gently, and Patrick bit back his first instinct, which was to object to her caution and seeming indifference. It seemed obvious to him that Freddie's death and Antonia Scott's must be linked, but he trusted Annie and her judgement so he kept quiet.

'I take it you've spoken to the police?' Bob asked.

'I've tried. They think I'm crazy, or grieving, or just in the way. They say my father had been ill and died of a heart attack, and that's that. They say, like you just did, that it's just coincidence that some of his work was stolen. Antonia's brother told them that the portfolio had been left quite close to the door because Antonia was going to go through it that morning. He'd left it next to one of the print racks so she'd know where it was, so the police just say it was

14

probably the first thing the thief saw. That the thief took a chance and grabbed it. But there were paintings hanging on the wall, just inside the door. What thief would go for a portfolio when they could see proper paintings?'

She had a point, Patrick thought.

'And was anything else missing?' Bob asked.

She shook her head angrily. 'No,' she said vehemently. Then shrugged her shoulders. 'I don't think so anyway; no one will tell me. I only know about the portfolio because Matthew Scott telephoned me to tell me it was missing. Technically, you see, it was mine. My father left everything to me. The portfolio had been dropped off so that Matthew Scott could value it. The Scotts specialized in selling my dad's drawings, I don't know if you know that?'

Bob nodded. 'He was a tremendous draughtsman.' He smiled. 'The Scotts liked his drawings because Freddie could knock one up in the morning for them, if he felt inclined to do so. For Freddie that was effortless. His paintings took a lot longer and you could never be sure—'

'He'd given all that up,' she said quickly. 'He promised me. He'd make copies but he always signed his name to them these days.' She looked anxiously from Bob to Annie and then to Patrick and this time the tears spilled over on to her cheeks.

'Freddie was a lovely man,' Bob said quietly, 'but you have to understand something. For him it was an addiction. It wasn't to do with the money he might make or getting one over on the art world, it was more like . . . more like the need to climb

15

the next mountain just because it was there. When Freddie discovered another artist he liked and thought he could, shall we say, emulate, it was as if someone had breathed fresh life into him. I've no doubt he told you that he was on the straight and narrow and I've no doubt he almost believed it. Freddie didn't lie – he was just economical with the truth, even to himself.'

'He was my dad, you didn't know him like I did.'

'Forgive me, but I had known him for a lot longer. Freddie was my mentor when I was a young artist starting out. He taught me so much and I will always be grateful to him. Freddie was also unreliable; your mother knew that, which was why she withdrew from him when she was pregnant with you. Believe me, I stayed friends with both of them all through that and neither had a bad word to say for the other, but your mother was wise enough to know that if she was going to give you any kind of stability it would have to be on her own, and on her own terms.'

'My father loved me. I know I didn't know who he was when I was growing up, but he always provided, and when we finally met . . .'

'He was so happy,' Bob told her. 'So happy that you wanted to get to know him and that you actually *liked* him when you did. Freddie was never sure you would. He thought you might bear a grudge. Bee, I'm not saying anything against your father. He was what he was and we all loved him because he was a very easy man to love. But the other thing you need to know is that

16

Freddie told people what he thought they wanted to hear because he knew that's what would make them happy.'

'You're saying he lied to me.'

'No, I'm not saying that. But I have a painting in my studio that Freddie probably created about ten years ago and evidence that he was making another version, and probably intending to apply the same provenance to it.'

'I told you he was still copying things.'

'Not this one. Someone – probably Freddie – had gone to a great deal of trouble to give this one a provenance and a history, and it was sold for a great deal of money on the basis that it was done by an artist who was not Frederick Albert Jones. I'm sorry, Bee, but there are signs that he was still up to his old tricks, whatever he might have said to you to the contrary.'

'And if he was, what difference does that make to what I'm telling you? Someone killed him. He was scared, he told me that. And Antonia Scott was murdered and his portfolio was stolen. Why doesn't anybody believe me?'

She again looked from one to the other and there was a beat or two of silence. Then Patrick said, 'If Freddie Jones was producing forgeries, and someone found out, doesn't that make it more likely someone might have killed him? It's happened before, hasn't it?' He was thinking particularly of the death of Eric Hebborn, widely believed to have been suspicious. His classic, *The Art Forger's Handbook*, was in Bob's library.

'It has,' Annie conceded.

'But is there any evidence of anything untoward

17

happening to Freddie, apart from his being a little more paranoid than usual?' Bob asked.

Bee glared at him. 'I thought you were his friend.'

'I was; that's what allows me to say these things. Entitles me. You can still be friends with someone, still care about them, even if you open your eyes and see exactly what they are and what they're capable of. Friendships happen *despite* all of that, not because the other person is perfect.'

It was unusual, Patrick thought, for Bob to be this harsh with anyone and he wondered at it, alongside Annie's reticence.

'I'd better go,' Bee said. 'It's obvious no one here is going to listen to me.'

'No one here can really help you,' Bob pointed out. 'We can't force the police to make these connections. We don't know what they're thinking or what they know and they aren't going to tell you.'

'Maybe Naomi could help, or Alec.' The words were out almost before Patrick realized he was saying them.

Annie frowned slightly. 'I don't see how,' she said. 'Neither of them are in the force any more. Though I suppose talking to Naomi might help Bee get a handle on how the investigation would proceed in a case like this.' She turned to the girl. 'She might be able to help you put your questions in a way that the police would take notice of.' She looked questioningly at both Patrick and her husband, and Bob shrugged.

'Who's Naomi?' Bee asked.

'She's a friend. She used to be a detective inspector,' Annie told her.

'I want to see her.'

'We will *ask* her if she's willing to talk to you,' Annie said gently. 'But you have to understand, she has no influence; all she can do is perhaps put your mind at rest about how the investigation will proceed. You do understand that?'

Bee nodded but Patrick could see that Annie's words were just feeding her anger.

'I'd better go,' she said again, and this time she stood up and shrugged off the blanket that Annie had wrapped around her.

Patrick opened his mouth to offer to drive her back to her car but a look from Annie silenced him. He frowned; there were undercurrents here that he didn't understand. Again, he told himself that he trusted Annie and that she must have her reasons.

Bob walked Bee to the door and Patrick watched as, hunch-shouldered, she started back down the long path to the main road. Bob returned to the kitchen.

'So,' Patrick said. 'What's going on, then?'

'What do you mean?'

Patrick sighed. 'Look,' he said. 'I've been around both of you for a while now and the way you acted today tells me something is going on that she doesn't know about. I mean, I know it's none of my business but . . .'

'You expected more sympathy from us,' Annie said.

'Something like that, yeah.'

'Patrick, it would not surprise either of us if Bee was right,' Annie said. 'Freddie played some dangerous games with some very dodgy

19

people and we are, quietly, looking into that possibility and have been ever since we heard the news of Antonia Scott's death. It is, as Bee says, just too much of a coincidence, so we are having someone look into it.'

Patrick nodded. Annie had some unusual connections, two of whom he had come to know. Nathan Crow and Gregory Mann, people he now considered to be good friends, were not the kind of individuals most people would encounter happily. Sometimes life took you in strange directions.

'Nathan and Gregory?' he asked.

She shook her head. 'No, this isn't their field.'

Bob laughed. 'We don't actually want to get anyone killed,' he added. 'And that includes Bee. If she's right, and if her father was frightened, maybe he'd crossed the wrong people yet again. And believe me, Patrick, Freddie sailed close to the wind on a number of occasions. They are not the kind of people that you want a nineteen-year-old girl chasing down. Not the kind of people that you want to be anywhere near. You understand that?'

'You want to protect her; you think that talking to Naomi might satisfy her and stop her prodding and poking where she shouldn't be.'

'I wouldn't have suggested it,' Annie said. 'But since you did, it felt like a possible solution.'

Patrick shook his head. 'It won't work,' he said. 'What you think doesn't matter. The only people whose opinion mattered to her are both dead. Her mum and Freddie. The way she looks at it, she's got nothing to lose.'

20

'Only her life,' Bob pointed out.

'I don't think she'll even think about that – not because she's brave or anything, but because she won't think it's real. Until you've been there you don't think it's real, that asking the wrong questions might get you killed. She's just angry, and when you're angry you don't really see reason, do you?'

Bob and Annie exchanged a glance.

'You're not often wrong,' Annie said. 'Patrick, I hope you are this time.'

'I'd better get back to work,' Patrick said.

He set his coffee mug down in the sink and went back to the studio.

Three

Naomi Blake, now Naomi Friedman, lived with her husband, Alec, in the flat that she had first moved into when she had come out of hospital following her accident.

Both had been serving officers when a motorway pile-up had ended Naomi's career, though at that time they had not been married or even together.

Naomi had been blind ever since.

This little flat had become her sanctuary and though she had spent time living elsewhere, when it had come up for sale again at an opportune moment she and Alec had bought it and moved back. It was small, easy to manage and peaceful and though Naomi would have

21

liked a garden she was otherwise satisfied with the arrangement.

Alec was away. He had left the police force under slightly difficult circumstances some eighteen months before and, after mooching around unsure of what to do for a while, had accepted an offer to work for a private security firm and was now frequently absent two or three days a week. Naomi missed him, but Alec was evidently enjoying himself and – though she didn't like to admit it – she was also enjoying her alone time. She loved her husband deeply but the last couple of years had been difficult and intense and she now felt the need for some quiet and reflection.

And besides, she was never alone. Her big black guide dog, Napoleon, kept her company.

When Patrick arrived at her flat that evening, she was playing around with some new computer software that he had installed for her a few days before. Since losing her sight, Naomi had become a real fan of technology; it enabled her to use voice input to access the internet, to have documents read out to her from websites and also to access books that were not available as audio.

Patrick rang the bell and announced himself so that she would know who was coming up the stairs, and then let himself in. His father, Harry, had been an emergency key holder for quite some time but it was usually Patrick who actually had the key. He had known Naomi since he was fourteen years old and he counted her as one of his best friends, despite the age difference.

'So,' she said, glancing across from where she

sat at her computer screen – her sighted habits still prevailing when it came to body language. 'What can I do for you this fine evening?'

'Fine! Have you heard the rain?'

Naomi laughed as another gust of wind blasted a mix of hail and snow against the window. 'Winter hasn't let up yet, has it? You want to get the kettle on while I just finish here. I'm doing the grocery shopping and I'm worried it might time out on me.'

Patrick took himself through to the kitchen, followed by Napoleon. He bent to pat the big dog, ruffling his ears. Napoleon's tail beat against the cupboard doors. It was a small kitchen and crowded with both of them in it. Patrick filled the kettle and then stood waiting for it to boil, listening as Naomi completed her order. He guessed from the amount of meat she was ordering that Alec was due home. Naomi would happily have become a vegetarian, but Alec was a committed carnivore.

He made tea and set Naomi's down on the small round coaster on the windowsill. It was stuck in place with double sided tape, so she always knew the position of it.

'Is Alec home at the weekend, then?'

'Yes, home Friday night, back on Monday morning. Hopefully he'll be coming back Thursday next week.'

'He's away more than he thought he would be,' Patrick commented.

'He is, yes. But at least he's not moping any more and he feels as though he's being useful. Money isn't bad either, which is a help; the

23

savings have taken a right hammering over the last year. And we still can't sell the damned house.'

Patrick knew she was referring to Alec's old home, a lovely 1930s house set in a big garden. People were being put off by the fact that there had been a dead man found there.

'It's not like we've left the body amongst the fixtures and fittings.' She shrugged. 'I mustn't grumble though, we're doing OK. We've still got some of the legacy from Alec's uncle.'

Patrick studied her thoughtfully. It was unlike Naomi to worry about money and he knew that they were financially stable, so this was something else. 'It's not that, though, is it?' he said. 'Alec's been dependent on you for a long time now. You've been so focused on him and what he needs, and now he's getting all independent you're bored stupid.'

She laughed. 'You're probably right. Actually we're incredibly lucky to be as secure as we are. Anyway, what brings you here tonight? It's not one of your usual evenings. And how are Bob and Annie?'

'Good,' Patrick told her. 'When I was there today, this girl turned up and I kind of thought you might want to talk to her. Or rather, would you talk to her?' He paused. 'I didn't begin that very well, did I?'

'No, not really. Want to start again?'

Patrick nodded. 'Yes, I think I'd better. Her name is Beatrix, Beatrix Jones, but nobody calls her that. And she is the daughter of the late Freddie Jones, art forger extraordinaire.'

Naomi listened as Patrick filled her in on the day's events. She'd heard about Freddie Jones, of course, but not about the murder at the gallery. When he had finished she nodded slowly and said, 'I'm with Bob and Annie on this, too much of a coincidence, and it also sounds very dangerous. She is best kept out of it, but—'

'But no way is she going to stay out of it,' Patrick agreed. 'I mean, would you? Would I?'

'Unfair comparison,' Naomi told him. 'I think most people *would* stay out of it. Most people would just leave it to the police – and in this case very sensibly too – but I take your point. She does sound desperate, and she is all alone, and I'm not really sure what I can tell her that might help.'

'Probably not a lot,' said Patrick, 'but at least she'll feel as though someone's taking notice of her and sometimes that's really all that matters.'

'True. OK, I'll see her after the weekend. I want some time with Alec but I'll be happy to have a chat to her on, say, Tuesday? I'd rather she didn't come here. I could do without someone knocking on my door every five minutes and I have a feeling she might.'

'I'll ask Bob if we can meet there. I think they'd like to be in the loop anyway.'

'Sounds like a good idea,' Naomi agreed. 'And in the meantime, I'll see what I can find out. You never know, I might know the SIO.'

'Bob and Annie say they're trying to find stuff out too; they still have contacts here and there.'

'So we can compare notes. We could really do with talking to someone in organized crime. A

25

specialist in art and antiques. I'll see who I can dig up.' She sounded pleased to have been presented with a project.

'Thanks,' Patrick said. 'I'd best be off, Dad will be getting dinner and I've got an assignment to finish for tomorrow.'

He gave Naomi a hug and Napoleon another pat and then he left. Naomi imagined him running across the road to get into his car, the rain still pelting down. 'Drive safe,' she said. Then she turned back to her computer and began a search for Freddie Jones and his misadventures. Patrick was right, she thought, she was desperately bored. Having time to herself was rapidly losing its novelty. But having time to herself with something interesting to do, now that she could go along with.

Four

Bee had felt utterly bereft when she left Bob Taylor's house. She wasn't sure what she'd ever expected them to do, but she'd hoped they would do something or at least believe her. She got the feeling that Annie had but that Bob maybe thought she was making a fuss over nothing, and she also had the feeling that Patrick was more sympathetic. Patrick had taken her phone number and promised to ask his friend, the ex-detective woman, if she'd talk to her, but Bee was not optimistic. Bob Taylor had been her last hope and now she felt utterly alone.

She came to a junction and instead of turning towards home she went right, driving back towards her father's studio. She still had the keys and the landlord had told her that the rent had been paid for another three months. Freddie always paid six months in advance. The landlord had said that she needed to clear her father's things out within that time, but for the moment she could come and go as she liked. She had spent an awful lot of time there. It felt like a safe space where she was still close to Freddie.

When her mother had died, Bee had sold the house; Freddie had helped with the solicitors and stuff. For the moment she was staying in a little flat that she'd rented. It was little more than a bedsit but it was OK and she'd rather keep money in the bank until she decided what she was going to do next. Freddie told Bee to buy somewhere. 'You can't go wrong if you invest in property,' he said, which was strange advice coming from someone who had never owned a damn thing in his life apart from his paints and brushes and far too many easels. She'd counted ten in his studio but had only ever seen him use about three: one for whatever he was working on, one for whatever he was preparing to work on and one for whatever reference material he might be using. He'd put a big board on that easel and stick stuff all over it. Photos, colour swatches, fragments of information that he picked up from all over the place. She supposed other people might refer to it as a 'mood board', but it was far more than that.

Tears running down her cheeks, Bee was

27

reminded by the solid ache in her chest just how much she had loved her father. She had loved her mother too, but that had been a different kind of love. Solid and steady and utterly reliable. She'd had time to get used to the idea, if not to accept it – never that! – that her mother was going to die. And at the end her mother had been so ill and in so much pain that Bee was relieved when it was over. She'd sat beside her mother's bed in the hospice, hour after hour, and towards the very end Freddie had sat beside her. He talked about when he and her mother had been together. By that time Susie, Bee's mother, had been barely conscious but Bee was convinced she had heard and had taken pleasure in the reminiscences. She had seen her mother smile and the slender, wasted fingers had gripped her hand.

Neither of them had been there when Susie had finally died; it was almost as though she had waited for them to go away. It had been in the early hours of the morning and Freddie had finally persuaded his daughter to go and get some sleep. She'd been too exhausted to drive and he had taken her home, promising to go back and sit at Susie's bedside until the morning. The call came just as Bee was getting out of the car; she got back in, Freddie turned the car around and they had driven back together.

And now they were both gone and Bee was nineteen years old and feeling utterly and totally bereft.

She knew there was nothing she could have done about the cancer that had taken her mother but surely there was something that could have been done for Freddie. Someone had murdered her father; she was absolutely convinced of that, and murders were preventable. Weren't they?

It had begun to rain by the time she reached Freddie's studio, a cold sleety mix that almost blinded her, even though she had the windscreen wipers on full speed. She made a dash to the warehouse door. Freddie had sublet space on the mezzanine floor. Freddie had told her that the landlord, Mark Brookes, used the rest of the warehouse mainly for storing and repairing machinery that he bought and sold at auctions, and the air was always redolent with the smell of grease and paint. A part of the warehouse was divided off and the landlord and his two sons worked there, getting whatever it was they bought ready for sale.

Bee shouted greetings as she went through and climbed the stairs. Danny, the elder of the landlord's sons, shouted back that there had been some post and she told him she'd pick it up in a minute.

There was an old blue sofa in Freddie's studio and Bee threw herself down on it and pulled the old plaid picnic blanket that Freddie always left on the arm around her shoulders. It smelled of oil paint and turpentine and Freddie's cigarettes. Finally giving way to the tears, she curled up into a tight ball and wept.

When Bee woke it was fully dark. For a moment she was disorientated; she'd not switched on the lights when she reached the studio, even though the rain outside made the whole place dim and twilight grey. As she remembered where she was, Bee sat up and rubbed her eyes. Everything was very quiet; even the rain had stopped. So quiet she could hear her own breathing.

She had rarely been in the studio alone at night. The main light switch was across the other side of the studio, just at the top of the stairs. There were lamps set around and the closest one was next to the sofa she now occupied, but the bulb had blown before Freddie had died and had never been replaced.

With a sigh, Bee got to her feet and started to feel her way across the studio. As her eyes grew accustomed, she realized that it was not fully dark. The big skylight windows that made the place so perfect for Freddie now filtered in a little of the light pollution from the city streets beyond the warehouse and she could make out his layout table, his easels and the plan drawers in which he kept his drawings and much of his reference material. She glanced at her watch and discovered that it was after ten p.m. Danny would be long gone. Danny wouldn't have worried about her being in the studio alone, and nor would his brother or his father; it was her space, as it had been Freddie's before, and they knew that Freddie often worked late. She assumed that they would just think she was like her father in that regard. They would not have been surprised that she was still there when they left.

She reached the top of the stairs and put up a hand to switch on the lights, when a small sound caused her to pause. It was like the chink of metal on metal, the sort of sound she was used to

30

hearing from the workshop below, but she could see no light filtering out into the warehouse area. Usually when the brothers did work late she could not only hear them clearly but could see the square of light blocked out on the floor from the opening to the workshop. The main workshop itself had no separate door. There was a second area, separated by a fire door, which they used for welding and other hot work but the purely mechanical side, where they fitted everything together, was open.

Bee thought about calling out, alerting Danny to the fact that she was still upstairs. She worried for a moment that he might have assumed she'd already left and that if she suddenly switched on the lights or shouted for him she was likely to scare him as much as that little noise had just scared her.

She listened again and was almost sure that she heard a door open and close. Uneasy now, Bee took a mobile phone from her pocket preparing to dial for the police and then she switched on the light.

The light illuminated the studio and the stairs and a section of the warehouse. She saw letters on the layout table and guessed that Danny must have brought them up before he left, and seen her asleep. He would not have wanted to disturb her and so had simply left the post for her to find. She peered over the railings but from the mezzanine floor she could see nothing out of the ordinary. She went halfway down the stairs and called out to Danny, but there was no reply, and the workshop lights were out. Going all the way down the stairs

31

she checked the main doors that Danny and his brother and father used when they departed and they were evidently padlocked, as usual, from the outside. Freddie had the keys to a small side door that could be locked separately from the outside and bolted from the inside, though he used the main door to come and go most of the time. She checked that next. It was not bolted, but that in itself didn't mean anything. She had let herself out that way the last time she was here and more often than not no one else bothered with this extra line of security. Bee could only remember using the bolt on the odd occasions when she'd been alone in the studio and Danny had reminded her to slide it across when he had left.

That he had not reminded her tonight reinforced her first thought that he had not wanted to wake her up. Slowly, she made her way back up the stairs and stood on the landing looking into the studio. This had been Freddie's world, far more than his tiny little house with its yard full of plants and glorified shed-cum-studio at the far end. Far more than her mother's house had ever been, when he briefly lived there before Bee had been born, and the fact that she was now responsible for clearing it and dealing with his possessions felt overwhelming.

Her phone chimed to tell her that she had a text. It was from Patrick, the boy she had met that afternoon. Bee read the text. It told her that Patrick's friend Naomi was willing to see her and suggested Tuesday of next week. Why not tomorrow? Bee wanted to ask. Why not now? Tuesday was five days away.

She sighed, then sent a text back to say thanks and ask what time. It was something, she supposed, though what this woman Naomi could possibly do for her she was beginning to wonder.

Bee switched off the lights and made her way slowly back down the stairs, using her phone as a torch. She let herself out and walked round the building to find her car. The industrial estate was practically deserted; there were lights on in a couple of the factories and a few random cars and vans parked here and there. The rain had stopped and the sky was clearing. She looked up at the few stars blinking between the clouds.

'Oh, Freddie,' she said. 'What the hell am I going to do?'

Back in the warehouse, a shadow detached itself and moved towards the stairs. He was glad that the girl had gone. He didn't want any trouble, he just wanted what had been promised to him. He'd been to the studio three times already and still not found it and he supposed it was possible that Freddie had hidden it at his house. He hoped not: the studio was deserted for much of the time but the house was down a farm track and anyone going to it had to drive through the farm yard to get to it.

He knew for sure it hadn't been in the portfolio stolen from Scotts. *He* already had that; though of course he could have lied about the contents. Toby wouldn't have put it past him; it would be just his style to keep demanding that Toby bring him something he already had.

He stood at the top of the stairs and waited ten

minutes, fifteen minutes before putting on the lights, not sure how long it would take the girl actually to leave the site. He'd been horrified when he spotted her asleep on the sofa and even more horrified when she started to wake up. Quite how he'd made it down the stairs and into hiding he wasn't sure. Then she had passed within feet of him when she'd come down to investigate the tiny noise he'd made. He wasn't sure what he'd have done if she'd seen him.

He didn't dare risk the main lights but he needed more than a torch to illuminate the search so he moved slowly around the room switching on one lamp at a time. The slow burning anger he had felt for Freddie Jones was in danger of bursting into new flames.

Maybe the girl knew what he was looking for; maybe she knew where it was. Maybe Freddie had confided in his daughter. Maybe he should just have confronted her.

Eventually he just sat down on the sofa where Bee had lain and stared around the room, much as she had done. If he didn't get it back, then he was a dead man. Freddie had promised him and Freddie had broken his word, and now that might cost another life.

Knowing he had no choice, he took his phone from his pocket and made the call.

'It's not here. Definitely not here. I've searched the place so many times now.'

He paused to listen to the response. Could feel his whole body begin to shake as the panic grew.

'I've tried everything, everywhere. Freddie promised . . . Look, maybe the girl knows. She was here again tonight, she's been in and out of the place . . . bound to know. That's it, she's bound to know.'

Words fell over one another. He knew that whatever he said now would count for nothing. He was a dead man.

Five

'You didn't have to kill her. You could just have threatened her and taken what you wanted. It's just . . .'

Sian stared at the photograph. She could say these words to it that she could never hope to say to him. Binnie was not somebody you questioned, not to his face. Binnie was somebody you didn't talk to, didn't say anything to that he didn't want to hear. But it hadn't always been like that.

She remembered when they'd both been kids, playing together in the fields behind Binnie's house. Sian had been faster climbing trees and he'd always been faster running down the black pad between his house and hers. They'd been such close friends for such a long time and she couldn't really believe what he'd turned into. She still couldn't get her head around how it had happened. Though, she supposed, it had been something that had happened over long periods of time and she'd only really noticed it when she'd gone away and then come back. She'd gone away to university, Binnie had stayed behind and

35

by the time she'd returned he'd changed almost beyond recognition.

The sort of trouble that Binnie got into, the sort of trouble that had changed him, that wasn't supposed to happen in a tiny village like this. It wasn't supposed to happen in rural middle England. That was the kind of thing you heard about in the big cities where there were gangs and ghettos – not that this sort of thing had even happened in the city where she had gone to university and done her degree in fine art. Not, she admitted privately, that she'd have been likely to have noticed even if it had. All her time had been taken up with her university friends and they had gone only to those places frequented by other students.

When she'd come back that first summer she had heard that Binnie's mother had gone off to live in Spain, leaving Binnie alone in the family home, and Sian had gone over to see him but he wasn't there. He didn't return from wherever he'd been until after she'd gone back to uni.

The second summer she'd been away on a placement and then stayed with friends. They'd texted a few times but that was all. Binnie was part of childhood; now Sian was embarking on her adult life it seemed there was no space for him and she realized with a shock that she had ceased even to miss him.

Degree over, no sign of a job and no sense of where she wanted to go next, she had come back home. Her parents, realizing that she no longer fitted into their household, had allowed her to move into what had originally been built as a granny annexe but had in practice been used mainly for storage and the occasional guest. It was actually quite a tiny space containing a small bedroom just big enough for a queen size bed and a built-in cupboard, a living room-cum-kitchen and a tiny shower room, but truth be told Sian thought it was wonderful. No one disturbed her and she had use of what her mother called the summerhouse (actually a glorified garden shed) for her painting – not that she'd done much lately; her mind had been too preoc-cupied. She had managed to pick up a bit of work at the local pub and her parents weren't charging her for the use of the annexe, just telling her she would have to buy her own food and contribute to bills, though the truth was her mum helped out with groceries and Dad always made sure there was petrol in her car. Sian knew how lucky she was but even so, coming back had felt like a betrayal of the past three years. Returning home had seemed like a step back into childhood and reconnecting with Binnie had been like putting a seal on the box that she had gratefully, if a little reluctantly, packaged herself inside.

On bad days she wondered if she would ever leave again. On other days, hearing from univer-sity friends about their struggle post-study, she was incredibly grateful to have this bolthole and this much security and a little job at the pub, even if the pay was crap.

She picked up the photograph of Binnie. She had been about fifteen, she remembered, when this had been taken, and Binnie just a year older. It was taken by friends when they had all visited the funfair. She could see the big wheel in the background and she and Binnie grinned out at the camera, heads close together. Happy. Uncomplicated. Kind Binnie – not the one she knew now.

She'd asked her mum what had made him change and her mother just shrugged and said cautiously, 'Sometimes people just do. I know you were friends once, love, but perhaps it's best you keep away from him now?'

Sian knew her mother would never try and insist; she knew that Sian was too headstrong for that. Tell her not to do something and guess what would come next? But now she wished that her mother had delivered much stronger advice, had given her more than a suggestion. That she had been able to lock Sian in her room or something.

If her mother had done that, Sian would not have seen someone die. She would not have seen Binnie stick the knife into the woman's ribs and then step back, watch her fall and smile that weird smile as though what he'd just done was the most wonderful thing in the world.

And Sian knew she couldn't tell anybody about it because this new Binnie, this Binnie who had changed, wouldn't hesitate to do the same to her or to her family.

She could hear her mother calling, standing at the back door and telling her that dinner was ready. It was Friday night and most Friday nights Sian's dad got back late from work and he brought fish and chips in with him. This Friday night was no exception.

She thrust the photograph back in the drawer

and closed it with a bang. One thing was for sure, she needed to get away from here, and soon. Binnie already had her as an accessory to murder; fuck knew what else he had in mind. She thought, briefly, about confiding in her parents and then dismissed it. They would tell her to go to the police and then who could possibly know what might happen? The people Binnie ran with these days, they wouldn't take kindly to that. Even if Binnie was arrested that would not make Sian safe, and it certainly wouldn't make her parents safe. She knew her mother could sense that something was wrong and that she and her father had discussed this at length. They'd suggested she go and stay with her aunt for a few weeks, she'd barely left the village since she'd come back from university last June. Or, to be more precise, she'd barely left the village under her own volition. Binnie had taken her away a couple of times and the second time, he killed that woman.

Sian took a deep breath and readied herself for an evening with parents and fish and chips and television. An ordinary, normal evening. It might even be a bit boring. Sian had never realized before just what value there might be in such predictable and ordinary things as fish and chips and tea and a night in front of the telly.

Six

When Alec returned on the Friday evening he found his wife engrossed in research, a half dozen tabs open on her computer and the Dictaphone in use as she recorded notes.

'Hello,' he said, bending to kiss her. 'What's all this, then?'

Naomi stood so she could greet him properly, settling contentedly into his embrace. Napoleon's tail beat steadily against Alec's leg as he waited for his turn.

'Mmm, it's good to be home. This has felt like a long week. And I could eat a horse.'

'Sorry, the supermarket doesn't deliver equines but there's steak in the fridge. Or do you want takeaway tonight?'

'Steak,' he said. 'And some of those big fat chips, if we have them?'

'We do. You want me to cook?'

'No, I'll do it. Help me relax into the weekend. You can sort out some salad? I'll go and get the kettle on. What is it about hotel tea? It never tastes the same. What are you up to, anyway?'

Naomi laughed. Giggled, more like, Alec thought. 'I'm investigating,' she said. 'Patrick brought me a puzzle to look at and I've got to admit I'm rather enjoying it.'

'Well, bring your investigating head into the kitchen while I cook and tell me all about it,' he said. 'Sounds more fun than my week. You know what, I've decided that most rich people have more money than sense. And talk about penny pinching. My God, do some people want the earth for nothing.'

He'd wandered off to the kitchen and Naomi, smiling to herself, followed him. She'd let him rant about his week first and then fill him in on her little bit of investigation – that sounded better than research, she thought. One really interesting thing she had learnt was that the SIO in charge of the Scott murder investigation was someone she knew. Naomi had very fond memories of Karen Morgan, now DI Karen Morgan, and she hoped Karen would recall her with the same pleasure.

She opened the fridge and started to remove the makings for the salad. She passed the package of steaks over to Alec. 'So, what have you been up to down there in glorious Bedfordshire?' she asked.

Over dinner she filled him in on the Scott murder and the suspicions Bee Jones had about her father's death. 'I called Bob and had a chat,' she said. 'He thinks Bee may be on to something but he doesn't want her to pursue this, just in case it leads her into trouble.'

'Sensible,' Alec commented. 'The assumption is that Freddie Jones was creating forgeries to order, I suppose?'

'Not sure about that. But Bob said his feeling was that Freddie must have stumbled into something that wasn't on his usual radar. Freddie did

41

fake, there can be no doubt about that, but Bob said his usual MO was to create work, just to see if he could, then let it go into the wild and see what happened. He'd put something into auction or maybe sell to a minor dealer or, as he got to be a bit too well known, he'd get someone else to do it for him, with a story about dead relatives and house clearance, usually. Bob said he got away with a lot twenty years ago but it's got much harder now because everything is so interconnected, what with the internet and so on. Years ago no one knew who Freddie was and he could take himself off across the country, sell his stuff through provincial auction houses and the like. These days it's different, with catalogues for art auctions being online and no one being more than a mouse click away. Bob says Freddie mostly reinvented himself as an expert in old master techniques. Bob even got him consultancy work from time to time and he was lucky enough always to have sold OK in his own right. Bob reckons he never made a fortune, but he made a decent enough living, and that's rare enough for an artist. He thinks Freddie started to reform when Bee was born. He wasn't involved in bringing her up but he undoubtedly cared about her and made sure she never went without.'

'But he still wasn't *there*,' Alec said. 'He wasn't a father. If I had a child I'd want to be involved, you know?'

Naomi nodded cautiously. They'd talked about having children from time to time and it was a bit of a sensitive issue; one she'd rather not get into just now.

'Anyway,' she said, 'when Bee was fifteen she demanded to meet him and so her mother arranged it. She and Freddie hit it off. They became very close. But you'll never guess who's SIO on the Scott murder.'

'Surprise me.' She could hear the smile in his voice.

'You remember Karen Morgan?'

Alec laughed. 'Who could forget? Seriously? I never thought she'd stay the distance.'

'Well, she did.'

'Karen Morgan. My God. All ginger hair and freckles and, boy, she could drink anyone under the table.'

He sounded far too impressed and far too fond, Naomi thought. 'Yes, well, she's now a DI, and *that* was a long time ago, Alec.'

'Yes, of course it was,' he said, obviously making an effort not to smile, but she could hear the grin that must have spread across his face at the thought of their old friend.

'You go and have your shower,' Naomi told him curtly. 'I'll see to the dishes.'

But Naomi couldn't feel too mad with him. Her own reaction had been similar. Karen had seemed like anything but officer material back then. She'd admitted she'd only joined the police to please her father and that she'd no intention of seeing it through. 'Wild' was probably the best word to describe her. Wild and funny and very pretty. She and Naomi had been close for a while. Naomi had to admit she was looking forward to making contact again. She just hoped that Karen would have equally happy memories of her.

43

Seven

The owner of the Madonna that Bob had been tasked with studying had called Bob on the Sunday. He was back in the country, between business trips, and thought he'd check in with the artist. Suspicions about the painting's origins had only arisen after Freddie's death when the police had become involved. The attending officers, not knowing if Freddie Jones had died of natural causes, had followed procedure and treated this as a possible suspicious death.

Photographs were taken and the landlord and his sons questioned as a matter of routine. It was a chance remark from Danny that had raised initial questions. He'd been asked to take a look at the studio, see if he thought anything had been disturbed, and he had spotted the Madonna and child, half finished, on an easel.

'So, he's doing another one of those, is he? You should have seen the last one, awesome.'

That alone might have meant nothing but a routine background check had revealed that the deceased had a record for forging old masters. Documents in the studio led to several galleries and a couple of auction houses being alerted and eventually to the owner of the so-called Bevi Madonna. The painting that now sat in Bob's safe.

Derek Bartholomew was a collector Bob knew

well. He had occasionally gone with Derek to view potential purchases or to bid at auctions and so Bob had been first port of call when the suspicions had been raised.

The two men exchanged pleasantries. Derek asked after Annie and told Bob that he'd just come back from Kuwait and was about to fly out to Canada.

'So, have you reached a conclusion, my friend?'

'Almost,' Bob told him. 'Or I *had* almost. Derek, did you ever meet Freddie Jones?'

'No, never did. I knew him by reputation, of course. But I believed he was out of the game, and from what I could ascertain the provenance of the painting was rock solid, so . . .'

'We all thought that – his friends, I mean. His family too.'

'I didn't know he had family. Confirmed bachelor, I thought?'

'He had a relationship some years ago. Fathered a child. She's now nineteen and made contact with him properly a few years back.'

'That must have been a shock.'

'No, he knew about her but the mother made it plain she didn't view Freddie as stable father material. She knew full well he'd start out with the best of intentions and then something would distract him and he'd forget he was supposed to be a family man. Freddie contributed financially but left the rest to his ex.' Bob paused. 'I'm making the arrangement sound very cold; it was anything but.'

'Must be very difficult for the family,' Derek said.

'Yes, but that's by the by. What I do want to run by you is, have you had any unusual enquiries about the painting? Anything you'd view as suspicious, I suppose. Phone calls, emails, anyone hanging around . . .'

'Bob, you're worrying me! What's this about?'

'In truth, probably nothing. The daughter came to see me, said that her father was very worried in the weeks before he died. Frightened, even, as though someone had threatened him.'

'You think someone he conned?' Derek chuckled softly. 'Can't say he didn't deserve some of that. A lot of people might lose a lot of money if it turns out they've got Freddie Joneses in their collections. He potentially pissed off a lot of people.'

'People who might threaten to kill him? Who might actually go through with the threat?'

There was a beat of silence. 'You think someone might have?'

'Derek, I don't know. Let's just say that his daughter is convinced of it, and I'm starting to wonder. You heard about Antonia Scott being murdered?'

'Of course. I was due to meet with her last week. She'd said she had some new work I might be interested in. Lovely woman. You think there's a connection?'

'Derek, I don't know. The truth is, all this that I'm telling you might turn out to be just wild speculation, but what is true is that a portfolio of Freddie's work was stolen from Scotts Gallery. The police are keeping quiet about what was taken, but I'm willing to bet money that was all that went missing.'

Again that moment of silence while Derek absorbed this. 'I have a couple of his drawings,' he said finally. 'Antonia sold them to me a couple of years ago. That man could draw and no mistake. But why take the portfolio? I paid a few hundred each for the drawings; you're looking at a few grand, tops, for a portfolio. When you think what Scotts regularly have hanging on their walls . . .'

'My thoughts exactly. Anyway, as I say, it's probably coincidence, but I've got to admit it's got me thinking about the painting. I'd like to hang on to it a little longer, if that's OK.'

'No rush, Bob. I just thought I'd touch base today, I'm off again in the morning and if you try and get hold of me in the next few days it could be difficult. I'll be picking up my emails, of course. And my secretary can let me know if you need to talk.'

Bob thanked him and Derek said his goodbyes.

Bob replaced the phone on its cradle and stared at it thoughtfully. He hadn't intended to talk to Derek about the things that Bee had told him; he had acted on impulse. Something about the coincidence of the phone call coming so close on the heels of Bee's visit had niggled and he'd wanted to prod. He hadn't known that Derek owned any of Freddie's drawings or realized he had been so interested in the man. Had he knowingly bought one of Freddie's false provenances? Freddie never called them fakes; he would always just claim that the attribution was misinterpreted. As far as Freddie was concerned, it was always a case of 'buyer beware'.

One thing he now knew about Derek Bartholomew that he'd not been aware of only weeks before was that Derek had been party to some very suspect business dealings. The enquiries that Bob and Annie had quietly set in motion had turned up a number of occasions when Derek had stepped across the line.

Bob shrugged. Paying bribes didn't equate to knowingly buying stolen or forged artworks and for all Bob knew, that might be just an everyday way of oiling the business wheels in some countries.

But it had got him thinking.

Bob had always got along fine with Derek Bartholomew but he knew Annie had no time for him – though she'd been pleasantness itself the odd times they had met. Bob had asked her why.

'The man is a predator and a liar,' she had told him. 'I wouldn't trust him as far as I could spit.'

Derek Bartholomew was equally thoughtful when he ended the phone call. He hadn't known about the portfolio; that probably meant that there were some Freddie Jones drawings ready to come to the market and probably at a cheaper rate than he'd reckon on paying, once you took the gallery commission into account, and there was one man he could think of who would be in the know, who always had an ear to the ground.

As he'd told Bob, he'd only spent a few hundred on the Freddie Jones drawings, but that had been years ago and the prices had risen dramatically in the intervening decade. Not only that, but since

48

Freddie's death – inevitably a well established dead artist generated far more revenue than a living one – the prices had shot up.

He picked up his phone and called his old friend, Graham Harcourt.

'Graham – Derek. How are you? Good. Now, I've got a bit of a delicate question for you. Just got off the phone with Bob Taylor. No, actually, I don't know what he's working on at the moment, heard he has another exhibition planned for next summer, though. But the thing is, Bob just passed on an interesting bit of gossip. Told me that when Antonia Scott was murdered, one of the things that was stolen was a portfolio from our old friend Freddie. Now I know you always keep your ear to the ground—'

He listened for a moment. 'Oh, you've heard about it. Thought you might have done. Well, you know, if anything should come up . . . Good, yes, do keep me in mind. It's a sorry business, I know, but nothing we can do to change that, is there? Poor old Antonia. Poor Freddie, for that matter, but every cloud, as they say.'

Derek said his goodbyes and rang off, well satisfied. If Graham heard of anything coming up for sale, he'd act as middle man. There'd still be commission, of course, but he could stand that. It would be less than the gallery would want, that was for sure.

Eight

Monday had been frustrating for Naomi. She had tried to get in touch with DI Karen Morgan but had only been able to leave messages for her one time colleague. She'd had to be satisfied with leaving her mobile number and email and hoping that Karen would choose to call back.

Tuesday afternoon found her at Bob and Annie's house, for her promised meeting with Beatrix Jones. Patrick had driven her over. Harry, Patrick's father, had suggested he then bring her back for dinner and maybe a film. This was something they had done every couple of weeks since Alec had started his new job. Sometimes Mari, Patrick's grandmother, joined them too. Harry had been older brother to Naomi's best friend when they had all been children. The sister hadn't survived to adulthood but Harry and his family were close and very much valued friends.

'So, what do you make of this Bee?' she asked Patrick. 'Have you talked to her since meeting her at Bob's?'

'Only on text and Messenger. I think I like her, but she's a bit single track at the moment.'

'I suppose that's inevitable. She's got a lot on her mind and she's got to get this all out of her system, one way or another. I doubt she's even had time to get over her mother's death, never mind her father's on top of that.'

'Oh, I know,' Patrick said. 'But it makes it hard to get to know her, if you see what I mean. We just keep circling back to the same questions and as I can't answer those questions . . .' He shrugged. 'But I think she could be nice, you know? And I want to help her.'

Naomi reflected that Patrick's instinct was to help everyone. She heard Patrick indicate and take the sharp turn on to the narrow track leading up to Bob's house. 'I saw a couple of hares running down here the other day. Had to stop the car.'

'Did you get any photographs?'

'A couple of shaky ones on the mobile. They can really shift. It's good to see them, though. Annie says there were loads when they first moved in but the farmer at the time used to shoot them. The new guy's a bit more into nature, apparently. Annie goes on to his fields to shoot rabbits – she reckons they really do damage – but they leave the hares alone. Looks like Bee's here already,' he added, as they pulled up in front of the house.

Somehow, Naomi was not surprised about that.

Once in the kitchen, Napoleon settled down with Annie and Bob's two dogs and introductions were made. Naomi could feel the young woman's curiosity. Patrick had told her that Naomi was blind but being told and being confronted were, Naomi knew, two different things. Patrick was so used to her, knowing what she could do for herself and what she might need a bit of assistance with, that he didn't even think about it any more. Annie and

51

Bob had long since got past the anxious stage but Bee oozed uncertainty.

'I'll put your coffee just by your right hand,' Annie said. 'Bee, could you get me some biscuits? That cupboard behind you, grab a couple of different packs and put them on a plate so everyone can help themselves.'

Naomi heard the cupboard door open, the rustle of cellophane and the clink as the plate was set down.

'Um, the biscuits are just in front of you? Is that OK?' Bee said to Naomi.

'It's fine, thank you.' Naomi smiled in the young woman's direction. 'Patrick's told me a bit about your problem but maybe you'd like to fill me in properly?'

'Right. OK. Look, maybe this isn't such a good idea. I don't want to bother you, I mean . . .'

Naomi sighed. 'I lost my sight in a multi-vehicle pile-up on the motorway. It ended my career but I was already a detective inspector and I've not lost my interest in other people's problems nor, I hope, any of my skills. Just my sight. I might not be able to *solve* your problems but I might be able to talk you through so you can ask the right questions, find out what you need to know.'

'Sorry,' Bee whispered. 'I didn't mean—'

'I know. Nothing to be sorry for. Now, you believe that your father was afraid of something before he died. What did he say to you? How did he behave? When did you first become aware that he had something on his mind?'

She reached for a biscuit while Bee gathered

52

her thoughts. Discovering from the texture that it was oaty, she dipped it into her coffee and then sat back, enjoying the taste of coffee-soaked, sweet, flaky biscuit.

'There are more of those,' Annie said. 'I'll turn the plate around.'

'Thanks,' Naomi said. 'But I'm supposed to be cutting down. Since Alec started this new job I seem to be finding too many excuses for tea and biscuits.'

'This is coffee,' Annie said. 'Maybe it doesn't count.'

Naomi heard Bee shift in her chair and then lean forward, as though she wanted to shut out the others and speak more directly to Naomi. 'It was about eight weeks before he died,' she said. 'I got to the studio one day and he just seemed . . . odd. The phone kept ringing and he kept ignoring it, said it was marketing calls and he didn't want to know, then when I went off to the loo he must have answered, because I could hear him talking when I came back up the stairs.'

'Did you hear what he said?'

'I stood on the stairs and listened,' Bee admitted. 'He was angry, telling the person that he didn't have something or other. That even if he did he wouldn't get involved with anything like what they were suggesting. I waited until he'd finished and then came up to the studio. He was upset, I could tell that. He was just standing there, staring at his work but not seeing it, you know? He hardly noticed I'd come back.'

'And did you ask him about the phone call?'

'No, I just asked if he was OK and he snapped

at me and asked why shouldn't he be. I got annoyed then and said there was no need to snap and he apologized and tried to pretend to be his usual self, but he couldn't manage to. Not properly.'

'And after that?'

'He just seemed nervous, anxious. The only time he seemed happy was when he managed to immerse himself in his work, and he was finding even that difficult. I kept asking him what was wrong and whether there was anything I could do but he just kept saying it was nothing.'

'And did you get anything else out of him?'

'Only once. Look, you've got to understand, Freddie wasn't the most organized of people. He'd remember to pay his bills when the red one came, he'd wash up when he couldn't find a clean cup, he'd eat when he suddenly realized he was ravenous – but where his work was concerned he was absolutely different.'

She must have looked at Bob for confirmation because he agreed.

'Never missed a deadline, so far as I know. Never gave anything less than his absolute best. He had a little blue book – actually he had a lot of them, always blue and roughly the same size. They were his journals where he'd log work in, log it out, keep numbers for galleries and a record of what he had where. Including prints; he must have supplied a dozen galleries and he licensed a few of his designs for cards and the like. His best paying work was through Scotts and a couple of other places that dealt in his originals. Freddie always had fingers in as many pies as he could.

He knew, successful as he was, he couldn't rely on just one thing. I think the only thing he didn't do regularly any more was teach.'

'He'd do occasional workshops,' Bee said, 'but Freddie was all about drawing and learning what he called the basics. He was into old master techniques and he said most of the art schools didn't bother with that sort of thing any more. He did summer schools at Ruskin and he'd go to Florence once a year to do a week at . . . I can't remember the name of the school. Sorry.'

Naomi, thinking of Patrick's experience in his first year of art school, understood Freddie's sense that he didn't fit into such seats of learning any more.

'You told Bob and Annie that Freddie insisted he was only producing legal work now. Do you think he was being pressured to go back to his old ways?'

'Of course I do. Bob doesn't think he ever stopped,' she added bitterly.

'I knew what drove him, Bee. He'd have found it hard to give up the challenge, but – and please let me finish,' he added, as the girl tried to interrupt – 'Freddie never did anything with what *he* saw as criminal intent. Freddie's way was to produce something, then let it into the wild to find its own place. Oh, he might suggest a provenance for it, but it was rarely anything specific or even really traceable. At least not recently, so far as I know.'

Naomi was intrigued. 'And previously? You say not recently.'

'Freddie made money any way he could in the

early days and part of that challenge was to, shall we say, create history, back story for his pictures. Freddie was careful, clever, assiduous. No one knows for sure what he got away with or how many times but eventually he found himself in court and did a few months in prison about sixteen or so years ago. I think that was enough for him. He swore off the fakes and lies after that – at least he said he had.'

'You never believed him.'

'As I say, as far as I know he stopped creating the provenance; there's no law against producing something in the style of, or doing a copy or near copy of a known work. There's no law against researching a lost picture and creating something that looks like the description, and Freddie rarely went for the big names.'

'Lost pictures?' Naomi asked.

'Most established artists have their work listed in what's called a catalogue raisonné,' Patrick told her. 'It's like a master list, compiled by an expert. For some artists it's a bit sparse but contemporary artists might have something that fills several big books. Usually the list includes works that the expert knows were produced but which might have been mislaid or destroyed or sold on, and no one knows where they are or even what they looked like.'

'And Freddie liked to fill in the gaps?'

'Sometimes, yes,' Bob confirmed. 'He saw it as a personal challenge. These days I think most of his work involved making legitimate copies for the collectors who either already owned the originals or wanted a close copy.'

56

He must have looked to Bee for confirmation because she answered grudgingly, 'Yeah, that's right.'

'And there are perfectly legitimate reasons for that kind of work. Sometimes owners wanted the picture on their walls, but didn't want to risk taking the original out of the bank vault. Other times, they might actually have sold the original but not wanted to go public about that. And some people just like the frisson of having a really good copy of something they know they could never afford to own. Something better than even the best print.'

'So, why do you think he made that painting you're talking about?' Bee wanted to know.

'Because I saw a half-finished picture he had on his easel, just a few days after his death.'

'You went to the studio? I didn't know that. Why didn't I know that? Anyway, he might have been making it for the owner. Or maybe Freddie just wanted to make a copy of the Bevi Madonna for his own pleasure? Maybe he wanted to own a copy?'

'Totally possible,' Bob agreed, 'and I spoke to the owner to see if Freddie had asked him about it, but the owner of the Madonna had never made direct contact with Freddie Jones. He had no suspicions about the painting until after Freddie's death and I'm afraid the fact that he began to entertain those doubts in the first place was down to me.'

'Oh?'

'Yes. As I said, I went to Freddie's studio shortly after his death. Antonia Scott was concerned. Freddie had a couple of pictures at the studio that he'd been restoring for her. She contacted the police, and after a couple of calls from her solicitor they arranged for her to go to the studio and I went with her. The Madonna Freddie had been working on was still on the easel at that point. We collected Antonia's property and I took a few photographs of the studio, and of that particular picture, and then we left.'

'You recognized it,' Naomi said.

Bob laughed. 'I know it well. The owner of what we believed to be the original is someone I've advised on occasion. I know his collection.'

'But you didn't advise on that one?'

'As it happens, no. It came up for sale as part of an estate clearance in a provincial auction house. The owner at that point was a retired solicitor. His heirs took what they wanted and left the valuation of the rest to the discretion of the auction house. There was nothing suspicious, Naomi, and there was a receipt for the purchase that led back to a now defunct gallery somewhere on the south coast. Might have been Bournemouth, I don't recall.'

'A defunct gallery?'

'Again, nothing suspicious. I think the owner retired, sold up. It was bought by an antique dealer – again, all above board.'

'But Freddie's MO was to sell through provincial auctions or small galleries.'

'It was indeed.'

'You said,' Patrick interrupted, 'at that point. *At that point* the picture was still on the easel.'

'I did,' Bob agreed. 'Because by the following

day it had gone. We only know that because the solicitor representing Bee's interests contacted us and asked if we'd removed it. He had the original police photos and had gone along to check that we'd only taken what was on the list Antonia had sent to him.' He laughed. 'Antonia was not best pleased. She felt he was accusing her.'

'I didn't see him working on a Madonna,' Bee said. 'The last thing I saw him do was a landscape with horses. He was reproducing one that had been damaged in a fire, one of a pair. He was working from photographs.' She shrugged. 'That was about a fortnight before he died. I didn't see him after that.' She sounded terribly sad about that, Naomi thought.

'What I don't understand,' Patrick said, 'is why was Freddie working on a copy of the Bevi Madonna now? Bob, how long ago was the original – or whatever it is – bought?'

'By its current owner, about nine years ago. But you're right.' He sounded surprised that he'd not considered this before. 'Why decide to produce another one now? That's assuming Freddie produced the one I've got here.'

'And who took the half-finished picture, and why would they bother?' Bee sounded really puzzled now. 'I mean, if someone wanted to hide the fact that Dad had been working on that picture, they'd have had to remove a whole load of other stuff. He'd sketch everything, then work the sketches up into preliminary drawings and . . . well, you know how he worked. He was meticulous.'

'Then maybe we should go and get whatever

59

we can find from the studio,' Patrick suggested. 'See if his preliminary work casts any light. It might be as simple as someone seeing the Madonna and wanting one of their own. It might all be dead simple. And you don't even know that the picture Bob saw is really missing. It could have been moved, put away. The police and Bee's solicitor have been in and out of the studio. Someone might just have wanted to keep it safe.'

'It's possible,' Naomi agreed. 'But the police and CSI would not normally move things out of position.'

'Even if they'd photographed everything?' Patrick asked. 'Anyway, Naomi, you're thinking about a crime scene. So far as the police are concerned Freddie died of natural causes, so the normal rules might not apply.'

'I don't remember seeing it,' – Bee was stead-fast about that – 'but I think it's a good idea to go and collect anything that looks important. And I'd be glad of the company,' she admitted. 'I don't know if I'd be sure what to look for.'

'When do you want to go?'

Naomi smiled at the sound of Patrick's eagerness.

'I can't do anything for a few days; I've got to go to a wedding. A cousin of my mum's. Her daughter's getting married and I'll never hear the last of it if I don't turn up. I'm heading to Sheffield tomorrow. I'll be back on Saturday.'

'Sunday, then?'

'Yes, OK. Sunday afternoon. I'll pick you up and we can drive over in the one car and then bring everything back here. If that's OK?'

Bob made no objection to his home being used as a rendezvous point, Naomi noted. She figured he was as interested as everyone else and besides, he knew Freddie's work and practice better than anyone.

And so it was agreed and Bee left only a little after this, obviously more content than when she had arrived.

'Thanks for coming over to meet her,' Bob said.

'Welcome, but to be honest, I don't think I did anything.'

'You took an interest. I think that's what she needs at the moment.'

'Hmm, maybe. But I've discovered one thing that might be important. To you and Annie anyway. I happen to know the SIO of the Antonia Scott murder. We've been playing phone tag since yesterday, but I'll catch up with Karen eventually. Maybe I'll be able to find out how the inquiry is really going.'

'You think so? That would be good. So far as we can see it all went cold very quickly. There was nothing on the news after the first few days, anyway.'

'And the investigator we employed doesn't think the police have made any progress,' Annie said. She'd been very quiet while Bee had been present.

'Patrick said you were having all this looked into,' Naomi said. 'Any chance I might have a chat with your investigator?'

'Do you really want to get involved?' Bob sounded doubtful.

'I feel as though I am already, in a small way.

61

And as I told Bee, I still have the skills I used to have.'

'I'll set it up,' Annie promised. 'His name is Alfie Kounis. He used to work for my guardian.'

'Ah, right,' Naomi said, thinking about the man who had raised Annie after her parents died. A man of great influence, it turned out, and whose guidance and protection had come at a very heavy cost to Annie.

'Alfie's a good man,' she said. 'You'll get along fine, I think. I'll give him a call tomorrow. You might have caught up with your inspector friend by then.'

Naomi agreed that she might, and she and Patrick left soon afterwards.

'You really do like her, don't you?' she asked Patrick as they drove away.

'Bee? Yes, I do. She's a bit strange, but I suppose people say that about me too.'

It had been a while since Patrick had had a relationship, Naomi mused, and the last one had proved to be problematic. But it was time he tried again. Though he had some close female friends at university, Patrick was quite shy around girls as a rule and never good at making the first move. She hoped that Bee wasn't *too* strange.

She was looking forward to talking to DI Karen Morgan and also to meeting this Alfie Kounis. She felt as though half of her brain had been asleep for far too long.

Nine

It was good, Naomi thought, to be with friends and looking forward to a relaxing and unpressured evening, nothing more complex to think about than the choice of film and pizza topping. This was a habit she had fallen into since Alec started his new job. A couple of times a month she joined Harry and Patrick for a film and pizza evening and they took turns to choose the film.

She found that people were surprised when she told them of her love of film. 'But you can't see it!' was the usual objection, and most people failed to get it even when she explained that she could get as wrapped up in a good story now as she ever could before. Fortunately, Patrick and his dad needed no such explanation and had both been trained to provide extra commentary when a visual was particularly important.

Tonight's choice was the latest *Star Wars* film and she'd gone for a Four Seasons pizza and a couple of glasses of wine. It was late by the time the film was over.

'You want to stay?' Harry asked. 'The spare bed's made up.'

It always was, Naomi thought. The tiny little box room didn't have space for much more than a single bed and a chair, but Naomi often did stop over on film nights.

63

'Yes, I think I will, thank you.'

'Good,' Harry approved. 'I'll let Napoleon out the back to do his business.' They'd taken the big black dog out for a walk along the promenade earlier in the evening and he too was now ready for bed, sprawled out on the blanket Harry kept for him.

Patrick's phone chimed, letting him know he had a text. 'Bee,' he said. 'She says thanks for today, and confirms about Sunday.'

'Good. She's off to the wedding tomorrow?'

'Think that's what she said, yeah. She seems to have come round to the idea that her dad might have been up to his old tricks.'

'I think she has to,' Naomi agreed. 'The only way she's going to get to the truth is if she's open to it being something she might not want to hear. Freddie Jones sounds like a fascinating man. Though I'd think he'd be frustrating too. I'm not surprised Bee's mother took the stand she did.'

'I get that,' Patrick agreed. 'What I don't get is why she kept his identity secret all those years. It wasn't like she'd had a one-night stand or didn't know who he was, or that he didn't keep in contact. Lots of kids have absent fathers but at least they know who they are and where they are. They still get some contact.'

'They still get birthday and Christmas presents, you mean,' Naomi teased.

'That's important, when you're a kid,' Patrick argued. 'Kids are mean. They'll ask you at school what you got from your mum or dad or whatever.'

64

'I suppose they will,' Naomi said. 'Not that you ever had to worry about that, did you?'

Patrick laughed a little self-consciously. 'No, but I worried about maybe *having* to worry about that, you know. When Mum and Dad split up and I had to go and live with her, I really thought maybe Dad would, you know, not be there. Stupid, but when you're a kid you think about these things a lot.'

Naomi nodded. 'I suppose you do.' As it happened, Patrick's sojourn with his mother and stepfather had been short. His mum had taken him to live with the new family in Florida and Patrick had hated it. He'd decided that he also hated his mother and his stepfather and his new step-siblings and that she, with her new family, didn't need him any more. After about eighteen months he'd come to spend the summer with his dad and simply refused to go back. He'd been eleven at the time and Naomi hadn't been reacquainted with Harry at that point, but she'd heard about the arguments that had followed his decision. In the end, the new stepfather had intervened and suggested they give it until Christmas and then see how everyone felt. Naomi had the suspicion that he'd made the suggestion as an attempt at reverse psychology; Patrick would want to do exactly the opposite of what the hated stepfather suggested. If that had been his intention, it had backfired spectacularly. Patrick had stayed with Harry. Patrick's mother had been furious and hurt.

The following summer Patrick had agreed to go to Florida, provided he held on to his passport and his open return ticket. In the end he had stayed for the summer and come home with a much more accommodating attitude. Phone calls to and from the States – now replaced by Skype chats – happened twice a week and included all the 'steps', father and siblings. Harry had even been over to stay on occasion, though he had insisted on getting a hotel. The fact that his ex-wife had run off with Harry's now ex-boss still rankled, Naomi knew, but they rubbed along in what she thought of as a civilized manner.

'That first Christmas you moved back must have been difficult,' she said.

'It was. I'd changed so much in the six months Mum didn't know what I was into any more and when Dad told her to give me vouchers so I could buy art stuff, she though he was deliberately trying to trip her up. But she kind of listened to him and I was really happy. I called her up on Christmas Day and she cried on the phone but it was the start of it all being better between us, you know. I've never been sorry about coming back here.'

Naomi nodded. Patrick and Harry had endured their moments of conflict, as she knew well. But they'd also grown incredibly close and Naomi was grateful that they'd drawn her into that closeness.

Harry came back in with Napoleon. 'It's starting to rain,' he said. 'I'll give him a rub down.'

Naomi smiled. This was second home for her canine companion. Harry kept an old towel handy to dry him off, dog food and bowls in the cupboard under the sink and a ready welcome for the pair of them.

Harry had once speculated that his relationship

66

with Naomi might progress further than friendship, and there had been moments when she
had wondered too. Harry was safe and familiar
and still her best friend's big brother but, in the
end, that had been the problem. She had loved
Alec differently and eventually he had been her
choice. Harry had slipped back into the role of
closest friend and she never ceased to be grateful
for that.

She often wondered if she'd be jealous, should
Harry find someone he could have more than that
with. She hoped she'd have the grace not to be,
but was honest enough to know that she probably
would.

Ten

Binnie had been watching Beatrix Jones's flat off
and on for several days, not as a spell of constant
organized surveillance but more because he
thought that was what he should be doing. It was
part of the role he was playing, staking out the
suspect, victim, whatever . . . he wasn't sure what
part Bee would be playing in this particular game
as yet, but he didn't really care. Binnie was having
fun and that was all he was bothered about. He'd
seen her come back the previous afternoon and
watched as she'd nipped out to the corner shop
for bread and milk – he knew that because she'd
not bothered with a bag, just carried her shopping
home, one item in each hand.

Later, he'd seen her lights go on and the curtains close and, through the sliver of a gap between the curtains, seen the flicker of the television. He tried to guess, from the pattern of flickers, what she might be watching. He checked the TV schedule on his phone and decided that the speed of flickers equated to one of two action films. It frustrated him that he couldn't narrow this down further. He wanted to know. Bruce Willis or Tom Cruise. Was she more of a Bruce or a Tom kind of girl? Sian would have gone with Bruce Willis, he thought. He wondered briefly what Sian was up to that evening, then remembered it was one of her nights for working in the local pub. He toyed with the idea of leaving his surveillance and heading back for last orders. It would be worth it just to see the look on her face. Binnie smiled, thinking of the pain he was causing to his one time friend and playmate. Stuck-up little snob she'd turned out to be. Just like all of them. Stuck up and living scared; Binnie had left all of that behind. Binnie had seen the light. Fear was for losers.

The lights went out just after ten but she left the television on, the flicker slower now – though, when Binnie checked, he could see that neither film had ended. It dawned on him that either he had been wrong – and that was something he could not accept – or she had turned over to watch the news in preference to watching the end of the film.

A slow fury rose in Binnie, starting in the pit of his stomach and rising through his chest and into his throat and then his head. His arms, resting on the steering wheel, shook with the force of it.

'Stupid bint,' Binnie said. 'Stupid, stupid, stupid bitch!' this time punctuating each word with a blast on the car horn. He should go up there, bash down her door and then bash her down as well. Didn't she know anything? You watched the film to the end. Anything else was disrespectful and just plain wrong.

The sound of the horn had attracted attention in the quiet terraced street. Light flooded out as curtains were drawn back – Bee's included. A man shouted at Binnie and Binnie's fury, relieved only slightly by his assault on the steering wheel and horn, escalated again. The need to hit something, the desire to inflict pain; for Binnie that desire overrode almost all other concerns.

Almost, but not quite. Binnie had a job to do. Mustn't blow it, mustn't get it wrong or it would be Binnie on the wrong side of the pain.

It was a logic he could understand, even het up as he was. He started the engine and drove away.

The next morning Binnie was back in position, watching the little flat once more. He was surprised to see a taxi draw up and the girl come out carrying a small wheelie suitcase. She was going somewhere, but judging by the lack of heavy luggage, probably not for long.

He followed the taxi to the station, cursed the lack of street parking that meant he couldn't follow her inside and then drove away, taking the route that led back past her flat.

Not so early now and people were up and about, taking kids to school and themselves off to work. Not the best time, Binnie thought; he could be cautious and logical when he needed to be. Tonight, then. He'd not been ordered to search her flat but sometimes it was good to use your own initiative and while she was away he might as well take a look around.

Binnie drove away, well pleased with the decision. He'd be careful to make sure she never knew he'd been there, but maybe he'd take a souvenir. He licked his lips in anticipation.

The following morning, Patrick dropped Naomi and Napoleon home on his way in to uni. She hadn't been awake enough to eat breakfast at Harry's so she made up for it now and checked her emails while eating toast and cereal. She'd been a bit slow to use assistive technology when she'd first lost her sight. It had felt like the final acknowledgement that her world had changed for ever and that, somehow, she was never going to be the person she'd once thought she recognized as Naomi, ever again. As time had gone on, however, sense had prevailed. Her phone and computer had been chosen for their inbuilt voice input and read back capabilities and for what software could be added easily and she had bought a reading machine for use at home. Patrick had put a couple of apps on her phone for her which harnessed the phone's camera and used it like scanning software. True, she sometimes got the positioning wrong and only scanned half a document, but she was getting better at it.

She instructed the computer to log on to her emails and read the headers and was delighted to find that she'd got an email from Karen Morgan.

Excited now, Naomi took another gulp of her coffee and then told the computer to open that email, wondering why Karen hadn't just texted or called her phone.

The reason was soon revealed.

Hello there Naomi. What a blast from the past you are! I tried to call you but kept getting number not recognized. This is the number I've got but it wouldn't surprise me if the idiot that took your message wrote it down wrong. I swear, he doesn't listen half the time.

One digit wrong, Naomi thought. At least the mysterious idiot had got her email right.

So, what can I do for you? Give me a call tonight. You won't catch me earlier, I'm in court all day but I'm looking forward to a good gossip! I hear on the grapevine that you finally married that Alec that kept hanging round? Wow, he must have upped his game. Nice enough guy but not what you'd call dynamic. Oh my God, I've just realized how long ago that was. Scary stuff, Naomi. Scary stuff indeed.

Looking forward to hearing your voice after all this time. After seven, OK?

Karen

Naomi smiled. She was a little frustrated at having to wait until the evening but she too was looking forward to hearing her friend's voice. Though even using the artificial voice of the read back she could hear Karen's tone breaking through. She'd forgotten Karen's low opinion of Alec. Strange to recall how shy he'd been around women back then. She wondered how Alec would feel if he should happen to meet up with Karen again. He'd been gracious enough – maybe even a tad overenthusiastic – when they'd spoken about her but, back when they'd all been in training together, Alec hadn't been all that keen either. Karen, he felt – and Naomi could not help but agree at the time – wouldn't have known serious if it fell on her.

Something must have changed, Naomi thought, for Karen even to be still in the police force, never mind to have made DI. But then, Alec had changed beyond recognition and so, she supposed, had she.

She finished her cereal and refreshed her coffee. 'You never know what life's going to throw at you, do you, Napoleon?'

The big dog wagged his tail, beating it steadily against her leg.

Eleven

Hot on the heels of the email was a disappoint-ment. Alec called and told her he might not be back until the Sunday afternoon. The company he now worked for ran high end event security and they were short handed for the weekend and wanted Alec to head up the control room. It was easy work, if long hours, at a private party that

72

sounded to Naomi more like a fully-fledged rock concert. He'd finish about six a.m. on the Sunday morning, grab some sleep and then head home. 'I've been offered double time and a bonus for unsocial hours,' he told her. 'Didn't think I could really turn it down.'

She agreed, though she was a little disappointed not to have him home as planned.

Her mood threatened a downturn but was rescued by Annie calling to say that Alfie Kounis had agreed to meet up with her on the Friday afternoon, if she could manage that. Maybe for a late lunch?

She named a restaurant that Naomi had heard about but never been to. 'Bob will try to be there to make the introductions,' she said. 'But he can't stop; he's off to an auction. He's spotted a couple of engravings he fancies.'

'More cartoons?'

'I think so, yes. Though where he's going to put them . . . he's already covered all the wall space on the upstairs landing and halfway down the stairs.'

Bob collected political cartoons, when he could get them. He sought out work from the eighteenth and early nineteenth centuries but he wasn't averse to later work either, engravings of original artwork.

'Are you OK for getting there and back? We can arrange for a lift.'

No, Naomi told her, it was fine, she could get her usual taxi. George Mallard, who ran a local family firm, was taking her to her regular slot at Citizens Advice, where she gave what legal advice she could to those in need of it. She could hang on there for an hour longer than usual and then get George to take her to the restaurant instead of straight home.

That sorted, and feeling both excited and rather virtuous in her independence, Naomi went to tidy the kitchen and then plan her day until she could phone Karen Morgan. More background research into Freddie Jones and the murky world of art forgery seemed to be in order. A good excuse to buy books too. And then a walk on the beach with her guide dog, who now knew the route so well he could probably manage it on his own.

Binnie studied the photographs he had taken of Bee's tiny flat. It was almost a bedsit, saved from that description by the fact that the broom cupboard of a kitchen had a separate door.

That she had chosen to live in a place like this – even your average student would think twice about it, Binnie reckoned – puzzled him. He knew she had money in the bank from when she had sold her mother's place and she'd be coming in for whatever Freddie Jones had left – and Binnie had good reason to believe that would be a substantial amount – so why choose to rent a dump like that?

He glanced round his own place and decided that even though he only occupied a small space in what had been the family home, he still lived better than she did.

Binnie's place had once been a farmhouse. His mum and dad had bought it and done it up before Binnie was born and he and his little brother had

74

the run of the place and the big garden and the fields beyond.

Mostly, his mum had raised them both. His dad had left for good when Binnie was ten and the summer after that Binnie's little brother had died. His dad had come home for the funeral and Binnie's mum had pleaded with him to come back permanently or, if he couldn't come back, at least to take Kevin with him. Binnie's mum was the only one who ever called him Kevin. Even his teachers called him by his nickname – when they got the chance. Binnie was bright, could have excelled at school but, to be frank, looking back he realized he just couldn't be arsed. There were other things he'd rather be doing – even though he hadn't found his true vocation then.

Binnie looked back at the photographs. He'd bought himself a Polaroid camera. He'd read somewhere that the Stasi, when they went in to search a property, took Polaroid pictures first so they could be sure to get everything back in exactly the right place. He liked that idea; it was neat and it was challenging. He'd also heard that sometimes they'd move something deliberately, something not obvious but enough to be unsettling, just to fuck with people's heads, and that was an idea Binnie liked even more. Everything had been really tidy in the little flat, everything in its place, and Binnie's brain had gone into overdrive. It was so perfect. What could he do here that was sure to be noticed?

In the end, after a couple of false starts, he'd settled for rearranging the bookshelves. Taking everything off the top and swapping it with everything on the bottom shelf. He'd taken before and after photos and he looked at them now, wondering whether he'd done enough. Whether she was an observant sort and would notice straight away or whether it would take her a day or two.

Either way, it should freak her out.

Binnie grinned. The fact that he'd found nothing of interest in the flat hadn't dampened his mood at all. He had been curious, that was all. Professional curiosity was another thing he'd learnt from his study of the secret police; he believed he should be thorough. Go above and beyond.

Binnie got up and put the photographs into one of the kitchen drawers, along with others he had taken elsewhere and the souvenirs he had taken. This time, a postcard someone had sent her from their holiday in Venice.

Binnie felt no actual need to take objects as souvenirs but it was another thing he had read about in the true crime books his mother had liked so much, and which she'd left behind when she had gone away. Killers like to take souvenirs so they can remember what it felt like when they committed their crimes. He'd read that and he'd added it to his magpie's nest of a brain, his list of stuff he wanted to emulate. He felt it was like playing the role properly, but he couldn't say that the urge had ever actually been a part of his modus operandi – another thing he'd learnt from those books, and from watching the telly, of course. Binnie was certain he had never felt the urge towards what those who claimed to know called 'ritualistic behaviours', even though he now played the game of doing so. It was never something he had actually felt in his bones. Not even that first time. Not even when his little brother had died, his head held under the water, his neck clamped in both of Binnie's so much stronger hands – not because Binnie had any particular grudge against him but because Binnie had wanted to know what it looked like to see someone die.

Twelve

Naomi called Karen Morgan just after seven.

'Naomi Blake! My God, what is this? I never thought—'

'It's Friedman, now,' Naomi laughed. 'I married him, remember.'

'Oh God, so it is. You know I really can't get my head around that. Is he still in the job?'

'No, left the force coming up for two years ago. Thought it was time for a change.' That was the diplomatic way of putting it; the reality was a little more complex. 'He mooched about for a bit and he's now working for a private security firm. Events management and such.'

'Oh, not another one,' Karen complained. 'And I'll bet the money's a damn sight better.'

It was that, Naomi thought. And generally better hours too. This weekend being an exception.

'Ask him if there are any jobs going for a very

jaundiced female DI,' Karen joked. 'I'll swear, Naomi, I'm drowning in bloody paperwork, I'm short handed and I'm getting nowhere with this blasted murder.'

'The Scotts' gallery?'

'That'll be the one. Why? Is that why you're calling?' She sounded amused and only a little surprised. 'And here's me thinking you've been missing me.'

'Actually, I have,' Naomi said, surprised to find it was actually true. Now she'd been reminded of her friend the glow of nostalgia burned much brighter than she'd anticipated.

'OK, I'll believe you. So, what's your interest in the Scott case?' There was a shift in tone, Naomi noticed. She could almost see Karen reaching for paper and pen. 'Because if, by some strange fluke, you bumped into the killer in a café and they confessed, I want to know about it.'

'Not quite that,' Naomi told her. 'My interest has more to do with one Freddie Jones.'

Slowly and carefully, sure now that her friend really was taking notes, Naomi filled Karen in on everything she knew, had been told or suspected. At the end of her tale she was terribly aware that it wasn't a lot: fragments and snippets and maybes, but . . .

'What's your take on this, Naomi? You think she's on to something?'

'To something, yes. There are too many coincidences to be, well, really coincidental. And Freddie had form. Was sentenced to two years for faking, served ten months. It was in Fenton Open Prison, and it was years ago, but who knows

78

who he might have bumped into? Bee says her dad told her he was a reformed character but Bob Taylor, who's known him for a very long time, reckons otherwise and even she's coming round to the idea.'

There was a pause on the other end of the phone. Naomi waited, suddenly knowing that elements of this were not new to Karen.

'You know there was a portfolio missing,' Karen said at last.

'I do. Drawings by Freddie Jones, apparently.'

'The thing is, Naomi, that was the only thing taken. No other artwork, no cash, no cards, and Antonia Scott was wearing a necklace worth about five grand and a bangle worth another two. Why didn't the killer bother with those? They were high carat gold, could have been melted and disappeared.'

'Maybe they didn't know what was what.'

'Any fool can recognize gold. And even if the folio was the target – and I don't get why it should have been – cover your tracks by taking other stuff. If he'd snatched the jewellery and maybe a painting or two, it might have been an age before even the brother noticed the portfolio was missing. It was almost as though whoever it was wanted it to be noticed. They were pointing it out. Look, I wanted this, I took it. No more, no less.'

'Disciplined, maybe. I've heard art is often stolen to order.'

'Apparently not as often as you might think, according to the specialist crime unit. And it's not sold on as often as you might think either.

The weird thing is, it becomes a status thing, almost like a currency in its own right. It can get passed around for years, sold or given as a gift or a reward. Organized crime works on its own rules and it's a very incestuous world, in some ways.'

That chimed with what Naomi's research suggested.

'Interesting that it was Bob Taylor who raised the alarm on this. Considering he was a friend of our Mr Jones. He could have maintained his loyalty to his friend and not said anything.'

Naomi hadn't actually thought about that. 'He had Antonia Scott with him at the studio,' she said. 'She might also have known the Bevi Madonna. But in any case, I think Bob is essentially honest, and he has a reputation to maintain. If it once got out that he'd suspected something but kept stumm, it could have massive repercussions on his career.'

'Hmm. True. What was Antonia Scott doing at Freddie's studio? I didn't know about that.'

'Freddie Jones had quite a reputation as a restorer. In fact that's who gave Bob his start in the business. Antonia Scott had left a couple of pictures with Freddie, to be restored or something. She contacted the solicitor who was dealing with Freddie's estate and they got permission from the police for Antonia to go and collect the paintings. At least, I think they were paintings.'

'Right, and the solicitor . . . you have a name for him?'

'It's not come up in your enquiries?'

'No, it has not. Odd, that.'

Naomi didn't know the name but said she'd find out. 'Bee lost her mother to cancer about a year ago, I'd bet she used the same solicitor who helped her out with her mother's estate. She had a house to sell and bills to settle, that sort of thing. She said a solicitor helped her out with that and I get the impression she's using the same one for Freddie's bequest. My guess is you'll find a common or garden local guy from a firm that deals with conveyancing and will writing. Bee's only nineteen, she won't have gone looking for anything fancy. Most like it'll be someone recommended by friends or family. There'd be no reason for him to come up in relation to anything else Freddie was doing.'

'True, probably. Get me the name, if you can, will you? Save me some leg work. You say the daughter's been raising questions with the local police?'

'Yes, but they've not been listening to her. Even after she tried to make the link between Freddie and Scotts Gallery, they were not exactly encouraging.'

'No, I don't suppose they would be. On the face of it, it's a stretch, but . . .'

'But?'

'But we've also been looking at Mr Freddie Jones, to start with because of the portfolio, but also because his name's come up elsewhere.'

'OK, and in what context?' Naomi asked.

She could hear her friend hesitating again.

'Let's just say there's evidence that Freddie Jones wasn't as retired as he claimed to be,' she said.

Thirteen

Sian's mother found her crying in the summer-house she'd been using as a studio. They were not childish tears or the tears of frustration her work sometimes produced. They were tears of pain and utter despair and it didn't take her mother long to realize that.

'It's Kevin Binns, isn't it? That's what you're crying over.'

'No,' Sian snapped far too sharply. But she allowed herself to be gathered into an embrace and buried her face in her mother's shoulder. Her mother was wearing an old cardigan, soft with wear and washing and permeated with her scent. For a moment Sian was small again, crying over a scraped knee.

'What is it, love?' her mother asked gently. 'I do wish you wouldn't see him. He's a bad lot, you do know that, don't you?'

Sian nodded and then shook her head. 'I know, but I can't not see him.'

'Oh, sweetheart.'

Sian could almost hear her mother going through all the possible responses in her mind. Considering all the possible interpretations of Sian's words.

'Do you . . . love him?' she asked at last.

Once upon a time the answer to that might have been yes. Sian had worshipped Binnie. He was

82

exciting and wild and unpredictable. Come to the fair with me, he'd said. Go on the fastest rides. Ride my bike with me; no one will see. Who cares if we don't have helmets, who cares how fast we go?

She'd been terrified that day as Binnie had thrown what she now knew was a stolen machine around the bends of the country lanes close to their home, her knee almost touching the tarmac as he'd leaned into the bends, her arms tight round his waist.

She'd finally understood that the more she screamed, the tighter she held on, the faster he went, but at the time she had convinced herself that she loved it. That fear was part of the excitement.

She knew better now. Fear was just fear, pure and simple and utterly consuming.

'I hate him,' she managed to whisper.

'Then why—?'

Sian pulled away. How could she explain? How could her mother possibly understand? 'Just because,' she said. Then, hoping it would sound more emphatic, 'Because he's my friend. Because I . . .' Sian wiped her eyes and stepped even further away, though all she really wanted to do was collapse back into her mother's embrace and ask her to fix it all, just like she used to. 'Forget it,' she said angrily. 'I don't want to talk about it any more.'

Her mother looked away and Sian knew that she too was blinking back tears. But what could she do? What could anyone do? Sian was implicated. Binnie had told her she'd go to prison

83

and had whispered in her ear what would happen to her there. But that was nothing compared to the threats he had made against those she loved. Threats she knew he'd have no hesitation in carrying out.

She wiped her eyes again and picked up her discarded brush. Dipped it angrily into the paint laid out on her palette. 'I have to work,' she said. 'I'm all right now. Don't fuss so much.'

Knowing she was going to get no further, her mother sighed and went away and Sian stared after her, willing her away; willing her to come back.

It was only after she'd watched her mother go back inside, through the kitchen door, that Sian looked at the canvas. She'd not noticed what colour had been picked up on to the brush and now an angry crimson streak spread from one side of her canvas to the other, burying the figure she'd been painting in a slash of red.

Binnie was several miles away. His boss had kept him waiting again, sitting on one of the uncomfortable hall chairs that were lined up against one wall in the square lobby. The floor was tiled in black and white and red and partly concealed by a finely knotted Persian rug.

It was usual for him to keep Binnie waiting; his way of letting Binnie know how unimportant he was in the scheme of things. Binnie had researched the psychology of this and knew exactly what he was meant to feel so he resolutely refused to see it that way. Instead, he caught up with his emails and took a look at the news. On one occasion, early in the relationship with his boss, he had walked over to take a look at the display cabinet that occupied the opposite wall and was packed with antiquities. Egyptian shabti, cuneiform tablets, tiny Roman bronzes, sitting beside examples of more modern glass. The owner, his boss, had of course chosen that moment to come down the flight of sweeping stairs and hold forth about his treasures and what they might be worth. It hadn't taken Binnie long to realize that was exactly what his boss had been waiting for, for Binnie to show an interest so that he could show off.

Binnie had never given him another opportunity. Now, he minded his own business or he considered the state of the world, skimming websites from the BBC to Al Jazeera to CNN and taking in some of the conspiracy sites along the way. He was with the guy on *Men in Black*, you had to read the worst of the tabloids if you really wanted to know what was going on and then you had to read the respectable press to understand what the majority – and their masters – wanted to believe was happening.

Today he'd been kept waiting for close on an hour. Had skimmed his emails and his Facebook account and then the main headlines. He was taking in one of his favourite truther domains when the man who reckoned to be his lord and master waltzed down the stairs.

'Good morning, Binnie.'

Binnie logged off and then nodded to the man. 'Morning.'

'Have you had lunch? I'm just about to.'

'No thanks. Got stuff to do.'

'We'll make this quick, then.'

Same questions every time, Binnie thought. Lunch, tea, supper – occasionally even breakfast, if Binnie had been summoned early. His opportunity to deliver largesse and Binnie's to refuse. A game they played. One day, Binnie promised himself, he'd shock the cunt by saying yes. He could imagine the shock – swiftly hidden, to be sure – and the awkward conversation over bacon and eggs or lobster or whatever the fucker ate. He lived alone and if he occasionally had guests – Binnie had sometimes seen a second car parked when he arrived – they never put in an appearance when Binnie was there.

'So, what's up then?' Binnie asked.

The man lifted a hand and a door opened close to the stairs. A woman emerged, carrying a set of overalls. Binnie took a good look at her – the first person, apart from his ersatz boss, that he'd seen in this massive house. She was middle-aged, greying hair and dressed in a smart blue dress. Like a secretary, Binnie thought. Or a PA. Respectable looking.

She held out the overalls and the boss took them, then she went away, disappearing through the wide wood-panelled door.

He likes his theatrics, Binnie thought.

'So?'

'So, for the job I had in mind, you might want to wear these. Your clothes are likely to get dirty.'

'I'm not a bloody cleaner, you know.'

'In a manner of speaking, you are, today. Come

with me. Nothing too onerous, I promise, and I think you'll enjoy it.'

Binnie took the proffered garment and then followed. They exited by the door through which the secretary, or whatever she was, had departed and Binnie noted with interest that the only door furniture was on the other side. There was no obvious means of opening it from the hall – which explained why he'd not taken note of it before. This had, he thought, probably been a service corridor so that the servants could come and go without being seen. He figured whoever wanted to build and own a house like this probably didn't want to be tripping over the hired help all the time. He wondered how many people *actually* lived and worked here.

Binnie was surprised to find that the corridor emerged outside. He could smell food so decided they'd emerged close to the kitchen. He followed the leader across the yard and into what he supposed had been a stable block but was now some kind of CCTV room. The man watching the cameras got up and left as they entered and Binnie got only a glimpse of someone with dark hair wearing a charcoal suit. It seemed his lord and master liked his staff nicely dressed. Binnie, currently dressed in jeans, a blue T-shirt and a warm jacket probably didn't fit the bill.

'Him.' The boss man was pointing at the CCTV screens, two of which were trained on an empty stable. Empty, apart from a man lying on a heap of straw. The other screens, which Binnie had noted were switched on as they entered, were now all blank.

'Who is he?' Binnie asked.

'Someone who was meant to get something for me. He failed. Someone who swears our old friend Freddie Jones must have concealed the thing I wanted or that the daughter must know where it is, but so far he's failed to find it. I'm not pleased.'

Maybe you should have held off killing Freddie, Binnie thought. Then you might have been able to ask him straight up. Freddie had been disposed of in what Binnie considered was a fit of pique – something he'd found interesting. It meant this man who liked to see himself as the big 'I am' was not as in control as he liked to think he was.

'So?' Binnie asked again.

'So, I want him to know that I don't like failure. Change your clothes, Binnie, have some fun.'

Binnie raised an eyebrow. Maybe the day was going to be interesting after all. 'You want me to find out what he knows?'

'I don't think he knows anything worth telling. I don't care what happens, Binnie. Do what you like and do it how you like. The mess will be cleaned up after you've gone. I'll just settle myself here and watch. I take it you don't mind an audience?'

Binnie looked long and hard at his boss and then long and hard at the man. He was small and fragile looking. Sinewy rather than muscular. 'He won't last five minutes,' Binnie said.

'Does that matter?'

'Not to me.' Binnie began to shed his clothes, folding them neatly and placing them on a chair.

It looked as if this was a surveillance room built for two. He stripped down to his underwear and then donned the overalls.

He was directed back through the door they'd entered by and given a key to the stable block below. The stall in which the man lay was bolted. Binnie slid the bolt and stepped inside.

'Hello,' he said. 'Got a message from our boss. Seems he doesn't like people letting him down.' Binnie glanced up where he guessed the camera would be, conscious that he'd have to put on a good show.

The other man cowered away from him, excuses and pleas rising to his lips. Binnie could hear him jabber but, after the first expression of sorrow and fear, was no longer listening to the words. A slow smile spread across his face. His boss had made no offer of weaponry but Binnie had fists and feet and that would be enough.

'Come here,' he said softly. 'Let's see just how sorry you really are.'

Afterwards, Binnie washed his hands and face in the cloakroom next to the surveillance suite and stripped off the overalls, tossing them aside. He dressed and then waited, wondering what to do next. His employer hadn't been in the control room when he'd come back. Once or twice Binnie had glanced at the screen, at the bloodied mess he had left behind, but he had detached from the incident and was simply waiting for whatever came next.

After a while the door opened again and the woman he had met earlier came in. She held a plain brown envelope in her hand and she laid it down on the console in front of the cameras.

'You can go now,' she said. 'If you go through the yard and follow the wall round, you'll get back to the front of the house.'

Binnie's eyes narrowed. He didn't like the summary dismissal but the woman seemed unperturbed. She opened the door and left. Binnie followed her down and watched as she crossed back into the house. She turned to glance at him before opening the door and going back inside.

Binnie paused, envelope clutched in his hand, thinking, then he returned to the CCTV room, or tried to. He'd been certain that the boss man had opened the door but now he could see that there was no handle on the outside and he recalled that when he'd come back from the stable the door had already been opened wide.

There must be some other way of getting inside. A remote control or gate fob or something.

Binnie pushed against the door and then slammed against it, hard. It didn't budge. It might be wood on the outside, he realized, but it was reinforced behind that.

'Fuck,' he said. It had dawned on him that when he'd followed the woman down the stairs, momentarily distracted both by her and by the brown envelope, he hadn't thought things through. The overalls. They were covered in the victim's blood and in Binnie's DNA.

Furious with himself, he went back down into the yard. No sign of a living soul, and a quick investigation revealed the doors to the kitchen and hall to be locked and similarly reinforced.

90

Binnie stomped his way back to his car and got inside. Then he opened the brown envelope and flicked through the notes. More money than he had guessed, simply from the thickness of the wad. And a typed note.

The world being what it is, we all have to have our insurance policies. I'm sure you understand.

Understand, Binnie thought, glaring up at the house and knowing he hadn't got a hope in hell of making it back inside, not until he was summoned at any rate. He couldn't do a thing.

At least, not yet.

Fourteen

The afternoon was overcast and heavily grey – she didn't need to be able to see to know that; the dampness in the air and the mild depression that seemed to pervade everyone's mood was enough. She stayed at the advice centre for the extra hour, seeing a couple of people who had just walked in off the street needing assistance in addition to the appointments. George Mallard came to collect her just before two. The restaurant was only fifteen minutes away and Alfie had said he'd booked for two fifteen.

Naomi was hungry. And curious. She hoped to satisfy both appetites.

'Shall I walk you inside?' George asked when they arrived.

'If you don't mind, that would be great.'

George was an old friend and Naomi had become very reliant on his taxi service. He and his sons all knew what she needed and how to help.

George made sure she exited the taxi safely and then placed Napoleon's harness in her hand. He took her arm. 'Two shallow steps up, then double doors,' he said.

'And you must be Naomi,' a voice said. 'Alfie Kounis. Pleased to meet you.'

She felt him shake hands with George and released her hand from George's arm so she could do the same. His grip was firm but not excessively so and there were calluses at the top of his palm that spoke of a hobby or activity more physical than she imagined private investigation to be.

'You'll be all right, will you?' George checked. 'Give me a call when you're ready to go and we'll come and get you, me or one of the lads.'

'I think that's me put on notice,' Alfie said, amusement in his voice.

'George is a good friend,' she said. 'He makes a point of looking out for me.'

'Well, I hope I passed muster.'

There was no sarcasm in the comment, Naomi noted. 'If you didn't, I'll be told,' she said.

Alfie laughed. 'I'm hungry,' he said. 'I hope you are. What do we do about your dog? Does he need anything?'

'He was sorted before I left work,' she said. 'He'll have his food when we get home. Don't worry, Napoleon is happy and he knows not to beg when he's on duty.'

Alfie took her arm, a little tentatively, and led her into the body of the restaurant. They must have entered through a reception area, Naomi thought, remembering that this was also a hotel. Alfie gave his name and they were led to a table. 'I'd like a jug of tap water, please,' Alfie said. 'And a beer, I think. What do you have? Naomi, what would you like to drink? Shall I read the drinks menu to you?'

'What beers do they have? That sounds nice.'

'Great.' He sounded happy about that. Naomi settled back in her chair, Napoleon at her feet. She felt disposed to like this man. She felt even more so when, having ordered drinks, he read the menu to her and told her what dishes he'd enjoyed here before. He was a man who evidently took his food choices seriously and hoped his guest would do the same.

'So,' he said, as they waited for their food to arrive, 'what can I tell you? Annie said I should be completely open with you, so maybe we should start with what you know already and go from there?'

'Sounds like a plan. You've known Bob and Annie for a long time?'

'Annie, yes. Since she was a scraggy teenager.' He sounded fond, Naomi thought. 'All long limbs and awkwardness. She's grown into an exceptional woman. But I'm sure you know that.'

Naomi smiled. Alfie's tone was friendly but there was an unmistakable warning there. He was here to tell her all about his investigation into Freddie Jones. Annie was off limits in anything but the broadest terms. 'I do,' she said. 'And

93

Patrick is really fond of both of them. They've been good to him.'

'Bob and Annie think he's got real talent,' Alfie said. 'And he's been through a lot in his short life, Annie understands.'

Naomi nodded throughtfully.

'So, Freddie Jones,' Alfie reminded her. 'Another very talented man. What do you know so far?'

Naomi was aware that she was probably going over what was old ground for Alfie but she started at what for her was the beginning, Patrick's encounter with Freddie's daughter. She kept as much detail in the telling as she could and then talked about her own research, such as it was, into Freddie and the Scott murder. She finished by telling him that she knew the SIO leading the investigation into Antonia Scott's death.

Food arrived and they were silent for a few minutes, giving it and their hunger full attention.

Alfie picked up the conversation again. 'DI Karen Morgan, I've read about her. She's got a good rep.'

'Deservedly so,' Naomi told him, feeling suddenly defensive about her old friend.

'But she's getting nowhere at the moment,' Alfie added. 'Not so much a matter of the trail going cold as there being no trail to begin with, from what I understand.'

'What do you look like?' Naomi interrupted him. 'Sorry, I'm still a bit stuck in pre-blind mode, I like to have an idea, you know?'

Alfie chuckled. 'I think I'd be the same,' he said. 'Well, I suppose I'm a bit of a mix-up. Dad was Portuguese and Mum was mixed race, so if you imagine a white British, Latin, African hybrid, you'd be near the mark. I've got my mum's brown eyes and my father's skin, olive rather than really dark, and his nose, unfortunately. Not the prettiest nose around. I'm getting a little thin on top – courtesy of granddad Fred – so I keep it cropped, but left to its own devices my hair is very dark and would curl. I grow a beard in winter but I've just shaved it off. I'm hoping to encourage spring to arrive; nothing else seems to be working.' He paused. 'Does that give you a picture?'

'That will do nicely, thank you.'

'I could be lying, of course. But no doubt you'll ask your taxi driving friend.'

'No doubt I will. So, what do you know that I don't?'

Silence fell again as Alfie considered this and they both enjoyed more of their meal. Finally he said, 'Well, I've prepared a dossier for you. Annie says you can use a hand scanner and then read back? Anyway, she said you've got the technology to deal with written documents, but I have also put things on a stick so you can use read back on your computer.'

Naomi thanked him, surprised.

'The long and the short of it is, in the early days Freddie was heavily involved not only in forging art objects and paintings but in faking the provenance for them. You probably know some of that but what I've pinned down is absolute proof for at least a half dozen objects. He was arrested, charged and eventually imprisoned

95

and he entertained himself in jail with drawing cartoons and caricatures of the other prisoners. No doubt that earned him an easier ride than he might have had. Once he got out he seems to have focused on his legitimate work and made his living doing restorations, copies and original work. Things changed about three years ago and I'm still not quite sure why.'

'Not money or any of the usual reasons, then?'

'No. Look, Freddie's never been brilliantly well off but he's always been comfortable. He's been assiduous in putting money aside for his daughter and he's lived very simply, almost frugally. At the time of his death he had about five thousand pounds in the bank and he had no mortgage on his house. The house itself is tiny, two up two down plus a bathroom in what was the coal shed. It's got a long yard, mostly paved, with a small brick building at the end that he sometimes used as a studio. Other than that he mostly rented studio space somewhere and he went for the cheap options. He wasn't one for working in artist communities. He wasn't one for working anywhere where people could take too much notice of what he was doing. Two years ago he set up in his present studio when he started to rent space in a warehouse. You know about that?'

'Yes, Bee told me all about it. She's not looking forward to clearing it out.'

'I don't imagine she is. From what I've seen of the house, the home studio and the studio at the warehouse, there's an awful lot of stuff to deal with. Bob and Annie will help her, I'm sure, and it sounds as though your Patrick's going to

96

get involved. I hope Harry has room for some more art materials at their place.'

Naomi raised an eyebrow. 'You do your research, then.' But she wasn't really surprised.

'Annie likes Harry a lot. She says he's one of the most honest and straightforward men she's ever met, and that's high praise.'

'And she's dead right about that. So what caused Freddie to go back to his old ways? You must have some theories.'

'Well, at first I thought it might have something to do with the daughter. He's always been financially responsible but that's not the same as having a young woman arrive on the scene, who needs her father to do things with her and for her. Teenagers are expensive.'

'You sound like a man who knows.'

Alfie just laughed. 'But I don't think that's the case. As I said, Freddie was not rich but he was comfortable enough and I looked back into his financial records and there is no sudden blip in what he was earning or certainly in what he was putting in the bank. Now it's entirely possible he had a cash stash somewhere, or reinvested it, and I haven't found the paper trail yet.' He paused and then said, 'You should know that my work has always been, shall we say, in the less active realms. I'm no Nathan or Annie. The work I did with their guardian was always forensic. I chase paper, not criminals. I look into shell companies, I examine people's financials. If Freddie was investing I will find out what he was investing in. If Freddie was being blackmailed, I'll find a trace of that too. I'm good at what I do, but there are gaps in what I'm able to discover. I'm sort of hoping that your friend Karen will be able to fill in those gaps. What I'm asking is, do you think she'd be open to a meeting?'

Naomi stared at him, or would have done if she could actually see him, but the action was the same. 'If you don't mind me saying, that's a bit of a cheeky question.'

'I don't mind you saying, and yes, it is. But I'd rather be straight. I'm getting insights that lead me to think that Freddie was in up to his neck or even over his head. That Freddie had some reason to be scared. He'd taken out additional life insurance, updated his will, added a new alarm system to the house, and Mark Brookes, the man he sublet his studio space from, said that he was jumpy, always checking the doors were locked all of a sudden, and that he asked him, a couple of weeks before he died, to keep an eye on the studio, should anything untoward happen. He wouldn't be drawn on what.

'Now, I can chase the paper so far, I can examine the figures and I can draw conclusions and I can even put names to transactions but what I can't do is investigate the criminality in a way that a police officer could. Or rather, I could, but Annie has instructed me that this investigation is to be totally legitimate and above board. I'm to do nothing that could not be used in court. I'm sure you can understand how that ties my hands, but she is right.'

Naomi considered. The waiter had come back with a dessert list and she listened as Alfie read it out to her. She laughed. 'Black Forest gâteau – does anybody do that any more? I'm amazed.'

'Haven't you heard? It's become fashionable again, alongside deconstructed prawn cocktail.'

'I think I'll have to have some then, won't I?'

Alfie ordered a crème brûlée and the waiter went away.

'I'd like a coffee after, would you like one too?'

Naomi nodded. 'Yes, I think that might be a good idea.'

'The restaurant area will be closing, but we can go through to the lounge. It's nice in there, big bay windows and comfy chairs.'

'I'll ask Karen to meet you,' Naomi told him. 'But you've got to understand, she'll probably consider you are duty bound to hand over any evidence regardless and also, I've not seen her in years. She'd be totally within her rights to tell me to get lost for trying to use her.'

'And as I said, I prepared a dossier that you can share with her and I'm very willing to talk through anything she doesn't understand. Naomi, I get the feeling this is more serious than any of us suspected. I get the feeling there is big – and I mean very big – money at stake here. Freddie obviously crossed someone, made somebody so angry that his usefulness was overridden, and they had him killed. His daughter is right, there does need to be a second post-mortem. The first just confirmed heart failure and as everybody was expecting him to die of heart disease some time or other that was no surprise. The only reason there was a post-mortem in the first place was that he'd failed to see his doctor as frequently as a man in his condition ought to have done.'

Naomi nodded. Dessert arrived and Alfie ordered coffee and told the waiter that they would take both through to the lounge. Once settled, Naomi asked him, 'And who might be responsible – do you have a name?'

'I have several, but that doesn't mean they are all involved. My money is on someone by the name of Graham Harcourt. He is a collector but also a businessman with a finger in every pie you could care to mention. He has a big house out near Otteringham, a posh Georgian place. I've done a bit of surveillance but the security system extends to the perimeter walls around his estate. Put it this way, I've seen Category A prisons with less security. None of it is obvious, but it covers every corner. A robin couldn't cross his garden without him knowing about it and if he could get away with putting notices on the gate telling people that trespassers would be shot, I think he probably would. There's a gatehouse at the main entrance, used to be occupied by the gardener. Since Harcourt moved in the gardener's gone and what looks like an extensive CCTV and security system set up in there is manned twenty-four hours. I had an associate of mine ask for directions and the guy he spoke to was polite enough, directed him back to the main road. My friend managed to get a couple of photos, one of the man and one through the window of the gatehouse, but he'd been told not to take risks and he didn't take any more. I've added those pictures to the dossier. I know they're not much use to you, but they might be of use to your friend. If she can make other connections.'

Naomi ate her dessert, deep in thought. It was very good, far more sophisticated than the cake of her childhood and so drenched in kirsch that she thought she might be over the limit, had she still been able to drive. She felt the edge of the table and set her plate down with a deep sigh. 'That was excellent; something that definitely needs to be revived. OK, I will talk to her and I think she'll see the sense in at least having a conversation. Can I give her your number?'

'My card's in the folder with the rest of the stuff. It has my business phone number on it and a brochure for the company I work for, so she can see I'm all legit.'

Naomi laughed at that. 'Anybody can create a brochure,' she said. 'Anybody can even register their business at Companies House. It doesn't make them legitimate.'

'What does?' Alfie asked.

But she knew he wasn't expecting any kind of answer.

They chatted over coffee, random things, tacitly acknowledging that their business was done and they could now relax. Naomi called for her taxi and Alfie walked her out.

'It was genuinely good to meet you,' he said. 'And I hope we meet again.'

Naomi smiled as she drove away. She was hoping so too.

101

Fifteen

Naomi called Karen just after seven on the Saturday evening. It had taken all her self-restraint to wait until after seven and not try ten minutes before, though she'd been impatient all day. She'd spent Saturday going through the electronic version of Alfie's dossier, using the read back facility on her computer. There was a lot of information, and it had taken her most of the day to start to get to grips with what he was finding out. She found it frustrating no longer to be able to take physical written notes which she could flick back and forth. The Dictaphone helped, but it wasn't the same.

Alfie described himself as a forensic researcher and that certainly fitted with what he had given to her. The level of detail was outstanding.

Alfie had tracked down five works, and a possible sixth, that were known to be by Freddie Jones, from his early days before his arrest. He had since identified a possible half dozen more and these were much more recent. All had come up for auction in the last two years and all had sold for high prices. Old masters, or their followers, but not the most well known names. No Vermeers, she thought. Alfie described them as 'second division' but still excellent. And in all cases the provenance could be tracked back at least a couple of centuries with only small gaps in the paper trail. All the works had been referred to in the catalogue raisonné for each artist and they were works that were believed to have been lost. All had emerged in ways that were plausible and had raised no suspicion. They had apparently been miscatalogued. Some had turned up in the attic of some big house. One, it seemed, had been hanging in a public library for years before someone had noticed it and recognized it as the work of a possible follower of Pieter Bruegel the Elder – though the strange thing was that Alfie had interviewed a long-term employee of the library who did not remember the picture at all, even though it appeared in an inventory list for twenty-five years before.

In each case, doubts seem to have been swept aside and only the evidence which supported provenance was emphasized. As Alfie had commented, there was a lot of money involved and no one wanted to believe that these paintings were anything less than genuine. Once appraised, reputations were on the line.

Karen picked up on the third ring. Hearing her voice, Naomi was reminded that they had actually had a lot of fun together and she was glad that she had made the decision to make contact again, even if it had been driven by external factors.

'It's so good to talk to you,' she said, genuinely meaning it. 'I should have done this long ago.'

'Nothing like the odd murder to rekindle a friendship,' Karen said. 'It's good to hear from you too. I've often thought about you. God, what a day! You and Alec are well out of it, you know that, don't you?'

'We regularly talk to ex-colleagues here,' Naomi said. 'I'm pretty sure Alec wouldn't go back now, even if he could. I don't actually have the option, but if I did, I'm not sure I would either. The workload seems to have got worse week on week. There seems to be a new form to fill in every month, and masses of paperwork to do. And people say that trying to get their TOIL time back is even worse than it was when we were in the job. There's been money for new recruitment, but it's getting the bodies. Nobody seems to want to know. And it doesn't help that we're pretty much in the back of beyond, up here; if you want a career path you go to one of the big cities.'

'Failing that, to one of the small cities,' Karen agreed. 'But no, it's not getting any better, although I think every generation of coppers must say that.' She laughed. 'But what else would I do? I came into this straight from university; I've never done anything else. And when I think about leaving I just hear the pension calling. I never thought I'd say this, Naomi, but I'm getting to the age where those sorts of things matter! Sad, or what? Anyway, down to business; what can I do for you? Or maybe what can you do for me?'

Naomi grinned. This was the opening she had looked for, the opening she'd hoped that her friend would provide her with. 'Well,' she said, settling back on to the sofa, Napoleon's heavy head resting on her knee, 'yesterday I had lunch with a very interesting man. I couldn't tell you if he was good-looking or not, but he had a nice handshake and apparently has dark curly hair

– that's when he lets it grow. But he's got good taste in restaurants.'

'And did he pay?'

'He would have done, but we went Dutch. He said he could pass it off as a business expense, but you never know where that sort of thing is going to lead, do you?' She giggled childishly, and Karen joined in.

'And does Alec know about this other man?'

'Alec is away. But yes, he knows.'

'So this is the private investigator you were telling me about?'

'Alfie Kounis, yes. He's been good enough to put everything he found out into a folder and has given me an electronic copy so I can email it. I've not quite got the hang of zipping everything together yet, so you might get several emails with different files, but I'll get it sent over later tonight. He's sort of hoping you'll agree to a meeting, pool resources. I've told him I'll ask you.'

'Have you now? I'm not so sure about that,' but Naomi could hear the smile in her voice. 'To be honest, if he's got something to offer, I may be able to bring him in on a consultancy basis. The fact that I'm saying that tells you I'm a bit desperate. There's been nothing, and I mean nothing. The only leads I've got have come from looking into Freddie Jones's background, and they're pretty skimpy.'

'Alfie reckons he was back to his old tricks,' Naomi told her.

'Alfie is probably right. I've come to the same conclusion. We've probably been chasing the same rabbits down the same rabbit hole, and believe me, it's definitely *Alice in Wonderland* out there. But I wonder if he's got this? I think Freddie was being blackmailed into it. I think he was being threatened and that it had been going on for quite a while and my sense is that he was ready to throw in the towel, maybe ask for help, but someone got to him before he could.'

'Really? That would probably explain a lot of things. But I'm not sure it explains why Antonia Scott was killed. And it's certain nothing else was taken?'

'No, only the portfolio. Which makes about as much sense as—'

'It does, doesn't it? OK, so what do we do now?'

'What do *we* do? Well, officially, you send me the stuff that you've got and *I* will look over it and *I* will decide what needs to be done.'

'And unofficially?'

'I thought we might have a meet-up, have a chat and maybe even meet this Alfie. Naomi, you realize—'

'What's it called?' Naomi said, 'Plausible deniability.'

'Oooh, I like that. Yes, definitely that. So, when are you free and what the hell do I program into the satnav to get to you?'

Naomi spent the best part of the next hour attaching files one by one and sending them to her friend. She felt excited, as though finally she was getting to do something she was good at again. She knew that there could never be anything but informal conversations about this, that they were off the record and Karen would have to be very careful about what she said, but she was still involved and that was important. Next, she called Alfie and told him that, in principle, DI Karen Morgan was interested in meeting with him and was now in possession of the information he had given to Naomi.

After that she sat back on the sofa, feeling slightly bereft. She was on her own again, on a Saturday night, and had done all she could do. Now she had a choice: an early night or a late film. She was relieved when Alec called. He didn't have much time but thought he'd say good night and ask about her day.

'Interesting,' she said. 'I spoke to Karen this evening. We might be meeting up next week.'

'And I take it this isn't just a social occasion?'

'You can take it that it's *also* a social occasion. Look, I'll tell you all about it tomorrow – you'll still be home tomorrow?'

Alec assured her that he would be, although it probably wouldn't be before five or six. He'd give her a ring the following morning.

She felt even more bereft when he'd rung off. 'Get a grip, Naomi. He'll be back tomorrow,' she told herself. She decided to combine the early night with the late film and took her tablet to bed with her, but fell asleep listening to explosions and gunfire.

Sixteen

Listening to the news on the Sunday morning, Binnie was interested to hear about a man who had been found on waste ground the night before. It was thought that he had lain there for quite some time; he was severely injured and in intensive care. Police were appealing for witnesses, particularly a woman who had phoned in anonymously to tell them about what she thought was a body. It was an area frequented by doggers, and it was thought that the woman had probably been involved in what the police referred to as 'illicit sexual activity' in the area. They assured anyone involved that they were not interested in this, but simply wanted to know what they had seen. They also suggested that the area was used by more innocent dog walkers in the daytime; had they viewed any suspicious activity or noticed what might've appeared to be a bundle of old clothes lying on the concrete, half concealed beneath rubbish?

Binnie knew instinctively that this was his man. He was quite impressed that he was still alive. Tough little bleeder, aren't you? he said to himself. Whoever the fuck you are.

He was, however, quite surprised that his boss hadn't finished the job that Binnie had started. He wondered if whoever dumped the body had assumed they were just disposing of a

108

corpse or at the very least someone about to become a corpse.

Binnie finished his second cup of tea and thought about getting some more toast. His phone rang. Binnie recognized the number and wondered if he was about to be rebuked for not actually killing the man in the stable but not a word was said about that.

'Job for you,' his employer told him. 'Listen up, this is what I want you to do. How is up to you.'

Binnie listened, smiled and hung up. He checked the time. More toast, then he would go and collect Sian. They would both go and see what Freddie's daughter was getting up to this morning.

Alec phoned just after eight and told Naomi that he was going to get a bit more sleep and then drive back. He would try and be with her for five o'clock and suggested they find somewhere to go and have dinner together. He'd be at home for all of the next week, including the weekend, and was clearly looking forward to it.

Patrick called to collect Bee at ten and they drove to Annie and Bob's. Bee told him she'd had a really good time at the family wedding, that it had been so good to reconnect with people. She seemed much more cheerful and Patrick was glad about that. He didn't have much in the way of family, but what he had he valued greatly and it was good to hear that Bee now felt that she had much more of a support system than she'd thought.

He noticed a blue car across the road from her flat, a Volkswagen Golf, with two people sitting in it. The only reason he noticed was that the street was still quite empty on a Sunday morning and the man turned to look at him as Patrick drove away, but he soon forgot about it.

They were going to go to Bob's first, to compile a list of things that Bob thought might be worth looking out for in Freddie's studio. He'd suggested going with them, but he was already way behind with work and Bee had assured him that she and Patrick would be fine, that all she needed was a bit of guidance on what to bring back. Patrick was really quite glad that he and Beatrix were going on their own, especially as she seemed in such a buoyant mood. He liked her anyway, but being with somebody who was totally introspective could be difficult and he felt that this morning he was seeing another side of her. He asked a lot of questions about the wedding, wanting to keep the mood alive.

The buoyant tone continued when they got to Annie's. Bee had a whole stack of photos on her phone and she and Annie spent a happy half hour looking through them and admiring the dresses and the cake and laughing at the drunk uncles and the daft hats. Bob and Patrick compiled the list and then they were off again.

They were halfway to the studio when Patrick noticed the blue car with two people inside, and there was something about it that bothered him. He realized it was because he'd seen a blue VW Golf, like this one, also containing two people, outside Bee's flat, and the coincidence seemed

110

odd but the car turned off a couple of miles before they had reached the studio and so he stopped worrying. He did make an effort to memorize the number plate, though. He parked up where Bee instructed and as they got out he took a good look around but there was no sign of that light blue car, or any similar ones, and so Patrick was able to reassure himself that he was imagining things. Even so, the back of his neck prickled and before they went into the studio he texted Annie and mentioned it to her. He knew she'd be out walking the dogs, so he probably wouldn't get a quick response. He told himself it probably wasn't even *worth* the response; there were a lot of blue cars and probably a lot of blue Volkswagens in the world.

As it was Sunday, the industrial estate was practically deserted. Here and there vans and cars were parked up but there was no sign of anyone working. Patrick assumed that there would be folk around, but there was no one in view. For such a built-up area it was astonishingly lonely and he was surprised to find how little he liked it; how uncomfortable it made him feel.

Lately, he had been very sensitive to the way places felt and more than a little suspicious of people. His recent experiences had taught him that even the most benign seeming individual might be hiding secrets he'd rather not know about and he had recently come into contact with someone who, although outwardly very respectable, turned out to be a serial killer. Patrick reflected that he had been shaken far more than he had at first admitted by his brush with death.

He had never felt uncomfortable around Gregory or Nathan, even though he knew exactly what they were and what they were capable of. Ridiculously, perhaps, they made him feel safe – though he supposed that was not so ridiculous, considering what he owed them: he would not have survived without them. But they were not people he talked about except to Naomi and Alec, and of course Bob and Annie. His was a strangely compartmentalized life, he supposed. Of course Harry, his father, knew all about Gregory and Nathan and even called them friends. A most peculiar state of affairs if you actually thought about it, Harry being one of the most truly respectable people Patrick could think of.

'Penny for them,' Bee said as they mounted the stairs to the mezzanine floor.

'Shouldn't you lock that door?' Patrick nodded towards the small side entrance they had come through.

She frowned. 'I never really bother. You can if you like, if it makes you feel better.'

Patrick went back down the stairs and threw the bolts top and bottom. He didn't like the fact that he couldn't see out.

'I think we should hurry up,' he said as he rejoined Bee in the studio. Then he took a look around and whatever nagging instinct had dominated his thoughts so far faded back into insignificance. This was Freddie Jones's studio. Freddie's work was everywhere: drawings, small paintings and art materials under the two great big skylights.

Bee laughed at him, recognizing what it was

he saw. 'I love this place,' she said. 'I'm dreading having to clear it out.'

'Bob and I will help you, we told you that.'

'I know, and I'm grateful. I suppose I just keep putting it off. Somehow it's like getting rid of Freddie if I get rid of all the stuff in this place but I don't have any option. My little flat is far too small to fit any of this stuff in and Freddie's house is much too far from anything for me to want to live there, so that's got to go too. I've got that to clear out and put up for sale as well.'

She bit her lip anxiously and Patrick took a closer look at the stacks of paper, canvases and panels propped against the wall, drawers filled with inks and pens and paints and jars of brushes set on the side. 'I think he might have been a bit of a hoarder,' he said cautiously.

She laughed. 'Just a bit. The thing is I don't know what to keep, I don't know enough about what he was doing. I'm not an artist and though I loved his work, to be honest I'm a bit more like my mum. She always wanted me to study medicine, like she had.'

That, Patrick owned, was his idea of hell, but he understood that everyone was different. He opened another drawer and began to rummage inside. This one seemed to be full of photo references, colour swatches and pebbles. He took out a stone and held it out to Bee. 'He's got enough in there to start a small rockery. What were they for?'

She took it from him, weighing it in her palm. 'He just liked to pick up stones,' she said. 'Wherever we went, he'd come back with a

113

pebble. Mum said he used to do it when she was with him, drove her mad. He used to pile them up in a big bowl and when the bowl got full he tipped them out into the garden. He was like a kid in some ways.'

Patrick nodded, thinking of his own collection of small pebbles, something he'd been doing since he was a kid. He had thought about it just as an artist thing, but Naomi did the same. Though she chose them for the way they felt and Patrick for the way they looked. 'We'd best get on and find what we came for,' he said. 'I've a feeling it might take us a while.'

She nodded. 'I think most of it's in those drawers over there. There's another portfolio and that has the sketches in for a Madonna.' She frowned suddenly.

'What is it?' Patrick asked.

'Did you knock those letters on to the floor?'

Patrick looked where she indicated. A half dozen letters lay on the floor near the layout table. 'No, I've not been around that side.'

'No, you've not, have you? Maybe Danny came up for something and knocked them over. I forgot to take them with me last time I was here.'

She picked them up and flicked through the envelopes quickly before laying them back on the table. 'They look like bills and junk mail. I'll have a squint at them and then give the bills to the solicitor. Thankfully Freddie made his solicitor his executor so I don't have to sort out all the financial stuff. I wouldn't know where to start. It was bad enough after Mum died, and she'd done most of it for me.'

114

Patrick stared at the letters for a moment, wondering if she was right and Danny had knocked them off the table. If not, then someone else had been here. Bee had told him about the night she was here when she thought she'd heard a noise downstairs. She'd brushed it off, but now that nag was back in Patrick's brain and he wondered again about the blue car that had seemed to follow them.

'Are there any windows here? I mean that we can actually look out of?'

'Um, yeah, in the ground floor office. They face out towards the front, not where we came in. The door should be undone.' Then she frowned. 'Why, you worried about something? You've been a bit odd since we got here. You thinking about that car again? It was probably just coincidence, you know. Why would anyone be following us here from Bob's place? You make it sound like someone followed me from home.'

She smiled at him, trying to reassure them both, and Patrick nodded. Maybe he was overreacting, he thought, and he said, 'You're probably right. I suppose I'm just being a bit nervy.'

She looked at him curiously and then came over to where he stood and opened one of the big plan drawers. She withdrew a cardboard folder and laid it on the table and then took out another stack of drawings. 'I think these might be what we want.'

Patrick touched the stack gently and then began to sort through it. 'These are beautiful.'

'Yeah, he was good, wasn't he?'

More than good, Patrick thought. The head of

115

the Madonna was sketched in sanguine with chalk highlights and there was a delicacy and sensitivity that reminded him of the greatest Renaissance artists. The drawings were made with such tenderness; Freddie must have loved creating this.

'So,' Bee said, 'how much of this stuff should we take with us?'

'I suppose all of it,' Patrick said. 'Do you have a spare portfolio? It won't all fit in the cardboard folder and anyway, we shouldn't risk these getting wet if it starts to rain while we're packing up.'

'There's probably one behind the sofa, but we could do with a box to put the smaller stuff in.'

Patrick went in search of a portfolio while Bee foraged for a box. He tried not to get distracted by all the treasures in Freddie's studio and had to admit to himself that even though he felt sorry for Bee with all her problems, he was actively looking forward to helping clear this place out. He hoped she'd remember her promise that any paints and brushes and stuff that she didn't need, or that Bob didn't want, Patrick could have. Art materials were expensive and he had seen equipment here that he could never have afforded and would be very reluctant to ask his father for, even though Harry would undoubtedly have bought it for him. Harry didn't really understand what Patrick did and how much he needed to do it but he'd been fully supportive. It was funny, Patrick thought, the way people turned out. In Harry's working life he had always been involved with figures and now he was a self-employed accountant. No one was quite sure where Patrick's artistic tendencies had appeared from. Bee had a father like Freddie and yet she took after her mother and, as she had once put it, couldn't draw for toffee.

He retrieved the portfolio and brought it back to the table. There were a few sketches already in one of the pockets, but he left them there and simply arranged the other drawings as carefully as he could inside. 'Shall I put the letters in here too, so you don't forget them?'

'Good idea.' She had found a box that had held printer paper and into this she put the smaller sketchbooks and some of the loose drawings. Freddie clearly had a tendency to scribble on anything and Patrick was amused to see that a study for the child Jesus had been made in biro on the back of an envelope.

'You think that's it?'

'I think so, but didn't Bob want samples of paints and stuff?' She looked around, somewhat bewildered. 'I wouldn't know where to start.'

Patrick studied the jars stacked on shelves. Some contained already ground pigment and others the minerals that Freddie would use to make his colours. He had a shrewd idea of which ones would be relevant, but unless he knew what oils and resins Freddie was mixing them with . . .

'I think Bob's going to have to come down,' he said. 'I can make a guess, but if Freddie made his own paints, then unless he was copying a standard recipe it's probably a bit beyond me. I've been grinding some of my own for my copy of the painting, but I'm still learning.'

She nodded. 'I think this will do for now. You

want to bring the car round the back so we can load things more easily?'

Patrick hesitated. 'Maybe you should come down with me.'

'Oh, for goodness' sake.'

He could see that she was going to accuse him of paranoia but then the unease grew in her eyes as she remembered that her father had also been afraid. She nodded. 'OK,' she said, 'I'll come with you to get the car.'

He followed her down the stairs, out of the side door and around the building. There was no sign of the blue car; no sign of anyone. The sky was a lowering grey but it was not yet raining and with luck they'd get the car packed before it did. He drove across the grass verge and the paving and into the little bay at the back where the rubbish bins were kept. The refuse lorry came in from the main road through the big gates, she told him, but they weren't usually unlocked apart from on bin collection day.

He'd suggested that she padlock the door when they left and was relieved that she had done so without further question. Patrick suddenly realized that he'd be glad to get out of this place, that suddenly that sense of uneasiness had increased. He looked around again but could see no one, and he tried to ease his anxiety by texting both Bob and Annie to let them know that he and Bee were on their way back. There had been no reply from Annie, as yet. She was probably still out. He reached to bolt the door as they went back inside.

'We're only going to be a minute,' she protested. But he bolted it anyway.

118

They fetched the portfolio and the box from the studio and paused on the mezzanine landing to look back and check they'd got everything they needed. Then they heard a sound. It was the same kind of sound that Bee had reported hearing the last time she was here. The scrape of metal on metal.

They looked at one another. 'It's OK, you bolted the door,' Bee said, but her voice was shaking.

'The sound didn't come from the side door,' Patrick said. 'It came from near the office.' He looked down over the railing of the mezzanine landing to try and see what might have caused the noise but a second later there was a pounding on the stairs as someone came running up. Neither Patrick nor Bee had a chance to react. Patrick was vaguely aware that Bee had screamed and that the box had been knocked out of her hands. He grabbed for the railing but he was already off balance, and then someone shoved him hard. Patrick knew he was falling.

Then the impact of the concrete floor, and he knew nothing more.

Seventeen

Annie hadn't read Patrick's text until she got back from walking the dogs. Bob had checked his phone and seen the message that the two young people were on their way back but they were both now getting a little anxious because

Patrick and Bee had still not returned. She tried phoning but got no answer from either Patrick's phone or Bee's. Bob was busy painting when she went through to the studio and he didn't notice her until she was right beside him and halfway through a sentence. Sighing, she plucked one of the buds out of his ear and started again.

'Something up?' Bob asked.

'Like I just said, Patrick and Bee haven't come back yet. Bob, it's been more than an hour since he texted. It's only about a forty minute drive.'

Bob shrugged. 'So? They're not babies, Annie. They probably got distracted, went off somewhere else. Went for a coffee or whatever young people do these days.' He'd meant to lighten the mood. He could see the anxiety in her eyes and realized that this wasn't just Patrick being late, this was Annie being worried, and those two things were quite different. Annie had an instinct for these things.

He washed out the brush that he was holding and wiped it on a rag. Then he wiped his hands too, spreading the Prussian blue paint over his palm.

'Oh, for goodness' sake,' Annie said. She picked up a clean rag and wiped him down again. 'That will have to do for now. Come on.'

Bob followed her into the hall and grabbed their coats. Annie ushered the dogs into the kitchen and closed the door on them. Dexter had a tendency to chew the front door mat, left to his own devices, but he was fine in the kitchen with his bed and his toys. Bob noted that she had taken the car keys, that she intended to drive.

120

'Best buckle up, then,' he muttered under his breath. Annie was a bit of a lead boot.

He slid into the passenger seat and they were off before he'd even fastened his seatbelt. 'So,' he said, 'what's got you in a tizzy?'

'I'm not in a tizzy. I told you, they've just not come back yet. I was worried. I *am* worried. And that text about the car. What if he's right, what if they were followed?'

'And you don't think they've gone somewhere else? You really think something's happened?'

She nodded. 'Patrick texted me before that, reckoned they might have been followed. Then he texted me again, said it was his imagination and the car had turned off and there was no sign of it when they got to the warehouse. But I could tell he was worried. When he texted to say they were coming back he . . . sounded relieved.'

'How can someone sound relieved in a text?'

Annie just looked at him and Bob shrugged. But her anxiety had infected him now. Freddie had been threatened, according to his daughter, and Freddie was now dead and so was Antonia Scott. 'I should have gone with them,' he said.

'We both should have gone,' Annie agreed. 'Bee has been to the studio so many times since Freddie died, it never occurred to me . . .'

'And they're probably fine.'

They drove the rest of the route in silence, Annie focused on keeping up her speed on a wet road and Bob's mind wandering between the painting he had left behind and the nagging thought that he had not cleaned the rest of his brushes – though he felt annoyed with himself that he should even be thinking about that. He kept telling himself that Patrick and Bee were fine, that there was nothing to worry about and that Annie was overreacting, but the other part of his mind, the part that knew his wife, told him that Annie never overreacted.

There was no sign of Patrick's car at the front of the warehouse so they got out and walked round the back. It was parked instead in a little yard, close to dustbins and a locked gate, but the small door outside the warehouse was open. They ran inside, calling Patrick's name.

'Oh my God!' Bob knelt at the young man's side.

'Don't even try and move him,' Annie warned. She was already on the phone, calling the police and the ambulance.

'He must have fallen from up there,' Bob said, indicating the mezzanine floor. 'That's a hell of a drop.'

'Fallen? More likely pushed.'

'You can't know that.' Bob was desperate for this to be an accident. 'I'll go up, check she's not there. Check she's not been hurt too.'

'OK, but be careful not to touch anything.'

She crouched down beside Patrick and took off her jacket. He was still alive but he was deathly cold and deeply unconscious. There was nothing she could do apart from lay the padded jacket gently over his chest. She rubbed her arms; her jumper was warm but the warehouse seemed suddenly freezing cold.

'Oh, Patrick,' Annie said softly. 'What on earth have we got you into? Harry will never forgive us. *I* will never forgive us.'

Bob clattered back down the metal stairs. 'She's not there. But the stuff they were obviously bringing back is scattered all over the landing. So if she's not here, where the hell is she?'

'My guess? Someone's taken her. Taken her and left Patrick to die.'

'No, no, no. That's not going to happen. He's going to be all right, Annie. He's tough, he can come through this.'

But Annie was looking at the blood pooling around Patrick's head and matting his hair; she had felt the coldness of his fingers and his pulse, slow and irregular. She knew there could also be heavy internal bleeding and hoped that the fact that he was still alive, maybe more than an hour after he'd fallen, was a promising sign. If he'd bled out internally, he'd already be *dead* and cold, not *alive* and cold.

'Sirens,' Bob said. 'Police or ambulance? I'll go and look.'

'Sounds like the paramedics,' Annie said.

Bob stood up and ran out of the building to meet them and Annie stroked Patrick's fingers. 'It's going to be all right,' she told him. 'Patrick, listen to me, you are going to be fine. You hear me? You are going to be fine.'

The paramedics came in and Annie stepped away so that she would not interfere with their work. Bob came to stand beside her and put an arm around her shoulders. 'You're freezing,' he said and took off his jacket, wrapping it around her.

Then the police arrived and Bob and Annie went and sat in the police car and gave the officers an account of what had happened, as far as they knew it. Annie could tell that the police were sceptical about her kidnap theory; she could see the idea forming in their heads that Bee and Patrick had maybe had some kind of quarrel, which had led to a more violent argument and maybe a shove that sent him over the railings. That the girl had then run off in panic. That they would soon find her. The officer cautiously put this into words as the most likely scenario.

'If that's the case,' Bob objected, 'then why didn't she take his car?'

'Maybe she panicked, couldn't find the keys. Maybe the keys are in his pocket. Sir, I don't know what happened any more than you do but it's possible, don't you think? Young people tend to act impulsively.'

'Someone took her,' Annie said slowly and precisely. 'Someone came and took her away.'

'And why would they do that?' the officer asked. He was distracted momentarily by one of the other officers tapping on the window and then pointing to the ambulance. 'Looks like they're ready to leave,' he said. 'Do you want me to drive you there – I know it's been a shock – or do you want to follow in your car?'

'We'll follow in our car,' Bob said. Annie nodded.

They had already spoken to Harry and told him what they could but kept it simple: Patrick had been involved in an accident at the warehouse, had fallen from a height and was now being taken to hospital. Annie called Harry again as they got in the car. She got no answer, and so assumed

124

he must be driving. She left a message on his voicemail telling him that they were on their way and would meet him there. Harry would be frantic, she thought. Harry and Patrick were closer than most fathers and sons.

Don't let him die, Annie thought. She was not a great believer in God but just now she was willing to take any additional help, even from an imaginary being.

Annie hated hospitals. She hated the smell, she hated the sound, she hated the kind of building that typically housed them, she hated the fact that being there always meant that something was wrong. The previous summer they had visited friends in hospital who had just had a new baby, and it had felt weird to Annie that they were actually going to witness something positive happening in the place she always associated with sickness and injury and death. And now they sat in the family waiting room, waiting for any kind of news. So far there had been nothing at all, apart from the offer of tea. Bob, always restless, paced up and down with slow, monotonous steps and Harry, positioned so he was facing the door, sat with his feet square on the floor and his hands on his knees, his back very straight. Annie had curled up in a corner of the long sofa.

After the first flurry of conversation when they had all arrived, and the first demands for information from medical staff who had been unable to tell them anything much, they had barely spoken.

Annie, and then Bob, had made statements and

arrangements had been made for them to go to the police station later – mostly at Annie's insistence. She had, by now, almost convinced the police officer they had met at the scene that there was more to this than just a girl having an argument and pushing a boy off the balcony. Bee had not turned up at home and, more significantly, her mobile phone had been found close to the warehouse. Someone had stamped on it and, taking a quick look at the partial muddy bootprint on the screen, one of the CSIs had surmised that the foot that had stamped on it had not been its owner's. A quick canvas of the area, a chat to people working in the next building (despite it being Sunday) gave the police the information that a blue car had driven away at speed with two people inside.

Patrick's text had mentioned a blue car with two people in it, a man and a woman, he thought. The coincidence was too much even for a sceptical police officer.

Annie shifted position and Harry glanced at her briefly and then returned his attention to the door. Annie got up. 'I'm going to find the ladies',' she said. 'You want some coffee? Maybe something to eat? Harry, you're going to need your strength. When Patrick wakes up he's going to want you with him.'

'Coffee, then,' Harry agreed.

Annie opened the waiting room door and stepped out into the noise of the corridor. A&E was off to her right and to the left were the toilets and the vending machines and another waiting area.

Annie sighed. She was bloody useless at just doing nothing. She had half a mind to go and get in the car and go searching for Bee, searching for anything. Just driving would be better than sitting, but she knew she couldn't. She had to stay put even though it made her feel utterly pathetic.

In the toilets she washed her hands and face. There was a smudge of Prussian blue on her thumb where she'd cleaned Bob's hands with the rag. It was one of Bob's favourite colours; Patrick, in contrast, preferred cerulean.

What if he was paralysed? she thought. What if he couldn't paint, couldn't draw? She knew people would just say, Oh, you're lucky to be alive, but would Patrick see it that way?

Annie shook the thought away and went back into the corridor, down to the vending machines. She bought chocolate and shoved it in her pockets and then managed to balance three squishy vending machine cups of coffee between her hands and walked slowly back to the waiting room.

Bob must have been watching out for her because he opened the door and she set the coffee down on the table. And then unpacked the chocolate from her pockets. 'Any news?'

'Nothing,' Bob said. 'Still nothing.'

'Surgery can take a long time,' Annie said, although she wasn't sure if that would reassure anyone. She wasn't reassuring herself, that was for sure.

The door to the waiting room opened and everyone looked up expectantly. Alec and Naomi came in, with Napoleon.

The conversation went round again. 'Any news?' And the inevitable 'No.'

Naomi sat down next to Harry and took his hand and for the first time he started to talk properly. He talked about Patrick, how frightened he was, what he would do if he lost his son and Annie, who had always known that Naomi and Harry were close, caught a glimpse of just how close and interconnected their lives were.

Her need to be doing something, anything, was overwhelming now and she leaned across to Bob. 'I'm going to take the car, swing by Bee's flat and see if I can see anything. I'll call Alfie and let him know what's going on and see if we can get some bodies on the ground out there. Alfie's got connections, we might be able to get some CCTV footage.'

Bob looked anxious and unwilling to let her go. Alec was leaning across, having overheard the conversation. 'If it's all the same to you, I'll go with you. We can take my car. There's not a lot I can do here.'

'There's not a lot *I* can do,' Bob objected.

'Please, Bob. Alec and I can be more use out there. Harry and Naomi are going to need somebody who can drive, or take messages, or do whatever needs to be done here. You're better at it than I am.'

From anyone else that might have seemed like a platitude, a way of fobbing him off, but Bob knew it was the simple truth, however much he might dislike or even resent it. He nodded. 'Go, then. But be careful.'

'Always,' she said.

128

Eighteen

Bee had been terrified and utterly bewildered. She had been aware of the figure rushing up towards her and knocking her sideways and the box she was holding spilling its contents on the landing and down the stairs. She had been aware that the man who had pushed her aside had then turned his attention to Patrick, shoving him viciously into the safety rail at the top of the landing. And then she saw him fall. Patrick had made a grab for the rail and as he fell his body had twisted. She'd heard him hit the ground and knew she had screamed his name. The next thing she was aware of was that her wrists had been grabbed and fastened with a cable tie behind her back. Tape covered her mouth and it wasn't like the movies, just a little piece across her lips, the man who had grabbed her had wound it round her head. She could feel it against her skin, pinching, and it pulled her hair when she moved. She was vaguely aware of these things but she was more aware that Patrick had not made a sound.

The man took hold of her arm and pulled her down the stairs. He moved so quickly she could hardly get her footing and she tripped and almost fell. He swore at her and then picked her up and threw her over his shoulder. As he turned across the warehouse, heading for the main door, she

129

got a glimpse of Patrick lying on the floor. He wasn't moving. There was blood, a lot of blood.

She realized that her assailant had come in through the little door that Danny and his father used. She knew that it was always padlocked on the outside but she supposed that a pair of bolt croppers could have dealt with that.

There was a car, and a girl and an open boot, and Bee was pushed inside.

She heard the girl screaming at the man. Heard what sounded like the man hitting the girl and telling her to get in the car. And then the car seemed to launch away at speed and Bee was thrown around the boot, helpless to protect herself. She curled up tight, wedging herself in the corner. She wanted to cry but she was terrified that if she did her nose would run and her throat would block up and she wouldn't be able to breathe. She was already having problems, and although she tried to tell herself that she could breathe, that it was only her mouth that was covered, that she would be all right, her chest and throat tightened so much she could hardly get the air to go in.

Tears ran down her face. Let Patrick be all right, she thought. Please let him be all right. And then, hot on the heels of that thought, he's going to kill me, isn't he?

After some time she felt the car slow and then turn and she was suddenly aware that the girl was yelling again, shouting at the man, and he was shouting back and threatening her. There was something in the girl's tone that told Bee

130

that she had gone almost beyond fear. That she was so desperate she was almost unafraid. She heard the girl cry out and then go quiet and guessed that the man had hit her again.

What was the girl doing there? Bee wondered. She wasn't driving, she wasn't any use to the man that Bee could see. She decided that this man just wanted the girl there on some strange whim of his own and there was probably no sense to it at all.

She tried to pay attention to the direction the car was going and estimate the length of time, but it was no good. She couldn't keep her focus. She felt the car slow again, almost to a stop this time, and the man spoke to somebody and then drove on but at a much more leisurely pace. They must be nearing the destination, Bee thought. After a few more minutes they stopped completely. She heard the door open and then the boot and then the man put a bag over her head and dragged her out. He didn't bother to make her walk this time, he just picked her up again, slinging her over his shoulder once more. She could hear boots on gravel and then on something more solid. A door opened and slammed shut. Another door opened and then there were stairs. She became aware of a second set of footsteps, following on behind but much more hesitant, and she guessed these belonged to the girl she had seen.

Finally another door opened and she was dropped on to the floor. The door closed again and she heard the lock. Bee began to struggle, trying to free herself from the hood.

131

'Keep still. Let me help you.' The girl's voice.

The hood was lifted from her head and Bee blinked in the sudden light. The girl, her face bruised and her cheek cut, was staring at her.

'You want me to take the tape off? I'll try not to hurt you.'

Bee nodded and braced herself. Again it wasn't like in films, it hurt like hell as the girl pulled the tape off her cheeks and her hair and her lips. She could feel little bits of skin tearing free and there was blood on her mouth.

'I can't undo your hands; he's fastened them with one of those cable tie things. I'm Sian; who are you?'

Bee stared back at her. 'You mean you don't know? Did you see what that asshole did to my friend? He fell – that bastard pushed him. Patrick fell.'

The girl called Sian was nodding. 'I know, I saw. I never saw him do anything like that before . . .' And then she stopped as though that was a lie.

Bee stared at her sceptically. 'No?'

Sian took a deep breath. 'I saw him kill someone. A woman in a gallery. I saw him stab her. I was there.'

'Antonia Scott.' Bee knew it must be her.

'I didn't mean . . . I didn't know. He said I should pretend to be this artist that she was expecting. He said it was some kind of joke. I knew it wasn't, but . . . Oh God, I've been so scared.'

Bee's look must have been scathing because Sian cowered back. 'Where the hell are we? And what the hell does he want with me?'

132

'I don't know. It's this big house in the middle of nowhere. I've never been here before. And I don't know who you are, so I don't know why he wants you.'

'I'm Freddie Jones's daughter,' she said. 'Does that make any more sense of it?'

If it was possible for the girl to get paler, she certainly did now. Her skin blanched beneath the bruises. 'Something about a painting,' she said. 'He took a portfolio from the gallery. That's all I know.'

'Help me up.'

Sian helped Bee get to her feet and they took a proper look at each other. About the same age, Bee thought, though Sian was small and blonde and a bit curvier than Bee was. On the terror scale, she figured they were about even.

'What the hell is this place?'

'It's a big house, that's all I know. We came in through what I think was a stable yard and up some stairs. I guess these are the servants' quarters, or were.'

Looking round, Bee guessed she was about right. The room was quite small and gave the impression, from the angle of the ceiling, that they were up in the eaves of the building. Cheap carpet on the floor, a single bed and basic furnishings. The curtains were closed. Bee went across to the window and Sian opened the curtains. They were cheap, chintzy and unlined, and the view out of the window told them nothing Sian hadn't already observed. Bee could see the corner of a cobbled yard, and the side of a wall with a door just visible. Opposite was another wall, red brick and blank. Even if she strained to see upward, there was not so much as a glimpse of sky.

'I get the feeling we could shout our heads off and no one would hear us,' she said. 'And no one would take any notice, even if they could.'

She tensed her wrists against the tie but there was little movement and if she didn't remember to keep wriggling her fingers her hands soon became cold and the pins and needles started. He'd bound her hands viciously tight, needlessly so, and she felt lucky that he'd not broken the skin. She took vague heart from that. Clearly, no one cared what happened to poor Patrick, but she got the feeling that the man, whoever he was, had been told to deliver her mostly unscathed.

'So,' she said, turning from the window and then going over to sit down on the bed, 'who the hell is that moron and who the hell are you?'

She wriggled her way back so she could lean against the wall. The bed had no headboard. Sian, clearly needing to do something positive, grabbed a pillow and shoved it between Bee's back and the wall. Bee wriggled again until her back and hands were in the best position she could find and then said, 'Well? You know more than me, so tell me. What are we up against here and what the fuck is going on?'

Sian perched on the edge of the bed. Her face seemed even paler and Bee wondered how that was possible. The bruising had darkened. It looked painful; one eye was swollen almost shut.

'Look through that door there,' Bee said. 'With any luck it's a bathroom or something. I'm guessing they don't want us to piss ourselves and spoil the decor.'

'You need to go? I mean, I can help . . .'

Bee shook her head. 'I'm hoping there's cold water and a towel or something. You need to get a compress on that eye before it starts to close. God, I sound like my gran.'

Sian managed what sounded like a laugh. She did as Bee said and opened the door. 'Toilet and wash basin,' she said. 'And a towel.'

'Good, soak a corner of it in cold water, then wring it out and hold it against your eye. It should help a bit.'

She watched as the other girl wet the towel and then came back to sit on the bed, the wet end pressed against her bruise as hard as she could bear. Her face half covered, not looking fully at Bee, she seemed to find it easier to talk. 'His name is Kevin Binns, but everyone calls him Binnie. He used to be a friend of mine but now . . . now he's just a monster, and I don't know what to do.'

Abruptly she burst into tears and sat sobbing, face buried in the towel.

Oh great, Bee thought. I'm the one who's been tied up and kidnapped, my friend is probably dead and now I've got to turn on the sympathy. She took a deep breath and told herself that she'd got to calm down. That this girl, Sian, had obviously been stretched to breaking point by whatever that animal had done and that she had to take it slow if she was going to find out anything useful.

'OK,' she said at last. 'He was a friend of yours.

135

So what the hell happened? You've got to tell me everything you know and then we've got to work out how the hell we're going to get out of here.'

Alive, she added to herself, how the hell are we going to get out of here alive?

Nineteen

'Where are we going?' Alec asked.

'Head towards the coast road and I'll give you the address in a minute. I've got to make a phone call, make sure he's home.'

'Who?'

'Alfie, the private detective Naomi will have told you about?'

'She's told me a bit,' Alec said. 'But I wasn't even home when we heard about Patrick. We came to the hospital as soon as we could. We've not had much time to talk.'

'Right,' Annie said. 'I didn't think about that.'

She was holding her phone to her ear, waiting for a response. Then she spoke briefly and gave Alec an address. 'It's about a forty minute drive. If you want to go back, I understand. I can take myself there.'

'We're on the way now. I'm no better at hanging round in waiting rooms than you are. I'm not good at hospitals, if I'm honest. When I thought Naomi might die . . . . after the accident, I practically haunted the place. Naomi's sister and I took turns to be there.'

'You weren't together then.'

'No, but it suddenly hit me how much I wanted us to be. You know the ironic bit? I had to play it even more carefully afterwards. Naomi can't take pity. If, for one minute, she'd thought I felt sorry for her, it would have been over before it began. So, we took things slow . . .' – he paused – '. . . and then Harry came back on the scene and I thought I'd blown it again. Harry has a much longer standing claim on her affections than I have, you know?'

Annie nodded. 'Does it bother you now? That they are still so close?'

Alec laughed. 'I get the odd moments of jealousy,' he admitted. 'But no. Ninety per cent of the time I'm just glad she's got such good friends. Ten per cent of the time I'm telling myself that I'm being stupid; that Harry is *just* a friend. A better friend than most people ever find – to me, too.'

He paused again. 'Truth is, I love Patrick and Harry a great deal. They're my family – but that doesn't stop the little green monster poking its nose in occasionally.'

Annie laughed. 'And then when you had the car accident . . . more hospital.'

Alec nodded. It hadn't exactly been an accident but he wasn't going to quibble.

'You came through it,' Annie said. 'So did Naomi. She lost her sight but I'm guessing she's no less the person she ever was. So far your unit has survived. The run of luck will continue, Alec. Patrick will be all right.'

'Unit.' Alec laughed. 'Very military.'

'Old habits and all that,' Annie said.

'And is this Alfie part of your old habits?'

'Um, yes. Though he was always freelance. He did some work for Gustav, my guardian; he was first port of call for looking into anything like forensic accounting. That's why I called him in. Freddie Jones is a little left field for Alfie but he's your man for following a paper trail, identifying a scam . . .'

'And we're going to see him now because . . .?'

'Not for any of Alfie's skills, actually. He's got friends who might be able to give us access to CCTV cameras. There's nothing near us, but it's very likely there are cameras close to where Bee lives and also near the warehouse where Freddie had his studio.'

'And what are we looking for?'

'Patrick texted me. I didn't get the text until I got back to the house about an hour later. I was out walking the dogs and the mobile signal is so patchy up at the back of us that I rarely bother with the phone. He said he'd seen a blue car near to Bee's place, two people inside. He was sure he'd seen the same car following them to the warehouse. He got a partial plate, but my bet is they're false. Patrick said the numbers were partly obscured by mud.'

'You told the police this?'

'Told them, showed them the text. They took a lot of convincing. Their initial response was that Patrick and Bee argued, she gave him a shove and then fled in panic.'

'Sounds plausible. I can see why they would think that.'

'So do I, but the problem with having a strong initial idea is that you stop looking at other possibilities, especially when they sound as dramatic as a young woman being kidnapped. They started to come round to my way of thinking when they found Bee's mobile, stomped by a large booted foot. And there were witnesses in one of the other warehouses who saw a blue car drive away at speed.'

'So, if the police are already involved?'

'Nothing will happen until tomorrow. Nothing will happen until Bee has been missing for at least twenty-four hours and all her friends and family have been contacted. The initial obvious conclusion will still be the one pursued. Am I right?'

'Probably,' Alec admitted.

'And no CCTV footage will be reviewed until the initial theory has played out, will it? It takes time and manpower to sit and stare at a computer screen on the off chance. I just figured we might be able to get a head start.'

'And, if you find that information, what do you plan on doing with it?'

Annie just glanced at him and then looked away. Alec decided not to push the question. 'I can't imagine what Harry must be going through,' he said. 'When it's your child . . .'

'Have you ever wanted children?'

'We've talked about it,' Alec said. 'But . . . well, it's difficult. You and Bob?'

Annie shook her head. 'I don't want kids,' she said. 'Bob would make a terrific dad but I just can't bear the thought of it.'

'You'd make a great mother,' Alec told her.

'Would I? I'd be so overprotective the poor little chicks would never be able to fly the nest.'

'I think we all feel like that,' Alec said, but he knew there was more than the usual anxiety in her responses.

Annie shook her head. 'Children are just hostages to fortune,' she said. 'You can't protect them and they can't protect themselves.'

Alec made no comment. He knew that Annie had only been in her early teens when her parents had been killed. He could almost understand her vehemence but he was suddenly conscious of how little he really knew about Annie Raven. How much he would never ask.

'Who took Bee?' he asked. 'You have any theories on that?'

'Whoever was frightening Freddie,' she said. 'I've got one possible name but even Alfie's not been able to help me prove a connection. Not yet.'

'God help him when you do,' Alec half joked.

'I doubt God will bother,' Annie said.

It was late, dark outside, the wall no longer visible even though Bee thought it was probably only three metres or so away. The room too was dark. They had tried the light switch but the bulb was either blown or had been removed.

Improbably, they had both fallen asleep, lying close together for comfort. Bee woke to find that her arms had fallen asleep too and then realized that what had really woken her was the sound of footsteps on the stairs.

She struggled to sit up and that disturbed Sian, who was suddenly bolt upright and staring at the door.

'Help me sit,' Bee said. 'My arms are dead and I can't move.'

Sian grabbed her shoulders and hauled her up just as the door burst open and a bright light shone in their eyes.

Bee was grabbed and hauled off the bed. Seconds later, she was gone and the door locked once more. Sian leapt towards it, hammered on the wood. 'Where are you taking her? Don't take her away, don't leave me here. Don't hurt her!'

She could hear Binnie laughing at her and then the sounds subsided and the silence fell again. The room was dark and dead and Sian was alone.

Bee was hauled unceremoniously along a narrow corridor and into a lobby area and then up a flight of stairs. The door opened on to a hall. They were no longer in the service area, Bee realized, and must now be in the main house.

She made an effort to notice everything she could, commit to memory anything that might identify the house. If she got out of here – when she got out of here – she'd make sure she could tell the police as much as she humanly could.

She was taken through into a study or library and pushed down into a chair. Finally, the man Sian called Binnie took a knife, leaned her forward and loosed her hands. For several minutes Bee sat still, unable either to move or to take notice of her surroundings as the blood flowed back into her dead arms and hands. She let out

141

a sob, then, angry with herself, took a deep breath and looked up.

A man stood beside an ornate fireplace with a cut glass tumbler in his hand. The liquid in the glass glowed a rich amber. He's posing, Bee thought, the idea coming unbidden into her head. He wants me to be impressed.

Somehow, that was funny. Not so funny she was going to risk laughing at him, but funny enough for her to grasp it like a straw lifebelt and hang on.

He wasn't tall and she pegged him at maybe late thirties. Hard grey eyes and light brown hair that was thinning so he had the start of a widow's peak. His shirt was very white and his trousers very dark blue. They looked like part of a suit. He wore what she found herself thinking of as the obligatory gold watch.

She wanted to yell at him, to demand impossible things, like him letting her go or at least telling her what the hell he was doing, bringing her here. Instead she said quietly, 'That bastard killed my friend.'

The man looked from her to Binnie. 'Did you?'

Binnie shrugged. 'Probably.'

'OK. It doesn't matter. Miss Jones, Beatrix. Though I understand no one calls you that? Bee, then?'

He sounds like a bad Bond villain, she thought. She had realized that as long as she could keep having these random, almost irrelevant thoughts, she might just about be able to hold it together – and Bee was very determined to try and hold herself together.

142

'I suppose he killed my father too,' she said.

'And what makes you think that? I understood he had a heart condition. He smoked and drank far too much, did old Freddie. Always had.'

'That's not what killed him,' Bee insisted. 'I know it was you.'

'You *think* it was me; there's the difference. Now.' He set the glass down and picked up a straight-backed hall chair.

Bee had noticed several of them out near the stairs when she had been dragged into the study. He sat down opposite her.

'Your father had something of mine. He'd been doing some work for me, but he failed to deliver the last piece. I'd like it.'

'Talk to the solicitor. He's the executor.'

'Funny,' the man said. 'Now, Bee, the object I'm looking for is a painting. Freddie didn't get the chance to finish it before he died, but no matter. I paid for it, I want it.'

He's nuts, she thought. 'So, if you'd paid for something, it would be yours, wouldn't it? All you'd have to do is ask for it. It would be in Dad's order book.'

'No, you're not getting this, are you? I ordered something "off the books", as they say. Freddie would not have a record of it. I think you might know where it is? Hmm?'

'If I don't even know what it was . . .'

'A painting. A Madonna and child with St Anne. Small, about the size of an A-four sheet of paper. On board. Poplar, to be exact, and with a border worked in gesso – though he might not have got that far. I only ever saw the preliminary

143

drawings. Ring any bells?' He paused, looking closely at her. 'Oh, I can see it does. Good.' He rubbed his hands together. 'I'm glad we're on the same page, singing from the same hymn sheet, seeing eye to eye.'

'What?'

'So, where is this picture? Tell me and I might see my way to letting you go. Or I might not. But I might at least see my way to not letting my friend here loose on you. No sense of proportion, our Binnie. None at all.'

Bee shook her head. She knew well enough that he'd never let her leave. That the best she could do was play for time and pray for help. 'I never saw it,' she said. 'The last thing I saw Dad working on was a landscape with horses, follower of Stubbs. He was painting a pair from an old photograph. He had a digital print of the other one in the studio and—'

'Yes, I know all about that. He finished that piece weeks before he died. The one I'm interested in—'

'I told you, I never saw it. I didn't see Dad for a couple of weeks, I'd been away. I never went to the studio after he finished the landscape.'

The man studied her for a moment and then got up and moved back to the fireplace. Posed once more with his whisky glass.

'Binnie,' he said, and gestured towards her.

'No!' Bee screamed and tried to get up, but Binnie was quicker.

'Just one should do it. She's not that brave or that tough.'

Binnie took her hand, separated out her little

finger from the rest. Bee screamed again as the finger broke.

'That will do.'

Binnie stepped back and the man poured a second glass of whisky. He resumed his place opposite Bee.

She cradled her damaged hand, sobbing quietly. She tried to summon one of those soothing irrelevant thoughts, but none came.

Instead, a half-remembered conversation popped into her memory. Sitting at the table at Bob Taylor's house, Bob had said something about a half-finished painting on the easel in her dad's studio. The day he'd gone there with Antonia Scott.

'Shall we try again? Here, drink this, it will take your mind off the pain.'

He proffered the glass. She shook her head.

'As you will.' He tipped the contents into his own mouth and set the empty glass down on the floor. 'Now, try again.'

Bee hesitated. An idea was forming but she was reluctant. How could she drag more innocent people into this? She had seen what had happened to Patrick. But the more she thought about it, the less of a choice she felt she had.

'Bob Taylor has it,' she said. 'He went to the studio with Antonia Scott to fetch some paintings my dad was restoring. He saw the painting, that it was half finished and unprotected. He took it for safe keeping. I think it's in his studio. But I've not seen it. I didn't go into his studio when I went to his house.'

'And why did you go to his house?'

'He was a friend of my dad's,' she said, on safer ground now. 'I've got to clear my dad's house and studio, and the studio he had at home. I didn't know where to start or what to keep or what might be valuable. I thought if I asked Bob to help me . . .'

He thought about it. 'That sounds plausible. And what were you and that boy doing there today?'

This time the lie was based on truth so it was also easy. 'Bob said he wanted any preliminary drawings for the Madonna. He said he wanted to get a feel for what Freddie intended. He worked with my dad, knew his style. I think he wanted to finish it for him. In his memory, you know? He didn't know it was yours. How could he?'

'How could he indeed? Well, that's a nice thought. I'll have to bear that in mind. You see how easy things can be when everyone just cooperates.'

Twenty

Alfie Kounis lived in a clifftop house on the outskirts of a small village. Alec did not recognize the name of Inscliffe, but then the settlement was so small you might have driven through it and never noticed it. Alfie's house was small too, just a very small cottage built in local stone and almost overshadowed by a second building that was revealed when the security light came on. It

146

looked, at first glance, like a double garage, but without the up-and-over doors.

The door opened straight into the living room and Alfie, barefoot and wearing tracksuit bottoms and a loose shirt, motioned them to sit down. Alec glanced at his watch and noted that it was almost one in the morning.

'Sorry about the time,' Annie said. 'But as I said on the phone, we need a bit of help.'

'Sit down. I'll get some coffee and you can tell me what you need.'

Alfie seemed unperturbed by his nocturnal visitors, Alec thought.

Alfie set a tray with coffee and cake and sandwiches on the low table in front of the settee on which Alec had flopped. He suddenly realized how tired he was.

'I thought you might be hungry,' Alfie said. 'Unless Annie's changed a lot,' – he turned to address Alec – 'she never turns down an opportunity for food.'

Alec suddenly realized that he was starving. He had grabbed something quickly at lunchtime but had then driven home, and there'd been no time afterwards to eat or even to drink. He took advantage now, while Annie filled in the details for Alfie, telling him about Patrick and the blue car and her encounter with the police at the warehouse.

'When you told me you needed CCTV access,' Alfie said, 'I made a few calls. If you give me the addresses I can go and set things up, and we can piggyback on one of the security systems close to the warehouse. We're lucky, it's quite a

147

large area of real estate and the owners have a centrally controlled system that can be remotely accessed. My friends have managed to hack into that and I think we should be able to pick something up from the main system near Bee's house.'

Alec must've looked sceptical because Alfie said, 'People think CCTV is a closed system and the camera systems themselves are, but the data is most often saved to a hard drive and that hard drive is usually on a networked system. Most computers have internet access so ultimately all of the systems are linked to a mainframe or central hub somewhere. All you need is access to the main computer network. It's like . . .' – he paused, thinking of an analogy – 'it's like once you're on the main motorway system, one way or another that links to everywhere else.'

Alec wanted to ask about the legality of that but he bit down on the question. He didn't want to know and he found he was eager to see what Alfie was actually capable of.

Alfie disappeared for a while and Alec guessed that he'd gone into the building that wasn't a double garage. He and Annie finished the sandwiches and the coffee and started on the biscuits and cake. Alec made a few calls of his own; he still had good friends and ex-colleagues in the local force who might be able to get things moving at their end.

Annie was watchful, listening to the one-sided conversation.

'I'm grateful for the food. I've not had time to eat anything,' Alec told her. 'I've just managed to get hold of DS Dattani. He's a good man and

148

a good officer. Apparently there's a CCTV camera just across the road from the warehouse where Bee was snatched. He's arranging for someone to start reviewing that now. He's going to give me a call.'

Annie nodded and picked up another biscuit. 'Alfie believes in feeding people. It's a habit he picked up from his mum. You can't go to Alfie's mum's house without being fed. Frankly, I think it's a habit more people should cultivate.' Annie grinned at him. 'And he's right, I am always hungry.'

Alec looked sceptically at her; she stood about five feet six, slender and willowy. Her mass of dark hair, tumbling past her shoulders in thick waves, looked almost too heavy for her slim frame.

Alec called Naomi at the hospital again but there was no news. She too promised she'd ring as soon as she had anything to tell. Alec hated waiting.

Alfie returned and motioned them through to what he termed his workshop. Inside the brick building were separate areas, clearly laid out for different activities. Alec recognized the soldering station and in the corner a professional looking computer setup with multiple screens and a control console that would not have looked out of place in a recording studio.

Annie had given him the approximate times that they were looking for, estimating from journey times and when Patrick had picked Bee up that morning. There was nothing available in the narrow street but the lights on the corner had a camera mounted above them and that was the first time they saw the blue car. Patrick's little red hatchback came into view and then a few seconds later the blue car followed.

They picked both cars up again a couple of streets away and then the sightings became more frequent as they headed through the centre of town. They were lost when they turned off the main road and on to the B roads towards Annie and Bob's house.

Alfie had been busy grabbing any promising looking frames from the video and was now examining them. As Patrick had reported, the number plates were partly obscured by mud and there were definitely two people inside the car. A heavyset man and a small blonde woman, but it was hard to see their faces.

Picking up the action at the warehouse, they watched as Patrick parked and then later as he drove over the verge and into the yard at the back. They saw both young people leave the car, go inside and close the door.

'Is there any way we can shift to the front of the warehouse?' Annie asked.

'I think we might be able to pull up another camera feed,' Alfie said. 'But the quality is not good. It's just a basic system someone installed across the road to watch the front of the building. The different systems are all networked, but each building is responsible for supplying its own kit, from the look of it.' He ran the two images side by side on different screens. The second one was grainy, black and white, but even so the blue car was unmistakable as it moved around to the front of the warehouse.

The occupants got out and Alfie was able to grab images of their faces as they walked to the main doors. The man evidently had bolt croppers because the padlock fell at his feet. He handed the implement to the girl – they could see now that she was very young, late teens or early twenties at most, and that she looked exceedingly unhappy. She was, Alec guessed, under some kind of duress.

The door was opened and the two of them went inside. Alec realized he was almost holding his breath. This must be the moment when Patrick was attacked.

About a minute later, though it seemed much longer, man and girl came running out and the man had Bee thrown over his shoulder. The girl opened the boot of the car and Bee was dumped inside. The boot was slammed closed and the man and the girl got back into the car and drove off at speed.

They followed the camera trail for about another mile, but after that it was country roads and no CCTV.

No one spoke at first, all immersed in their own thoughts and shocked by what they'd seen.

'I'm going to call Vin back,' Alec said. 'Alfie, can you package this up, with the timestamps and the frame grabs. I'll take full responsibility for it. Your name doesn't have to come up, but we do need to get this information to the police as fast as we can.'

Alfie nodded. 'Take me about ten minutes. If you've got an email, I can send it direct. Just tell your friend that it's on its way.'

Alec nodded. He wandered to the other end of the workshop to make his calls and then came back to Alfie with some email addresses. 'DI Tess Fuller, and copy in DS Dattani. Tess is local and a good friend. And DI Karen Morgan,' he said. 'She's heading up the Antonia Scott inquiry. Tess and Vin will make sure it gets to whoever is in charge of looking into the attack on Patrick.'

He sat back down. His phone sounded an alert that he had a text. He read it. 'Patrick's out of surgery,' he said. 'He's in the ICU. Bob is taking Naomi home but they're going to see Mari first.' Mari was Patrick's grandmother. 'Bob says he'll take her to the hospital if she wants to go. I imagine she's itching to get there but Harry's told her to get some sleep and wait until there's something she can actually do.'

'I don't imagine there's been much sleeping going on,' Annie said. 'Bob will do whatever is needed, you know that, don't you? So will I.'

They waited until Alfie had sent the emails. He sent them from Alec's personal account. A lot of questions would be asked, Alec thought, but that didn't mean he had to answer any of them. If necessary he could use his own work for a security firm as cover for Alfie's activities.

He was yawning as they drove away. 'I can drive,' Annie said.

'I'll be all right, just take it slow.'

'Poor little Bee,' Annie said. 'Nothing in her life so far has prepared her for this. Alec, we've got to get her back.'

* * *

152

Harry watched his son. Watched the breath going in, the breath coming out, and knew that Patrick was responsible for neither. Induced coma, they called it. He wasn't being allowed to breathe on his own for a few days, they told Harry. His brain and his body needed time to recover. There was some swelling on the brain . . . and a fracture to the skull and a shoulder that had to be pinned in five places. He might not have full mobility in that joint again. The surgeon speculated that the shoulder was what hit the ground first, that he might have twisted when he fell, trying to save himself, and that it was probably a good thing. Had his head hit the ground first there would be no hope. Patrick would probably have died at the scene.

There were broken ribs as well, and a fractured pelvis and a ruptured kidney. He could live with one, the surgeon said. Many people did.

He was lucky. Internal bleeding was far less than had been thought and because most of the initial impact had been down his left side, he had not broken his back.

The way he fell, the surgeon said, might have wrecked his shoulder, smashed his collarbone and his ribs. Punctured a lung. But it had probably saved his life.

He was sitting alone, having sent everybody else away because he couldn't bear to see the looks of sympathy or their anxiety. Sitting alone, watching his son not breathing. Watching a machine breathing for his son. Harry kept telling himself that Patrick was lucky to be alive. That Patrick would heal. And he could hear Patrick's voice in his head saying, *Dad, I was bloody rubbish with my left hand anyway. I'm not going to be much worse now, am I?*

Harry realized that he was crying when the tears fell on his hands. He wiped them away with his palms and searched his pockets for a tissue. The door behind him opened and he renewed his attempts to wipe away the tears, not wanting the nursing staff to see him cry.

'Oh, son.' His mother's voice behind him. 'Oh, my darling.' Harry was suddenly a child again as Mari gathered him into her arms.

'What if he dies, Mum, what if he dies?'

'Hush! He'll hear you. He'll think you're doubting him.'

She pulled up another chair and they both sat watching Patrick not breathe. Mari might not have been at the hospital before but she had been busy. She had called Patrick's mother and step-family and both his mother and stepfather were on their way. They both sent their love to Harry and told him that it would be all right. That they were coming and would soon be with him.

Oddly, Harry drew strength from that. From his estranged wife telling him that she was going to be there; from his old boss, now her new husband, telling him the same. They both loved Patrick and somehow, Harry thought, if weight of love could make a difference, then Patrick would make it.

'Bob took Naomi home and then he came to fetch me; he's sitting in the waiting room. He's all in, poor love; when I left him he was nodding off in the chair. And Annie and Alec are on their

154

way back. They found some things out but I'll leave them to tell you all about it when they get here. Alec said to tell you that the police would probably want to speak to you again, see if Patrick had said anything that might be important. Alec said that it was going to be a case of attempted murder and kidnapping. There's film of some man taking Bee from the warehouse.'

'Film? I don't understand.'

'It was caught on one of those CCTV cameras. Annie took Alec somewhere. To see someone called Alfie? Anyway it seems they found recordings. You mustn't mention Alfie, he's not supposed to be doing this sort of thing, apparently. It was all Alec, if anyone wants to know. He sent the footage to one of his colleagues. Ex-colleagues, I suppose they are now. But you know what I mean.'

Harry stared at his mother, not quite grasping what she was saying, and then he nodded. 'Someone took the girl away? But that's terrible. It's what Annie thought had happened but, you know, I almost wish she'd been the one to push him. At least one of them would be safe then.'

'Hush, boy. It's all going to be all right. She's got a lot of good people fighting her corner, and so does Patrick.'

She took his hand and held it tight but Harry knew how she was really feeling, despite the optimistic words. Her own daughter, Harry's sister, had been taken away and killed. She'd been snatched and, despite there being good people then, fighting her corner, she'd never come back to them alive.

'Do her family know?'

'I think there's an aunt they've got hold of. The police, I mean. Annie said she'd mentioned going to a family wedding so I assume she might have told Annie where that was or something.'

Mari reached out and touched her son's hand. 'You'll be just fine,' she said. 'It will all be just fine.'

Alec and Annie arrived back at the hospital to find Vin Dattani talking to Bob. A uniformed officer hung round in the corridor outside the waiting room.

Bob looked relieved to see them. Vin and Alec shook hands and Alec made the introductions. Vin wasted no time.

'Got your email. I'm not going to enquire too closely as to how you got that information, but fortunately we can duplicate it. I've got people examining those cameras now and with the timecode we can be very precise, track most of the journey. We're also running images of the two people in the car through the system. But as you know, that can take time. Hopefully we'll get a match. In the meantime, I'd like Mr and Mrs Taylor to come with me to the police station and make a full statement. There are also some items I'd like them to take a look at. There were drawings and letters that Patrick and Beatrix seemed to be taking away from the studio and Mr Taylor informed me that they were bringing them back for him to look at. So if the two of you could do that now, that would be very helpful.'

'I'll come along with them,' Alec said.

156

Vin shrugged but didn't object.

They made quite a procession leaving the hospital, the police car and then Alec and then Bob and Annie.

'Have you had anything to eat?' Annie asked her husband.

'One of the nurses directed me to the café. I grabbed some sandwiches and a drink. You?'

'Alfie was his usual hospitable self. So Patrick's out of surgery? Do we know any more than that?'

'Not really. Harry went off to the ICU and I stayed behind in the waiting room but I've not heard from him since.'

They arrived at the police station and Vin led them into an interview room and sent for tea and coffee. 'This is just informal,' he said. 'I'll get somebody to take an official statement in a bit but I wanted to have a chat first. You've both known Patrick for a while now? But I understand that Beatrix Jones is new to you?'

'I knew her father really well. I'd met Bee maybe two or three times. Three times, I think, once at Freddie's studio and twice at a couple of different gallery openings. He brought her along as his plus one.'

Vin nodded. 'But you don't know her well.'

'Not well, no. She turned up on our doorstep about a week ago. Her father had died, and she wasn't convinced it was of natural causes. She'd told the police, and she'd made quite a bit of noise about it, especially after Antonia Scott was found dead.'

'That's the gallery owner.' Vin was checking

157

through his notes, obviously trying to bring himself up to speed.

'That's right. And apparently the only thing that was stolen was a portfolio of Freddie's work. I'm assuming it was drawings; the Scotts sold a lot of his drawings.'

'And why was she suspicious about her father's death? I'm presuming she was anxious about it before Antonia Scott's murder?'

'Apparently so,' Bob said. 'But Antonia's death, I think, put the tin hat on it for her. She was convinced he was murdered and to be honest we've been anxious too.'

'Oh?'

'Freddie had been behaving oddly, even for Freddie, in the months before he died. I talked to him a couple of times and he almost told me something and then backed off. Then when Antonia died, that really seemed strange. Frankly, we were wondering what Freddie had been up to, what he'd got himself into. He's got a record, as you know, and though he told Bee that he was out of that game I never really believed him.'

'You mean art forgery?'

'Art, documents, Freddie was a bit of an all-rounder. He was amazingly talented both as a legitimate artist in his own right and . . . well, everything else.'

'And you thought he'd got himself in too deep? That he'd gone back to his criminal activities and—'

'That he was up to his neck in something. You see, Freddie never went for the big time, he wasn't that ambitious. As long as Freddie was making

158

enough money and life was interesting he had no ambition beyond that. Freddie was an artist. Whatever it took to make sure he could earn his living as an artist, that's what he did. I don't think he drew many lines, if you see what I mean, not between what was legal and what was a grey area and what was downright criminal. And the problem with that, as I'm sure you can appreciate, is that there is always somebody around to take advantage.'

'We thought someone was threatening Freddie, possibly even threatening Bee,' Annie said. 'But until we had evidence of something, no one was going to listen to us. Bee had proved that when she went to the police about her father's death. So we employed a private investigator. And I don't mean your getting evidence for divorce cases type. He's more of a forensic accountant. He was looking into Freddie's finances and any business links he had. Freddie was scared and Freddie didn't scare easily. He wasn't afraid of petty crime, he wasn't afraid of going back to prison, though he surely wouldn't have wanted to. He was one of those people who just took life as it came, the good with the bad. So for Freddie to be frightened, it had to be serious.'

Vin took some notes. He looked thoughtfully at Annie. 'And has this private investigator come up with much so far?'

'A few possible leads. I've instructed him to send everything he can as electronic copies to your email. If you want to talk to him he's perfectly happy to do so. DS Dattani, this is totally above board. We were worried about a friend and we were worried about his daughter and it seems that we were right to be so.'

Vin nodded. He glanced this time at Alec and then said, 'I'd like the three of you to look at this CCTV footage.' He made no mention of the possibility that two of them might already have seen it. Vin was concerned now with maintaining a clean chain of evidence and though it had been Alec and Alfie who had alerted him, Vin knew that his officers would have found the same evidence. It might just have taken them a little longer. It was police evidence that mattered now.

He opened his laptop and turned it so that they could see. Annie, Bob and Alec watched the film in silence. The first part Alec and Annie had already viewed, but there was further footage from two other cameras.

'He made no attempt to hide his face,' Bob said. 'He doesn't care who sees him. I think he's enjoying himself; he wants people to know. Kind of nihilistic, isn't it?'

'Takes all sorts.' Vin nodded. 'There are criminal exhibitionists, just as there are exhibitionists in every other walk of life. But it does mean he's pretty confident, overconfident even, and that will probably make him very unpredictable. Not to mention dangerous.'

'Do you know who he is?'

'Face recognition is still running. Nothing yet. It can take a while, as you know.'

Alec nodded.

'You said there were things you wanted us to look at,' Annie said.

160

'Yes, there are. Give me a minute.' Vin left them briefly and returned with two large cardboard boxes, stacked one on top of the other. He placed them on the table and opened the lids.

'I can't take anything out of the evidence bags; not everything has been processed yet and there might be fingerprints, DNA. But take a look through, see if anything looks familiar, and if you can tell me why they were bringing these things to you, that would be a big help. We're going to be getting a specialist team involved and they may well want to talk to you again. They can probably ask you better questions than I can.'

Slowly and carefully Bob and Annie examined the contents of the boxes. If they had a comment to make Vin noted it down, along with the reference number of the evidence bag. Bob told him about the unfinished painting, and that he thought these were reference works for it, but looking at them, he realized they could just as easily be reference material for the Bevi Madonna. Both Bob and the owner had hoped that Bob's connoisseurship and knowledge of Freddie's work would be enough to decide the origin of the piece but more and more Bob was realizing that it would have to go for laboratory tests. What he had initially thought would be an easy question to answer was becoming more and more complex. Bob's opinion pulled this way and that until he no longer knew what to think.

'If he did paint that one you've got,' Alec said, 'why do another one right now?'

'We asked ourselves the same thing,' Bob said. 'Someone must have seen the original and wanted one, perhaps. It's not a question I can answer. It just adds to the confusion, to be frank. One thing, though, Freddie kept records of everything he painted. In little blue exercise books. There might be an explanation in there.'

'Records?'

'A lot of it was just about pigments, recipes, reference material.'

Vin looked through his notes. 'I'm going to hand Mr and Mrs Taylor over to one of my officers,' he told Alec. 'You'll need to make a formal statement, covering everything you can think of from the moment Bee knocked on your door, and your worries about Freddie and the events of today. Sorry, I know it's going to take a while. We'll make sure you're well supplied with coffee and we'll rustle up some food from somewhere.'

Annie nodded. 'No problem.'

'Can we just phone Harry at the hospital first?' Bob asked.

'Of course. It'll take a few minutes to arrange another room and a couple of officers to take statements. You have to do it separately, you understand that?'

Bob nodded. Vin left them and Bob and Alec both took the opportunity to make phone calls, Alec to Naomi and Bob, in the end, to Mari, as Harry's phone seemed to be off. Bob brought her up to speed on everything they knew, and what was going on at the police station now.

Vin returned with a uniformed officer who was

162

to take Bob's statement and he led Annie down to another room.

'You off home?' he asked Alec.

'I think so. Unless you need me for anything.'

Vin Dattani grinned at him. 'I think you've done enough for one day,' he said. 'Have you met this private detective?'

'Yes, I have. And I don't think he's a private detective in the way you mean. Like Annie said, he's an investigator. Not your common or garden sort; corporate and probably government work, I'd guess.'

'Well, I look forward to meeting him.' Vin rubbed his eyes and Alec was reminded that he'd probably got his ex-colleague out of bed when he'd called him at two in the morning. It was now almost seven and Alec really wanted his sleep.

'Give my best to Naomi. Tess will be sorry to have missed you but she is away on a course. And we've just had a phone call from DI Karen Morgan saying that she'll be coming up from Mallingham. Now it looks as though all investigations really do cross over. She said she knows the pair of you.'

'Yes, Naomi and Karen used to be very close.'

'Quite a reunion this is going to turn out to be,' Vin said.

Twenty-One

Bee had been taken back to the room and it had been Sian's turn to mother her, wrapping the towel round her hand and trying to comfort her.

'What did they want?' Sian's voice shook.

Bee, sobbing now but fighting for control, told her everything that had happened. All she'd said.

'Who's Bob Taylor?'

'An artist friend of Dad's. He said he'd seen the painting on the easel so Dad must have been working on it, but he told me it had disappeared. He doesn't know where it went. That's what he said, anyway.'

'But you don't believe him?'

'I don't know what to believe. Bob and Annie – that's his wife – Bob and Annie were trying to put me off when I said I thought Dad had been killed. I think they wanted to keep me out of trouble. So Bob might have lied about the painting going missing. He might have done what I told that man he'd done and taken the picture back to his place. My dad meant a lot to Bob so maybe he wanted to look after it.'

'Maybe.' Sian shrugged her shoulders.

'But I shouldn't have done it, should I? I've sent them to Bob and Annie's place and if anything happens to them it's going to be my fault, isn't it?'

Sian wasn't sure what to say. She couldn't deny

164

the truth of that and if she tried Bee would know she was lying. It wouldn't make her feel any better.

'You couldn't help it,' she said, hugging Bee close. 'You had to think fast. He broke your finger, for fuck's sake; who knows what he'd have done if you'd said nothing?'

'But I could have made something up. I should just have made something up. It was just the first thing that came into my head.'

She dissolved into tears again and Sian released her long enough to go and get more tissue from the cloakroom. Outside it was getting light again. She could just about see the brick wall. Neither girl had a watch but Sian guessed it must be after six. She sort of remembered it being this kind of light around then. Sian hadn't slept well lately and she'd often seen the dawn these past few weeks. She wondered if anyone was going to bring them food. They'd drunk water from the tap in the cloakroom but that was all. Apart from when Binnie had come for Bee and then brought her back, they'd not heard another sound from the rest of the house.

What now? Sian thought.

'How long have you known this Binnie?' Bee asked her.

Sian sighed. She didn't want to go into that right now, but she supposed Bee had a right to ask. 'Since junior school,' she said. 'We moved into a house about a mile away. Binnie was ten and I was nine. His little brother had just died. He'd drowned in the garden pond. Binnie seemed kind of lonely and Binnie's mum was really nice,

165

though losing her other little boy seemed to have made her a bit dippy. We both went to the same village school.

'Binnie went up to big school ahead of me and when I went . . . well, I got bullied that first term. Then Binnie found out and he did something to the bullies. I don't know what. I just know they left me alone after that and I was grateful, you know. We started to spend time together, and because we lived so close I saw him in the holidays as well. There were ponies in the field next to Binnie's house and the farmer let us ride them. We'd help out at the farm, that sort of thing. He taught Binnie to drive the tractor.'

'So how did he turn out to be like this? Like he is now?'

Sian shook her head. 'I don't know. I went away to uni and when I came back, he'd changed.' Or maybe, she thought, I started seeing him like he really was all along.

She couldn't quite believe that. Binnie had always been nice to her. There'd been a time when she'd wanted them to be proper girlfriend and boyfriend but Binnie had said he didn't have time for that sort of thing. What he really meant was that he saw her as a kid, she'd realized soon afterwards, when he'd started seeing a girl several years older than himself.

She was glad now; that would have been one more thing to regret.

'I guess it was always there. This other side,' she said at last. She remembered the rumours that had gone around, about Binnie's kid brother. She recalled that the farmer had told them they were not welcome when one of the horses had gone lame after they'd ridden her. She'd not understood, they'd always been so careful. Her mother had told her sternly not to go anywhere near the farmer again. But she'd never really explained why. Two weeks later the man's barn had burned to the ground with twenty of his milk herd, newly calved, inside.

It had never occurred to her that this had anything to do with Kevin Binns.

He was fun once, Sian thought. A bit wild, but he'd just been Binnie, and both of them had lived so far from their other friends – or, at least, Sian's other friends; looking back she couldn't really recall Binnie having that many – that they'd naturally gravitated towards one another.

'Mum never liked him,' she said. 'Dad worked away most of the week so he didn't really have much of an opinion. But Mum always felt that he was bad.'

'Got to agree with her,' Bee said.

It was light enough now for them to take a proper look at her hand. Bee unwound it carefully. Her little finger was black with bruising and stuck out at an odd angle. The bone between the joints was obviously broken and the finger slightly twisted. At the base of the finger, the joint seemed out of alignment. It hurt more than the break.

'I think it's dislocated,' Sian said, 'as well as broken. If we can get that joint back in place, it might not hurt so much.'

'How do you know that?'

'I don't. Not for sure.'

Bee studied her hand and then nodded. 'OK, we'll give it a go.'

'What! Really? Look, I mean, I don't know.'

'You going to help me or what? OK, you pull on that bottom bone and I'll press.'

Sian looked sick at the thought of it and Bee surveyed her green-tinged pallor with a mix of exasperation and sympathy. 'OK,' she said. 'I'll try it on my own.'

'No, I'll do what I can.'

It hurt beyond the level it had when Binnie had broken her finger, but something in Bee made her determined that she was going to undo what he had done. She felt immensely resentful that he'd made her give in so easily; immensely pissed off that the man had been right when he'd said that one finger would be enough because she wasn't that tough. She wanted to prove them wrong, if only for her own satisfaction.

In the end, the joint relocated with a click that seemed to resonate throughout Bee's entire arm – though she decided that the sound was probably just in her head. She felt faint and sick, a red mist almost blinding her as she tried not to pass out. With Sian's help, she staggered to the toilet and heaved, but her stomach was empty of everything apart from a little water and, her whole body in spasm, she brought up only bile.

Bee sat down hard next to the toilet and leaned back against the wall, a sheen of sweat on her face. Sian wet the towel again and wiped her forehead, then looked at her hand.

'It looks a bit straighter,' she said.

Bee could hardly bear to look. She squinted at

the offending hand and decided that Sian was right, then she allowed the hand to be rewrapped in the cold, damp towel.

'I want to kill him,' she said. 'I really want him to die.'

Monday, dawn. Sian had not come home, her mother was sure of that. Usually she heard doors opening or saw a light go on in the annexe.

She generally tried to respect her daughter's privacy but worry caused her to go through to the annexe, via the door from the main house. She stood in the tiny kitchen-cum-living room and called Sian's name. No reply.

She went through to the bedroom. Sian had always been tidy and the only thing out of place was a cardigan, lying on the end of the bed. The bed itself was not slept in. She'd not been home all night.

Tracey Price went and woke her husband.

'She's an adult; she probably stayed over at a friend's place.'

'And didn't tell us? Anyway, what friend? She was supposed to work at the pub last night, it's not likely she went over to a friend after that, is it?'

'When she was away at uni you'd not have known where she was,' her husband, Richard, said reasonably. He stretched reluctantly. 'I'd best get up, then. Get myself off to work.'

Richard left on Monday mornings for a job a two-hour drive away. He usually stayed overnight on weekdays, coming back on the Friday evening. Tracey didn't like the arrangement, but she had learnt to live with it. 'Don't go,' she said. 'Phone in and tell them you won't be there today.'

'Oh, for Pete's sake.' He looked impatiently at his wife but could see that she'd barely slept. 'OK, I'll tell them I'll be a bit late. Will that do?'

'I suppose it will have to,' she snapped back.

'Tracey—' But she had already stalked out of the room.

He'd had his shower and dressed before she came back. 'She didn't turn up for her shift at the pub. No one's seen her since we did, yesterday morning. I've phoned all the friends I can think of. Now I'm going over there.'

'Over where?' He noticed she was wearing her coat and wellingtons. 'Where are you off to?'

'He's got her. She's gone somewhere with *him*. I just know it.'

'Kevin,' Richard said. 'You think she's with Binnie again?'

'Where else is she? Ever? I warned her off, I told her he was bad news. She knows how I feel but does she take a blind bit of notice? Does she hell!'

'OK, look. I'm coming with you. Let me get my coat.'

He was dressed for work in his suit and tie, but he dragged on his wellingtons, tucking his suit trousers into his socks. He was still inclined to think his wife was making a fuss over nothing but a little niggle of panic was starting at the back of his own brain.

They took the path across the field, over the stile and down the rough track towards the old

170

farmhouse. It was, Tracey thought, a long time since she'd walked this way. She often took the footpath but she never came down to what, long ago, had been called Weston Farm. Actually only the house and a large garden remained, along with the orchard. The rest of the land had been sold to neighbours when the Westons had moved away and Binnie and his parents and little brother moved in. She was shocked at how dilapidated the place was. The lean-to conservatory no longer leaned but was falling to one side and the house didn't look as though it had seen a coat of paint in years.

The grass was soaking with dew and so long that it saturated her jeans above her wellingtons, right up to her knees, but Tracey paid no attention. She was looking for her child and that was her only focus.

They went round to the back door (nobody used front doors around there apart from the postman) and she hammered on the rotting wood.

'Keep that up and you'll break it down,' her husband observed.

She seemed to take that as a challenge and hit the door even harder. It moved under the weight of her fists but no one came to answer it.

Richard stepped back so he could get a better view of the upstairs windows. 'I'd say there's no one home. You sure he still lives here? The place looks like it's been deserted.'

He came back and peered in through the kitchen window. Here, there was at least some evidence of life. Plates on the draining board and a loaf of sliced bread on the kitchen table. 'I can't see Sian wanting to be in there, the place is filthy. You know how fastidious she is.'

He realized he was trying hard to be reassuring, almost jokey, and his wife's glare told him it wasn't really working. 'So what do you want to do?'

She had a mobile in her hand. 'I'm going to call the police.'

Her finger was poised above the nine and he reached out and took it from her. 'You can't call this an emergency,' he said. 'She's a grown woman, that's what they'll tell you. Let's go back home; we'll call the local police and report her missing.'

She reached for the phone but he held it away. 'Please, Tracey. Calling out the cavalry won't get you anywhere. Sian will turn up and just be terribly embarrassed.'

'I don't care how embarrassed she is.' She turned back to look at the kitchen door and then, before he could stop her, Tracey aimed a kick which burst the door open.

'Tracey? What the hell?'

But his wife had already gone inside. Richard stood in the kitchen while Tracey went running around the house. He could hear her footsteps on the stairs and then in the bedrooms. He'd been certain there was no one else in the house, so had not bothered following her. The silence was too profound and there was that feeling of neglect and emptiness that spoke of only occasional and transient occupancy.

He looked around the kitchen. The fridge was working, and there was milk and cheese and

172

butter inside. And out-of-date steak. There were letters on the kitchen counter; they all looked like bills apart from one postcard. Richard picked it up, curious, and realized that it wasn't addressed to Kevin Binns or any of his family. It was addressed to a girl called Bee and was from a friend who was staying in Venice.

The sense that his wife was right to be afraid had been growing but there was no sign of his daughter ever having been in this house, or at least not recently. As a child, he knew, she had been in and out of the place. But not since Mrs Binns had left, he was pretty sure of that.

He tried to remember whether Kevin's mother had left a forwarding address. If she had, his wife would know. She'd left in a tearing hurry, he knew that. Binnie had gone off for a few days and when he came back his mother had gone. Tracey had said she'd gone to Spain but no one seemed to know that for certain and as far as Richard was aware, no one had heard from her since she had departed so precipitately.

He remembered that she hadn't been able to stand her son. He remembered too, vaguely, that there had been another boy. That he'd died when he was very small and that the father had left either just before or just after that. But even in those days he'd worked away a lot and Richard really couldn't recall clearly.

Tracey was back down the stairs and standing in the kitchen, staring at him. 'She's not here,' he said.

'No.' She took a deep breath and then coughed as though the air in the kitchen was infectious and she wanted to get it out of her lungs. 'I don't think he uses much of the house. There's one bedroom with a bed in it, the rest are just full of boxes.'

'We should leave,' he said. 'Go home and call the local police and report her missing. I'll phone her friends again, just in case. I'll get in touch with work and tell them I won't be in for a few days.'

'Yes,' she said. She led the way out and Richard examined the door to see if there was any way of fastening it closed and then gave up. He was mildly worried in case Binnie realized it was they who broke his door down but he had the oddest feeling that Binnie would not be coming back to the house, a feeling he could not account for.

His wife was striding ahead of him and he let her go, knowing she needed to work off her anger before she reached home so that she could think more clearly. She waited for him at the stile that crossed into the last field, the one closest to their house. She was looking back across the valley towards another farm. 'Do you remember the barn fire?' she said.

'Hmm, he lost a load of cows and calves, I believe. Switched from mixed farming to arable after that, didn't he?' Richard wasn't sure where that memory was dredged up from. Tracey was the one who knew the neighbours; he knew them from occasional visits to the local pub and the summer barbecue which most of the village attended, but that was about all.

'There were rumours, about Binnie.'

'This is a small community; there are always rumours.'

'There were rumours about his little brother as well. That he didn't drown by accident. And no one really knows where his mother has gone.'

'Oh, for fuck's sake, Tracey. We know he's a bad lot but you can't blame everything on the boy.'

Wrong thing to say, he realized as she strode off again. Richard followed on behind, keeping his distance, his wife's fury trailing like a banner in her wake.

They called the police when they got home and their details were taken but as Richard had predicted the police officer told Tracey that Sian was an adult and she'd not been missing yet for a full twenty-four hours. When Tracey objected that no one had seen her since the morning before, the police officer told her that she didn't actually know that. Only that *she* hadn't seen her daughter. He suggested that she call her daughter's friends and try her workplace again, just in case there had been a misunderstanding.

Tracey slammed down the phone and strode off to the annexe. Richard left her to it.

He made them both some tea and toast, guessing that his wife would probably refuse to eat but feeling that he should make the option available to her at least. He definitely needed his food. He phoned his office and let them know what was going on and then called the pub. From the pub landlord he got a couple of other names and phone numbers and he called them too, and one of those was able to give him a few more possible contacts. Richard started to work his way through those.

He didn't know his daughter's university friends. He'd met a couple of them when they'd visited her at the university, but that three years away had been almost a closed book to him. Sian had spent it growing up and he knew that, in a way, the worst thing that had happened to her was that she should have had to come back and live at home. She'd flown the nest once and she should have been able to keep on flying.

But what else was to be done?

His wife's breakfast had grown cold and he went over to the annexe to suggest she come back and at least have a cup of tea. She was sitting on Sian's bed, a small pink address book between her hands. He sat down beside her.

'This was in her drawer. It's got emails and some phone numbers in it. I think it must be university friends. I don't recognize many of the names.'

He told her who he had already contacted and how. But that nobody had seen Sian the day before.

'Something's happened to her, I just know it.'

He was beginning to think she was right. 'We go back to the house, you eat something. No, don't argue with me, you need to keep your strength up. And we work our way through the phone numbers. We'll take half each. If there's no phone number then we'll send an email. If anyone's heard from her, we'll find out.'

She nodded reluctantly and he took the pink book from her, flicked through to see if anything was familiar to him.

'And then if she's not come back in a few hours we'll phone the police again and we'll keep on phoning them until someone takes notice of us.'

176

Twenty-Two

'How can any place be this quiet?' Sian asked. The window wouldn't open, but she pressed her ear against it trying to hear sounds from the outside. Occasionally there were indications of life, footsteps, once the sound of something metal being dragged across hard ground, but that was all. No one had been anywhere near them since the night before and it was as though they were utterly cut off, not just from the world but even from the house itself.

Bee's stomach grumbled. Both girls were really hungry now. 'It's like they've just forgotten about us,' she said.

The silence surrounding them encouraged them to explore the room further, assuming that if they could hear nothing then no one could hear them either. They had looked for security cameras, hidden microphones – even though neither of them knew exactly what such a thing would look like – but had discovered nothing.

The window was small. Even if they smashed a pane they couldn't hope to squeeze through, and the transom itself was nailed shut. There was an empty built-in cupboard and Bee had become briefly excited when she discovered a wire coat hanger. Surely that had to be useful for something? The two of them had sat on the bed staring at it as though its use would reveal itself and Bee

177

had tried untwisting the coil of wire from around the hook, but her fingers were not strong enough.

They'd searched the chest of drawers, the only furniture in the room apart from the bed. And they both tried hurling their full weight at the door but it had not even rattled. It looked like an ordinary wooden door on the inside, but they'd come to the conclusion that it was reinforced in some way.

'Someone will come looking for us,' Sian said, sounding more confident than she actually felt. 'Mum and Dad will know I'm missing, they will have phoned the police.'

But where would they even start? she thought. They certainly wouldn't be looking for a big house in the middle of nowhere.

They guessed it was somewhere around midday because the light outside was quite bright, or comparatively so; the day seemed very overcast still. Once more they heard footsteps on the stairs, two pairs this time.

Binnie opened the door and both girls huddled in a corner, afraid he had come to take one of them again. He had a woman with him and she was carrying a tray. She put it down on the bed and then went out again. Binnie grinned at them both and then left, locking the door behind him.

For a moment or two both girls stood staring at the tray and the door, not quite knowing what to do. There were sandwiches on the tray, and bottles of orange juice and apples.

'Do we eat them?' Sian said. 'What if they're drugged or poisoned?'

178

'With Binnie around, do you think they need to resort to drugs or poison?' Bee asked. 'I'm hungry. I'm going to eat.'

They both sat down on the bed and examined the contents of the tray. There was also a small blister pack which, when Sian turned it over, she discovered contained painkillers. 'These must be for you,' she said.

Bee took them and examined the packet carefully but it seemed to be just ordinary paracetamol and there was no sign of tampering. She extracted two and took them with the orange juice. Her hand was throbbing horrendously and the bruising had spread from the finger across the back and the palm.

They ate in silence, both surprised at how much better it made them feel. 'At least they don't want us to starve to death,' Sian said. 'Is that a good sign?'

'I don't know,' Bee said.

They stared at one another. In the hours they'd spent together they had discussed every possible permutation that they could think of, but worst of all were the possibilities they didn't want to think about.

By early afternoon Naomi's little flat was looking rather crowded. Alfie had already had a formal meeting with Vin and both had then come on to meet Karen at Naomi's. Karen was going back with Vin later for a proper briefing but they had all agreed that a couple of hours of pooling resources would be useful.

Alec had managed to grab a few hours' sleep,

but Vin had not yet been home and the weariness was beginning to show.

'So,' Karen began, 'what can you tell us about this Graham Harcourt?'

'According to Companies House,' said Alfie, 'he owns an investment company going by the name of AltInvo. Essentially he takes other people's money and invests in various businesses; they get the profits after he's taken his cut. It's not quite a hedge fund, and it's just on the right side, legally, of becoming a Ponzi scheme. Often these businesses are quite high risk but they are also high return. We're talking oil, precious metals, art – which is what is relevant to us here – and some more exotic resources. More recently he's been investing heavily in palm oil, for instance. Essentially, he doesn't care what the commodity is as long as the return is fast.

'Now there's evidence that AltInvo is a shell company, and that within that shell company are nested other more specialist businesses.

'As you can imagine, the deeper you dig into the shell, the more layered it gets and the more difficult it is to track down exactly who is doing what or who owns what. I got a list of names, directors of these other companies, but it's far from complete and I don't even know that the names are genuine. All I can do is work through them one at a time. The evidence I have seems to indicate that family members are often used to front what look like different companies but are actually the same institution. And of course we're into the area of offshore tax havens, and we can assume that money laundering is going on.'

180

'And have you linked Freddie Jones to this?'

Alfie paused. 'Yes and no. We know that Graham Harcourt is an art collector and also an art dealer. We know he owns one or two Freddie Jones pieces because he bought them from Scotts. Unusually, alongside a couple of drawings, there's a large painting. Scotts normally only dealt in Freddie's drawings but on this occasion they handled the commission for Freddie. Now I've not seen this piece, I only have a description of it and it's described as "a woodland scene in the style of Nicolas Poussin". Now exactly what's meant by "in the style of" here is something of a moot point, considering Freddie's past. But as Scotts brokered the deal we have to assume that, on the face of it at least, this is an original artwork and not a copy – or a fake.'

'You said "yes and no", and that sounds like a definite yes, so what is your possible no?'

'It seems Freddie Jones did some work for Graham Harcourt, off the books. I found a series of emails that Antonia Scott sent to Freddie, and if you want to know how I got them, Bob Taylor was also copied in. They were emails expressing concern about rumours that Freddie was engaged in a series of commissions for Graham Harcourt and maybe another collector. Bob was copied in because Freddie was not replying to Antonia's emails and the thought was that Bob might persuade him to see reason. Her major concern was that, as Freddie's ersatz agent, she was missing out on the commission.'

'And how long was that before Freddie died?' Karen asked.

'Two, close to three weeks. I've brought copies of the emails, but in brief, Bob intervened and suggested that Freddie at least talk to Antonia. After all, she'd been very good to him in the past and he sold a good deal of work through Scotts. Freddie maintained that Antonia's representation was only for the one painting and that he didn't owe her a damn thing for the others he had agreed to produce.

'Apparently Bob finally pinned him down and Freddie said he didn't think Antonia would approve of his customer base. Antonia was, as Freddie put it, "legit and upmarket".'

'Which seems to imply that whoever he was doing the work for was not,' Naomi said. 'Though I thought that, on the face of it, Graham Harcourt was both legit and upmarket?'

'You'd think, wouldn't you? But apparently Freddie saw him otherwise and didn't want Antonia involved. At least that's what he told Bob. It was at that point that Bob and Annie contacted me and asked me to look into Graham Harcourt's affairs. Soon after that, of course, Freddie died, but sometime in the weeks beforehand Bob persuaded him to take the portfolio of drawings to Antonia. I guess it was a kind of sweetener to make up for her missing out on the other deal. Apparently the portfolio was dropped off at the gallery about a week before Freddie died, but Antonia, at that stage, hadn't seen the drawings. She'd been away in France or Belgium or somewhere and her brother had taken delivery. He was satisfied, but as far as the art was concerned Antonia was the brains of the operation. She had the eye.'

'And that's why her brother had left them for her to see on the day they were stolen,' Karen speculated. 'She was due to meet a new artist. From what we can tell, Antonia turned up at the gallery about half an hour before opening time. She saw a young woman with a portfolio standing outside the gallery; a few people spotted her beforehand and assumed that she was a new artist. In fact a café owner from a few doors down remembers speaking to her. He congratulated her on the fact that Scotts was interested and he remembers that she looked nervous and just smiled at him. But he assumed she was nervous because Antonia had quite a reputation.'

She'd set up a laptop on the table and now she apologized to Naomi. 'I'm sorry you can't see this, it's pretty interesting.' She turned it so the rest of the company could. 'Now this is from the CCTV traffic camera set up in the street just down from the gallery. You see, there's the young woman with the portfolio. She's standing around looking nervous, the image of a young artist about to enter the dragon's den. And here comes Antonia. She speaks to the girl and they both go inside. Now watch. Sorry, Naomi.'

'Bloody hell.' This from Alec.

'What?' There were times when her lack of vision really made Naomi grumpy.

'This blur, this guy, he comes out of nowhere. He charges into the gallery and only seconds later he and the girl come out, carrying her portfolio and another one. Bloody hell, he was fast.'

'Familiar, too,' Alfie said.

'While he's familiar in the sense that we've

183

now got another sighting of him, the man we saw at the warehouse, we still don't have a clue who he is. Or the girl – but she certainly looks like the girl that was in the car, the blue car on Sunday afternoon. Now look at her face as they come out.'

The man had his head down as though avoiding the cameras, but the girl either hadn't thought about that or was too shocked even to try. They'd had a clear view of her standing outside the gallery and they had a clear view now of her trying to pull away from the man. She was looking around as though trying to summon help and she looked terrified.

'Again, she seems to be under duress,' Alec commented.

'And then about ten minutes later the real artist arrives, finds her would-be patron dead and phones the police and the ambulance. And that is about as far as we got. Dead ends everywhere we look. Not a trace of criminality in the Scotts' dealings, not a trace of irregularity in any of their finances – or at least not as far as our experts can tell. Alfie, have you looked into the Scotts?'

'I have, and I concur. On the face of it, they're squeaky clean.'

'And *not* on the face of it?' Karen wanted to know.

'And *not* on the face of it, there are times when they sailed pretty close to the edge. When they may well have handled either stolen or misrepresented goods, but you'd probably find the same history in most upmarket galleries. It's not always possible to establish provenance for a piece and

184

until fairly recently, record keeping was often poor. The internet's made a big difference. You can see that in the high-profile cases where Jewish-owned art has been reclaimed after years of going from dealer to dealer, collector to collector after the Second World War. Most of the galleries and dealers involved dealt in good faith, because there was no paper trail. It's only when there are records of original ownership, and when those records can be verified and information about them disseminated sufficiently widely, that connections can be made. And for the most part, this is high-profile art. Big names, well documented paintings. Freddie Jones didn't get involved with that; he concentrated on "school of" or "follower of" works, so far as we know. Or the lesser known masters with gaps in their catalogues raisonnés. Paintings that were known to have existed but were presumed lost.'

'I've something else to throw into the mix,' Vin Dattani said. 'You might've heard on the news a couple of days ago about a man being found on waste ground, beaten half to death. Well, we've identified him.'

'Has he regained consciousness?' Naomi asked.

'No, not yet. But as sometimes happens when the doctors think someone may not survive, we took fingerprints. Sometimes it might be the only way of finding a next of kin in time for them to say their goodbyes. In this case, we found a match for the fingerprints and he turned out to have a record. His name is Toby Elden. He's been done for receiving stolen goods on a few occasions, and specializes in stolen antiquities.'

185

'I know the name,' Alfie said. 'It came up in some of my research. But not in connection with Graham Harcourt.' He paused and flicked through his notes and Naomi got up to make more tea while he was looking. It took him a few minutes but then he said, 'Right, I've got it now. For a brief time he owned a gallery. Eastbourne, heart of respectability. And he sold some of Freddie Jones's drawings and the odd painting. I've not got it here, but I know I do have a partial customer list back at the office. I'll let you have it, but I'll also run it by Bob. There's a possibility he may recognize a name or two on it.'

'OK,' Vin said. 'At least we can say some of the threads are being pulled together, even if we don't know who all of the players are. A shape of sorts is beginning to emerge.'

There was a murmur of agreement. It wasn't much, but it was a start.

Karen and Vin left fairly soon after this because she still had to have her official briefing and now they had more information.

Alec followed them out, heading for the corner shop to get more milk. Karen promised to call back later and they were going to take the opportunity to have dinner together and a proper catch-up. She'd booked into a hotel for the night.

'So,' Naomi said, 'what's your take on all this, Alfie? And what are you protecting Bob from?'

Alfie laughed. 'Not much gets past you, does it?'

'Oh, it does, all the time. But you see, I know a little bit about Bob that the others don't. I know that Freddie was his mentor and I also know that when Bob started out he had bugger all. Like a lot of artists, he struggled to make ends meet for the first few years. Oh, he's successful now, very successful, but that wasn't always the case, and when you're hanging around someone like Freddie Jones, well, I just wonder if—'

'If he succumbed to temptation,' Alfie finished. 'The truth is, Naomi, I don't know. And I don't want to ask. But I'm making the assumption that Bob may well, like the Scotts, have sailed a little close to the wind at times, or have more knowledge of those who did than is really comfortable for him. I know if I asked him straight out he'd tell me, but unless that becomes relevant . . .'

'Why poke tigers?'

'Indeed. Annie is my friend, my friend of long standing, and I do not wish any harm to come to her or her husband, not even just embarrassment. I owe her, you might say, so if I'm a little careful with the truth it won't be because I want to interfere with the investigation. Far from it; neither Bob nor Annie would ever stand for that. But what is long past can remain long past, I hope. There are a few of us who have not been tempted to bend the rules when we're desperate.'

Alec came back, and the conversation shifted easily to more neutral concerns. But when Alfie was about to leave, Naomi said, 'I'm bored, you know that? Getting involved, even peripherally, has been good for me. I can help with your research. I've been doing some of my own and all I need is a few pointers on what direction to take next.'

She heard Alec open his mouth to intervene and then think better of it.

187

'Then we'll have to have a think about you doing some research for me. I'll pay you the same rate I usually pay my researchers. Oh, don't worry, Alec, nothing she can't do sitting at a table with that laptop – and any bits of tech you haven't got, Naomi, I probably have.'

Alec saw him out. They'd obviously paused for a conversation at the top of the stairs because he was a few minutes coming back, but he sounded happier when he did. Alfie had obviously reassured him, she thought, and felt slightly resentful about that.

'Seems we've both got new jobs,' Alec said.

Twenty-Three

The girls were both sleeping when Binnie burst through the door and grabbed Sian by the arm.

Sian screamed in panic and Bee, forgetting her hand, hurled herself at the man. He shoved her aside so hard she bounced off the bed and hit the wall, and lay there stunned and winded. By the time she had struggled to her feet, Binnie and Sian had gone. Bee hammered on the door, almost relishing the pain from her broken finger. Then, as she realized this was a useless effort, she slid to the floor and wept angry, frightened tears.

Where had Binnie taken her? Would he bring her back? Bee had just about coped with the kidnapping and imprisonment because she'd at least not been alone. Sian had been with her, talked to her, shared the fear and, yes, the shame of walking into trouble. Both girls had felt, totally irrationally (at least on Bee's part), that they had been in some way to blame. Sian because she had let Binnie dominate her and Bee because she had drawn Patrick into her affairs and probably got him killed as a result.

Abruptly, she stopped crying and retreated to the bed once more. There were footsteps on the stairs, two sets, but lighter than Binnie's. For a moment she thought it might be Sian coming back but then the door opened and the woman they had seen the day before came in carrying another tray. A man stood behind her; he didn't fully enter the room, so Bee could not see him properly. Bee guessed he was just the hired muscle.

The woman put the tray down and then departed without a word.

Bee stared at the closed door and slowly she realized that her fear was being replaced by pure unadulterated anger. She was furious at the situation she was in. Scared, yes, of course, but she could feel a rage growing inside her and it was a good feeling. Somehow it made her feel less of a victim, however illogical that really was.

There were more sandwiches on the tray and some biscuits and another apple. Another little bottle of orange juice. More painkillers.

Not expecting any more, Bee had been rationing them. She counted the number in the blister pack; the idea had entered her head that there were now enough to kill herself, should things get really bad. She'd read somewhere that it only took nine paracetamol to bring about fatal liver failure. That didn't sound like much fun, but who knew what they'd got in mind for her and she found it oddly soothing to know that there might be another way out, even though reason told her she'd probably never take it. She allowed herself two paracetamol; hammering on the door had really hurt her hand, but it was good pain. Self-inflicted, and born of anger and not fear. Or at least not completely of fear.

She wondered about keeping sandwiches back for Sian, but there seemed to be only one portion so obviously the woman didn't expect Sian to be back any time soon. In the end, hunger took over and she ate everything on the plate.

There had to be a way out of here. She had to try and find one, at least, though she and Sian had spent hours yesterday studying the room and speculating and coming up with more and more outlandish ideas, so she wasn't sure what made her think today would be any different.

She went back to the door, pushing at it experimentally, even though she knew it wouldn't move. Running her hands around the edges, she couldn't even feel a draught. So that left the window. The panes, they'd already established, were far too small for them to get out of and it looked like quite a long way down, but maybe if she tore the bed sheets up and tied them together and then tied them to the leg of the bed?

Even as she thought of it she knew it was a silly idea but she felt she had to do something. Her thoughts went back to the coat hanger in the cupboard.

She tried again to unravel the wire but bruised and bloodied fingers soon told her this was a lost cause. But there was a second, wooden hanger with a metal hook, and with a bit of persuasion the hook came away from the wooden frame.

She took it across to the window and started to poke about, prodding around the frame and then the frame itself, and discovered that actually parts of it were completely rotten and could be picked away.

Bee stepped back and looked at it thoughtfully, wondering if she could remove the middle cross-piece and then pull the glass panes out. She wasn't even quite sure how windows fitted together or how the glass was fitted in but at least it would give her something to do, and since no one seemed to stay in the room very long – when they came in at all – it was quite likely no one would notice what she was up to until it was too late.

'Stupid idea,' she said. But she knew she was going to do it anyway. What else was there?

Slowly and carefully she began to work away around the panes of glass, loosening the old putty and half rotten wood. She was pretty sure that nobody could hear her inside this servant's wing – which was what she and Sian had decided it was – but she wasn't so sure about anybody hearing her from the yard so she worked slowly and quietly, pecking away, a fraction at a time.

When Sian gets back she can help, Bee told herself. It was unthinkable that Sian would not return.

Twenty-Four

Annie's phone began to beep but not in the way it would if she was just receiving a text message. She took it out of her pocket and stared at it. 'Turn the car round – we need to go home,' she told Bob.

He glanced at her and then looked for somewhere in the narrow road where he could comfortably swing the vehicle around. The road leading from their house was winding and narrow, not the place to do a U-turn. 'What's up? Was that the house alarm?' About six months before, after an incident at their home, they had installed a remote alarm that rang their mobile phones, and the police, if anything happened. He'd never actually heard an alert until now.

'It was. Look, there's a gate over there. The alarm company will have phoned the police.' She knew that the alarm itself was silent so whoever had broken in would not hear it and be warned, but she was worried about their two dogs.

Bob swung into the farm gateway and performed a clumsy three-point turn before pulling back out on to the road and putting his foot down. They were, he estimated, only about ten minutes from home. He wasn't sure how long the police would take to get there but, like Annie, he was worried about the two dogs and what might happen if the burglars confronted them. Not so much what would happen to the burglars, the dogs were soft as tripe, but someone breaking in might not realize that, especially if Dexter decided to make his usual 'I don't understand what's going on but I'm going to bark about it' racket.

'Don't worry,' he said. 'We'll be back in a few minutes. And the police shouldn't be long.'

'It could take them anything up to half an hour,' Annie said. 'One of the disadvantages of being in the middle of nowhere.'

Bob glanced at her. He knew that the suggestion that they might stay in the car until the police arrived would not be considered for a moment, therefore he decided not even to make it.

The road straightened slightly and Bob accelerated again, very much aware that had he handed over to his wife, Annie would have driven much faster and undoubtedly a lot better. He could sense her mild impatience but she didn't say anything.

He swung off the road and on to the track that led down to their cottage. It was single track with passing points cut into the verge at intervals and it curved gradually so that they could not see the house until they were almost there. Bob was surprised to see that there was no one parked.

'They must have come in through the back way,' Annie said. Behind their garden were fields and woods.

Annie got out of the car, the front door keys already in her hand. Bob followed, pausing only to take a tyre iron out of the boot.

* * *

193

'There are dogs, I can hear them barking.'

'They can't get in here. And besides, I've got a gun.'

Sian was horrified. 'You can't shoot dogs. You can't shoot someone's pet dogs.'

'Then you'd better hope they don't get in here, hadn't you?'

She swung round to stare at the door.

Binnie laughed at her and Sian stiffened. She hated it when Binnie laughed that way. It was cruel and cold and not like the boy she had grown up with.

'Why are you like this now? What happened to you?' She'd asked him that same question before and he'd just shrugged or grinned at her as though it was a stupid one.

'We get what we came for, we get out. Simple as that.'

'Why did you have to drag me along?'

'You could have said no.'

'Could I? From what I remember you didn't give me much choice. You kidnapped me, took me to that house, locked me up. What choice did I have?'

He laughed again. 'There's always a choice,' he said. 'You could have made it. You could certainly have made it earlier, before you agreed to help me out with that gallery owner.'

'I didn't know what you were going to do. How could I have?'

'You must have guessed you wouldn't like it. Pretending to be something you weren't, pretending to be someone else. Even you must have known that was wrong.' Binnie laughed at her again. 'You're even more stupid than I thought you were. You had a choice then, didn't you? You just wouldn't have liked what I'd have done afterwards, but the choice was still there.'

Sian blinked back tears. 'Let's just get out of here before they come back.'

The back of the house had been converted into a studio with windows all along one side and more windows in the roof. It was part room, part glorified conservatory, boarded and comfortable, and she could imagine it being cosy in the winter with a log fire at one end. The wall opposite the windows was partly panelled and covered with pin boards and pictures. Canvases, boards and frames were propped against it. She found herself drawn to one of the paintings leaning against the wall. It was a large work, very beautiful. A lone tree with its roots reaching down into the earth and what looked like another world beneath. The painting was unfinished but she could see how wonderful it was going to be. She was distracted by a yelp of triumph from Binnie. He was comparing a painting to a photograph he had in his hand. 'Is that it?' she asked.

'Sure to be. Look for yourself.'

Sian came over to the table and looked at the painting and then at the photograph. They did look the same, and yet . . . 'Binnie, I'm not sure—'

'Not sure about what? Look for yourself. It's a Madonna and fucking child, isn't it? Looks the same as the one in the photo, doesn't it?'

Sian stared at the painting. It wasn't the same, she was sure of it. This picture was lovely, but

195

there were differences – though she found it hard to say exactly what they were. Abstractedly, she found herself wishing that the photograph was clearer so that she could compare the way the brush strokes had been made and the colour applied. But there was no arguing with Binnie and she wasn't going to try.

The dogs were barking loudly but the tone had changed. Binnie was too absorbed to notice, freeing the little painting from its easel and shoving it into the canvas bag he had brought with him.

'I can hear a car,' Sian said. 'Listen to the dogs. It's them, they've come back.' She headed towards the French windows but Binnie, head cocked, stood still and simply stared at the door as she had done earlier but with a slight smile on his face. He wanted them to confront him, Sian realized suddenly. He wanted an excuse to fire his gun.

'Binnie, we have to go. Now!'

The car doors had slammed and the front door crashed open. Was it just because they'd heard the dogs that they knew something was wrong? she wondered. If there'd been something wrong in her house she would have sat in the car and phoned the police, she wouldn't have come bursting in like that. She could hear footsteps in the hall, running, and voices shouting, presumably to the dogs. Another door opened.

Binnie stood for a moment longer and then he turned and strode towards the patio doors as though he had all the time in the world. Sian turned as well. She wanted to run but suddenly a door opened at the other end of the studio and a woman appeared. Binnie swung round but the woman also had a gun. It was a shotgun, rather than a handgun, that she held, but at that moment Sian equated size with additional force and the armed woman seemed much more frightening, especially as Sian was standing between her and Binnie. Especially as there was nowhere logical for her to run.

Sian hadn't even known that second door was there. It was concealed in the panelling with a pin board hanging on the back and she had just not noticed it. All her attention had been on the main door through from the house and through this door a man now emerged, with two dogs.

Binnie turned and fired and the man swore and the next thing she knew the man had grabbed her and she was on the floor with her hands behind her back and the dogs barking at her. She heard the woman fire the shotgun and glass breaking. The man swore again and Binnie laughed.

'You've got her?' the woman called over, and then Sian was aware that she had run out in pursuit of Binnie. Sian wanted to call to her not to do it, to tell her that Binnie was a nutcase and would shoot before he even thought about it. She doubted Binnie thought about anything much any more.

'I've got her,' the man confirmed, though the woman was gone and could no longer have heard him. He had both of Sian's wrists clamped in one surprisingly strong fist and in the other he now had a mobile phone and Sian could hear him speaking to the police.

'I'm not going to struggle,' she said. 'I'm not going to fight you, but please, tell the police he's gonna hurt my mum and dad. Tell the police they've got to look after them.'

The man paused in his conversation and then said, 'Tell me who they are.' He stood up, pulling Sian with him, and sat her down in a chair by the wall. The dogs stood guard but the truth was all the fight had gone out of her, and she realized he must be able to see that. He leaned against the table and studied Sian carefully while he finished his conversation and put the phone back in his pocket.

'The police have promised to send a patrol car to your parents. And they're on their way here.'

Sian was just terrified about her mum and dad; she no longer cared what happened to her, she just wanted them to be safe. 'You sure?' she said. 'Because as soon as he's out of here, he will report back and he'll tell them . . . he'll tell them to go and hurt my mum and dad.'

The man regarded her solemnly, head slightly tilted to one side as though considering whether or not to believe her. In his position, Sian thought, she probably wouldn't have done. Something else occurred to her. 'Aren't you worried about your wife? She shouldn't have gone after him.'

'Annie can take care of herself. What's your name?'

'Sian, Sian Price. I didn't want to come here. But he said if I didn't—'

'Save it for the police,' he said.

Sian felt as though he'd slapped her in the face. She wanted to tell him, wanted him to know that

198

it hadn't been her idea. 'He wanted to damage things,' she said. 'I told him he couldn't do that.'

'And how would you have stopped him?'

Sian didn't know and just stared at the floor. Binnie hadn't actually said he wanted to do any damage but she knew he did. That was what Binnie was like now. Maybe it was what he had always been like.

The woman came back, the shotgun broken over her arm. 'He had a four by four parked in the next field, took off like a bat out of hell. I've got the number but the plates are probably false. Took Jeff's gate out on the way. Fortunately he has no livestock in the field at the moment or we'd be dealing with cows on the road too.'

She seemed oddly relaxed, Sian thought. As though this was almost an everyday occurrence, as though it didn't faze her.

'The police are on their way,' the man said. 'This young woman tells me her name is Sian Price and she's worried about her parents. The idiot with her apparently threatened them.'

'OK. Did the police give an ETA?'

'They said ten minutes when I spoke to the controller. They were already alerted by the alarm. But you know what their estimates are like.'

'Then I'd best get the kettle on,' Annie said. 'What did he take?' She glanced around the studio and frowned. 'He took Patrick's Madonna? Now why would he do that?'

'Presumably because the young man involved was not an art expert. He must have thought it was Freddie's.'

199

The woman called Annie raised an eyebrow but made no comment and absurdly Sian felt a moment of gratification that she had been right. That the painting had not been done by Freddie Jones.

'Patrick is going to be very upset about that,' Annie said. 'When he recovers.' She looked directly at Sian and said, 'I'm assuming it was your boyfriend who attacked him at Freddie's studio?'

'He's not my boyfriend. Yeah, it was him.'

'Well, you may or may not be glad to know that Patrick will survive.'

'I am glad. I'd no idea what Binnie was going to do.'

'Though how disabled he will be is anyone's guess at the moment.'

Sian swallowed nervously. The man that she now realized must be Bob Taylor seemed like a pretty ordinary sort but this woman, this Annie, was anything but. There was a coldness and sternness to her that Sian found frankly terrifying.

The police's sirens could now be heard and Annie went to welcome them.

Sian, overwhelmed now, began to cry.

Twenty-Five

There were two patrol cars. Two of the police officers came into the studio and looked around and Sian heard them talking to Annie as she was led away into the kitchen. One of the police officers was calling for the CSI to come. Another one bagged Annie's shotgun and she heard Annie saying that the licence was in the kitchen drawer. Sian gathered that because guns had been involved she was immersed in a whole new level of shit.

One of the police officers pulled out a chair and told her to sit down. She did, noticing how beautiful the grain was on the scrubbed oak table. It was as though her mind couldn't grasp the situation she was in and so her thoughts were bouncing around irrelevancies. But one thing kept breaking through. 'I need to phone my mum and dad, I need to tell them to get out of the house. They'll hurt them. Maybe worse. Binnie said he would.'

Bob had dealt with the kettle and was now retrieving Annie's paperwork from the kitchen drawer. He laid it out on the table. 'I promised that you'd have somebody going out to see this girl's parents,' Bob said. 'Could one of you just check that's happening? Better safe than sorry, don't you think?'

Sian could see that the police officers thought she was just making things up but one of them shrugged and asked for Sian's address again. She heard him calling control a few minutes later.

'Your mum and dad will be meeting you at the police station; they're on their way now.'

'I want to talk to them; I need to talk to them. I need to know they're all right.'

'Where's the harm?' Bob Taylor said. He unhooked a phone from the wall and brought it over to the table. Neither police officer gave permission, but that didn't stop her.

Hands shaking, Sian managed to dial her mother's mobile number. Her mother answered on the second ring, asking who this was.

'Mum, it's me. Are you all right?' She listened as her mother demanded to know what on earth she'd been doing, what was going on. Somehow her mother's anger was reassuring. It felt normal and balanced and told her that she was still cared for and Sian realized with massive shock that she'd come to doubt that. She had almost ceased to care for herself and had unconsciously assumed that others had stopped caring for her too. 'Are you going to the police station?'

Yes, her mother told her, they were on their way now, just turning in to the end of the road. They would be there, waiting for her to arrive.

'Stay there, Mum, please stay there. Don't go anywhere else, it's not safe.' Sian was crying again now though her mother was asking her things she couldn't manage to answer.

Gently Bob took the phone from her and Sian could hear him having a conversation with her mother. It seemed strange that the man whose house she had just broken into was now the one who was facilitating things for her, the one who was helping her.

Annie came into the kitchen accompanied by the other two officers. She glanced around, assessing the scene, and then went to pour tea and put the kettle on to boil again. 'If you look behind you, Craig, there are some biscuits in the cupboard.' The police officer she had addressed

202

turned and opened the cupboard door. Sian was amazed again at how at ease this woman seemed. What was it with her? She was as weird as Binnie.

'So what happens now?' Annie said.

'Two of us will take the young woman back to the station, two of us will wait here for the CSI,' the one called Craig told her. 'You think only the one thing was taken?'

'As far as I can tell,' Annie said. 'You'd better take Bob back into the studio. If anything else is missing he'll know.'

Craig grabbed a mug of tea and a couple of the biscuits and then he and Bob left the kitchen. Sian watched them go, nervously. She found that she was glad that the other officers were still in the kitchen and she wasn't alone with Annie. Sian had had a lot of experience, lately, with predators. Enough to know when she was in the presence of another one.

Bob stood on the threshold of the studio and looked around carefully. Nothing else missing, nothing damaged apart from the window that Annie had shot out. 'I hope she bloody hit him,' he said.

Craig laughed. 'Maybe you'd better hope she missed,' he observed. 'Make life less complicated, eh? Your wife says he probably took that picture by mistake, so what would they actually be after?'

'I think she's right about that. It's an excellent copy. It was painted by a young man who works as my part-time studio assistant; unfortunately he's in hospital at the moment. And in fact it seems that the bloke who broke in here today is responsible for that too – according to the girl, anyway.'

'So Mrs Taylor told me.'

'Raven; she didn't take my name. Her name is Annie Raven.' Bob found that he was smiling as he said this. He knew a few people took it the wrong way, that Annie had kept her own name, but Bob himself would have been astonished if she'd done anything else. It would have been as though he had tried to put a stamp of ownership on her – and nobody owned Annie.

'A lot of people seem to be doing that nowadays,' Craig commented. 'Friends of mine got married a couple years back, and they did a double barrel kind of thing, putting the names together. My cousin got married, she kept her own name too. You never heard about it a few years ago, did you? But our Sally, she's got her own business and everything, run it for years, so it made sense for her to keep her own name. So what you think they were after, then? Annie said there was another painting.'

Bob turned to the panelling and felt along the edge. It clicked open, revealing a space behind and a substantial wall safe. He input the combination and opened the door.

'That's quite a security system,' Craig commented. 'Just for paintings, is it?'

'I do appraisals and restorations,' Bob told him. 'Sometimes the artworks I keep here are very expensive so I have to have a security system to match. I upgraded the house alarm a few months back. Now we get a call if anything is amiss and so do you. There are cameras out front and back. I'll download what you need from the hard drive. Usually all we get is foxes and badgers.'

Bob withdrew a wooden box and set it down on the table, opened it up. Inside was a small painting in a beautiful gilt frame. A Madonna and child and St Anne, painted in colour that gleamed like gemstone. It was delicate and beautiful and caused even Craig to draw a quick breath.

'Wow, that's a bit of all right, that is. Valuable, is it?'

'That, my friend, is a moot question. Up to now I thought there was every likelihood that this was a forgery; but given that someone is prepared to try and steal it, I'm beginning to wonder about that one. I'm supposed to be making a decision about it, whether it's a genuine sixteenth-century painting or one that was made about a decade ago by Mr Freddie Jones. I was inclined towards the Freddie Jones theory but now I'm beginning to wonder.'

'Our thief isn't going to make himself very popular, is he? Not when he turns up with the wrong painting.'

'I suspect he's going to make himself very unpopular. I suspect it may not go well for him, let's say that.'

Bob repackaged the painting and put it back in the safe, closing the door and then the panelling.

They heard a car pull up on the gravel drive. 'That will probably be the CSI,' Craig said. 'We better get out of here so they can do their job. Sooner they do, the sooner you can have your studio back. I bet you're glad you had that alarm installed.'

Bob agreed that he was. He returned to the kitchen while Craig opened the front door and let the tech support inside.

Craig came back into the kitchen with his colleague, who had news for them. 'The girl reckons she and Beatrix Jones have been locked up together, the past couple of days. She's in the middle of nowhere, locked up in what sounds like servants' quarters in some big house.'

Bob exchanged a look with Annie. Who did they know who owned a big house? The name Graham Harcourt sprang to mind, but surely that was just too far-fetched? He decided to save it and talk to Vin later on rather than try to explain everything to these two police constables. DS Dattani at least had the background information already, or so Naomi had told him after the meeting at her flat the previous afternoon.

A few minutes later all four officers left, there being no reason now for anyone to remain behind now that the CSI were here. Annie set about a new round of tea and coffee making, leaving mugs and biscuits on the hall table and then retreating to the kitchen.

'So,' Bob said, 'did you hit him?'

Annie grinned. 'I winged him, but it didn't slow the bastard down. He was over the fence before I had the chance to fire.' She shrugged. 'Pity.'

'Maybe not. I'm not up to speed on body disposal and a dead burglar might have complicated life just when we don't want it.'

'Do we ever want it to be complicated?'

Bob smiled at his wife. 'Probably not, but I've learnt to live with a certain level.' He grew more serious again. 'So, what do you reckon's going on here, Annie? I mean, first Patrick attacked and Bee getting snatched, and now this.'

'Someone wants that painting. Either because it's genuine or because it's not. Or because . . . Bob, you've not taken it out of the frame yet, have you?'

'It's not in a frame, as such. There's a raised border that's actually built up with gesso on to the picture surface and then gilded at the same time as the detail on the painting itself. The only difference being that the frame is gold leaf and the detail on the Madonna and child is shell gold; that's why the detail is so fine.'

She nodded. She'd become familiar with the different technique, having watched Bob work. Shell gold was applied with a brush or a pen, on to a base of either fine clay or bole. It was a skilled technique that resulted in incredibly fine, brilliant details.

'And behind the backing board?'

'I've not removed it yet. I suggest you give me a hand as soon as our CSI friends have gone.'

Annie nodded. She glanced at the kitchen clock. It was just after three p.m. 'I'm going to check in with Harry,' she said, picking up her phone. 'Let him know we might not make it over today and bring him up to speed. He needs to be careful, now. We all do. I'll speak to Naomi as well, while I'm about it.'

The dogs, sensing that their humans were still

207

upset, ambled over and Dexter lay his head against Annie's knee. She stroked him absently, and Bob got up to wash the latest round of mugs. He'd been shaken by the day's events. He loved this house and his studio but it wasn't the first time that violence had damaged the peace. He thought about moving, to somewhere less isolated, perhaps, but the thought was fleeting. Annie hadn't run from a damned thing her entire life and Bob wasn't about to press her to start now. This was home; they'd just have to ride out this latest storm.

He dried his hands and turned to look at his wife. She was listening to Harry and nodding occasionally, punctuating Harry's conversation with little *hmm*s and sounds of agreement. When she put the phone down she had an expression of relief in her eyes.

'Some good news from that end, at least. They're talking about taking Patrick off the ventilator, tomorrow or the day after. It's not major progress, but it's something. And Harry sounds more positive, bless him.'

Bob sat down beside her and took Annie's hand. 'It's a start,' he agreed. 'Annie, he's going to be all right. I know he is.'

'He'd bloody better be,' she said softly. 'At least we know where Patrick is. Poor little Bee . . .'

Bob nodded. 'She'll be found. It will be OK, love.' Then he smiled. 'And I don't think she'd take kindly to being called "little". Bee is under the impression that she's all grown up.'

'None of us are all grown up, Bob. Not really.' She gripped his hand and then took hers back so she could use the phone again. 'Naomi next,' she said. 'You go and see if the workers want more coffee and when they're likely to be gone. I want to take a look at that picture.'

Twenty-Six

Sian's parents were in the reception area when she arrived and while her mother hugged her tight her father declared to anyone who would listen that he had phoned a solicitor and that his daughter had done nothing wrong.

The police officer Sian had heard Annie call Craig gently extricated her from her mother's embrace and said she must go and be booked in. She heard someone else offer them tea and the desk sergeant reassure her father that the solicitor would be able to see Sian as soon as she'd been through the usual processes.

Escorted through two more glass doors, she wondered what the usual processes were and where her father had found a solicitor. As far as she knew, the only solicitor he'd had any dealings with was the man who'd helped them when they'd bought a piece of land next to their house. He'd probably just googled solicitors or, more likely as this was her dad, looked through the Yellow Pages.

Her mind was rambling again, Sian realized. Grasping on to random thoughts because it couldn't cope with the important ones like what the hell was Binnie involved in and why the hell had she gone with him?

That last question was easy to answer. Fear. Not so much for herself but for her mum and dad and what Binnie said would happen to them if she didn't do what he said.

She twisted round to speak to the police officer following her. 'You've got to tell them not to go home,' she insisted. 'Please.'

'I doubt they'll be going anywhere,' he reassured her. 'Your mum looks set for the night. You're a lucky young woman.'

'Yeah,' she breathed softly. She was. They hadn't given up on her; they were here. Not like Binnie's mum had given up on him. Or was that even true? Maybe Binnie had just scared her so much she'd taken to her heels and run away.

The CSI had finally left. Their van had barely pulled away before Annie and Bob were back in the studio.

'We'd best do something to block up that broken window,' Bob said. 'There's some backing board in the cupboard over there, that should do it. Fortunately it's only a small window, not like last time.'

Annie went to get the board and some tape while Bob opened the safe. They had reset the alarm and the cameras and increased the sensitivity of the security lights around the house. The foxes were in for a shock tonight. Neither of them really expected Kevin Binns to return, or any of his associates, but you never knew. Someone would realize he'd gone away with the wrong picture. That might mean that they'd want to return for the right one.

Bob's thoughts were obviously travelling the same path because he said, 'Maybe we should book into a hotel for a few days, and maybe we should take the picture with us? Just until all of this blows over.'

He set the picture down on the layout table and came over to help Annie tape up the window. The glazier had promised to come over in a couple of hours which, Bob thought, was going to cost him an arm and a leg this time of night.

'If it will make you feel better, then yes, we'll do that,' Annie said.

Bob knew she wasn't patronizing him but it still felt like it, just a bit. 'I'm not scared.'

'Yes you are, and quite right too. These are dangerous people, Bob. First rule of defence is not to be there. We take a look at the picture, and we wait for the glazier. And while we're waiting, we store anything away in the safe that we can manage. There are some valuable materials here and I don't want to come back and find them squished all over the floor, just because someone couldn't find what he wanted. We pack a couple of bags, enough to keep us going for a few nights. We'll go and stay in town, close to the hospital. That way we're around if anyone needs us.'

'It feels like running away.'

'No,' Annie said, 'it's an organized retreat. Like I said, first rule of defence is not to be there when the attack comes. There's a good chance nothing will happen, but I suggest we also set the alarm

211

to maximum volume rather than leave it silent. We might as well at least give them a scare if they do come back.'

Bob nodded. It was a reasonable plan, though he hated leaving the studio and this house to the mercy of whoever might come and want to wreck things. 'What do we do with the dogs? Shall I give Jeff a ring? He's going to be pissed off about his gate, isn't he? What did he say when you phoned him earlier?'

'He jumped to the conclusion that it was someone green-laning,' Annie said. 'It's not the first time he's had problems with four by fours driving across his fields. He was a bit shocked when I told him we'd had a break-in, and that I had chased the bastard with a shotgun.'

'Which bit was he shocked about?' Bob asked. 'The break-in or the shotgun?'

Annie laughed. 'Only that I had missed; he reckoned I was a better shot than that. I'll give him a ring, see if he'll look after the dogs for a few days. They think of it as their alternative home anyway.'

For the second time that day Bob opened the box and withdrew the painting, laying it face down on a soft blanket. He looked closely at the backing board. It was old, strips of poplar that had shrunk with age but not warped. The board on which the picture was painted was laminated poplar. Boards laid first one way and then across the other, glued together with an adhesive that was made of casein. Patrick always referred to it as 'cheesy glue' because essentially that was what it was. It made for an incredibly stable

212

surface which did not warp and did not come unstuck even across centuries.

On the backing board were several labels. There were also two small brands burned into the wood. Labels and brands indicated previous owners, collections that this little painting had once been a part of – or at least that was the claim. This development of a cohesive provenance, Bob knew, had been a speciality of Freddie's. The most ornate label was the one which had given this picture its name, the Bevi Madonna. Giovanni Bevi was a known seventeenth-century buyer and collector. He had both created his own collection and curated for others. It was an important name.

Because of the weight of information on the backing boards Bob had been extremely reluctant to remove them from the painting, and that reluctance returned now. Annie could see him hesitating.

'Bob, if you don't want to disturb it, then don't. Look at it this way, if anything's been hidden behind the board, then it must have been slid in through that little gap there. I'll get one of the LED torches; we might be able to see something.'

She left him for a few minutes and came back with a very powerful but very small torch. The crack between the boards was just about big enough for her to get her little finger through and Annie did her best to angle the light to peer inside. They moved the picture this way and that. Nothing rattled, nothing moved; Bob would have noticed already if anything had been floating around loose inside, though if he had he might have put it down to a loose sliver of timber, broken free from the backboard. They could see nothing obvious and the only way to find out more would involve damaging the labels.

Bob ran his fingers across the faded paper and said, 'When you think about it, how long ago do you think these boards shrank? The first hundred years, the second? This label, this gallery label, purports to be nineteenth-century. You can see it's been stuck across where the boards join and there's a little gap beneath where the boards shrink back. And then there is this wear line, just down the middle, where you'd expect it to be with the tiny movements between those two boards, and all the dust is going to collect behind on that little sliver of paper. If Freddie did this, he really thought about it, didn't he? But I think we're barking up the wrong tree, love. I don't think he's hidden anything in the back of this.'

Twenty-Seven

Binnie seemed unperturbed to be returning alone. His employer asked where Sian had got to and he just shrugged. 'House owners came back, I scarpered, left her behind.'

'And that doesn't bother you at all? She knows exactly who you are and you don't know how much she can tell them about this place.'

Binnie shrugged again. 'Stupid bint's too scared to say anything,' he said. 'And if she does, she'll never be able to point them in this direction. And even if she does—'

'And if she does, my friend, this will be down to you.'

Binnie nodded acknowledgement, but he still didn't seem particularly bothered. He put the painting down on the table.

'Go and get the other girl. I want her to see this.'

Binnie went off and a few minutes later came back with Bee. She was yelling and struggling and demanding to know what he'd done with Sian.

'Your friend isn't coming back,' Binnie's boss told her. 'Forget about her and look at this.'

He had set up a small easel on the table and now he unwrapped the painting and placed it on the easel, then stepped back. He studied the work intently. 'He's taken a slightly different direction with this one, but of course it's still in the early stages. Who knows what he could have achieved? That is the sadness of it, such a tragic loss of talent.'

That's not my father's work, Bee thought. It dawned on her immediately that it was probably Patrick's; she'd not seen the copy he'd been making but that was certainly a logical assumption. Binnie had stolen the wrong piece.

But she wasn't going to say that. If this idiot couldn't tell the difference, she was not going to enlighten him.

Genuinely curious, she stepped closer to the painting and studied it. Bee was no artist, as she'd told Patrick – she'd rather have followed in her

215

mother's footsteps and gone for something scientific – but she'd been around Freddie for long enough to recognize quality when she saw it. To know that there was inherent skill here. And now that skill had probably been killed off by some moronic idiot, doing whatever he was told just for the money.

She turned away, suddenly utterly disgusted with it all, and glared at Binnie. 'Was it you that killed my father?'

Binnie just smiled at her. 'What do you think?'

'How? How did you do it?'

'That's for me to know and you to wonder about, isn't it?' He leaned closer and whispered in her ear, 'Smoking kills.'

Binnie's employer seemed to find that funny. 'You can take her back now,' he said.

'What are you going to do with me?' Bee had promised herself she wouldn't ask, but when it came down to it she couldn't help herself.

'As the man says, that's for me to know and you to find out.'

Binnie grabbed her arm and took her back to the room.

Sian hadn't waited for her father's promised solicitor. She just wanted to talk and to tell the police officer (who introduced himself as DS Dattani) anything he wanted to know. At first she found it hard, she didn't really know where to begin, and he kept having to make her go back and start again or clarify some point or other. The tape was running and a female officer who had said her name was Karen Morgan sat close by, taking notes.

216

Sian found it so terribly difficult, admitting the part she'd had to play.

'I saw him kill her. He had a knife and he just stabbed her and she fell. I realized she was dead.'

'At that point, it's likely she was still alive,' the woman said. 'When the real artist arrived about ten minutes after you left, Antonia Scott still had a little spark of life left in her. It's possible she could have been saved.'

Sian stared at her, utterly stricken. That made it even worse. 'I'm so sorry. I'm so, so sorry. I was just so afraid.'

'He threatened you?'

'He threatened my mum and dad.'

'You could have told someone. You could have told your mum and dad and asked for police protection. Did it never occur to you that you could have done that?'

Sian wiped away the tears that she didn't actually feel she was entitled to shed and nodded. 'I almost told my mum,' she said. 'She hated Binnie. Never trusted him. I almost told her and then at the last minute I just couldn't. I knew she'd hate me for it.'

'You mum and dad are here,' Karen Morgan pointed out. 'I don't think they're going to hate you.'

'They don't know what I've done, though, do they?'

'If you were truly under duress, then the courts will be more lenient. You have to tell us absolutely everything that went on. What he said, what he did. And anything you can think of that might help us work out where this house is or

217

who it belongs to. Remember, there's still another girl out there and her life is most definitely at risk.'

'You think I don't know that?'

Sian continued to talk. She wasn't always sure she was getting things in the right order. Thoughts tumbled over one another and sometimes a sequence of events seemed really confused and difficult to work out.

There was a soft tap at the door and DS Dattani went to open it. It seemed that the promised solicitor had arrived.

'We'll have a break now,' Sian was told. 'You can talk to your solicitor and we'll make sure you've both got drinks and something to eat. Then we'll resume the interview.'

'When can I see my mum and dad?'

'That will have to be later.'

They left the room and a man came in. He put his briefcase down on the table and reached out to shake her hand. Then he sat down and explained who he was and what they were going to do.

Vin closed the door on them, took Karen through to the main office and found her a chair next to his desk.

'And what's the betting this house belongs to Graham Harcourt?'

'I'd say the odds are good, but we need more than that if we're going to get a warrant. We need something that positively identifies the house; otherwise all it will be is a fishing trip.'

'We could arrange to take the girl there?'

'It might be possible, but she still might not recognize the place. She was scared, and the car she was in drove round the back of the house into the yard. She might not know it from the front. But if we can get some pictures to show her, just see if anything is familiar. I'm conscious of the fact that Bee Jones is still being held somewhere, probably at that house.'

'And in the meantime, do we assume that the family is definitely at risk?' Vin said.

'I would say so.' Karen paused and frowned. 'These are serious offences, but I'm wondering if it's still possible to release her under police bail. I doubt she's a flight risk and I think the whole family would be better off in a safe house than for the girl to be on remand somewhere. My guess is that she'll still be at risk and we don't want the added problem of losing a vital witness.'

'It would be an unusual step,' Vin said. 'But it's not without precedent. We'll have to see what we can do. She's not going anywhere for the best part of the next twenty-four hours, at any rate. And from the look of her mum and dad, neither are they.'

Graham Harcourt waited until everyone had left him before resuming his examination of the painting. According to that little tick Toby Elden, Freddie had concealed the information Graham wanted in the painting – though he'd been unclear as to how or where – and now, looking at the picture lying on his table, Graham was distinctly puzzled.

He had set great store by Toby's statement. After all, they'd had to threaten to beat him to a pulp to get that scrap of information out of him, and Graham knew that Toby had been looking for the exact same thing. He'd been picked up outside Freddie's house and, as the police would have put it, had clearly been going in equipped. Even once he'd let Binnie loose on Toby, he'd offered nothing more or different. Toby had been convinced because that was what Freddie had led him to believe.

The picture had been painted on board, which had been gessoed with a mix of rabbit skin glue and chalk. This technique took skill and patience; the aim was to ensure it was perfectly smooth and completely free of tiny pinprick holes left by air bubbles.

The surface was scraped and polished until it was completely smooth, pure white and silken to the touch. Absorbent and also resilient, it took colour beautifully, in thin layers, built up in either delicate cross-hatched strokes or impossibly thin glazes, so the light bounced back through the colours and the pigments glowed.

Graham Harcourt knew all of this; and didn't give a damn.

The board looked solid but it was hard to tell. To prevent warping, the surface had been gessoed on the reverse too. It had also been the intention of the artist to create a frame directly on to the picture. Layers of gesso had been applied and punched and stamped with tiny stars and open circles. It would eventually have been gilded and burnished and then aged – the most skilful part of the process in many ways. Un-aged gilding was, in Harcourt's eyes, ridiculously garish.

The first layers of the paint had been completed,

but the under-drawing was still visible, as were the tiny pinpricks delineating the halo of the Christ child and the Madonna. The work was careful and meticulous – he could see that. Maybe not up to Freddie's usual standard . . . but of course, he'd never seen his work in progress before. He knew some collectors were fascinated by process, liking to feel that they were in some way expert in their understanding of an artist's work; Harcourt himself had no such vanity. But then, he wasn't exactly an ordinary collector. He rarely kept anything for long; what would be the point in that?

He took out his pocket knife and began to prod at the edges of the picture. What if Freddie had concealed a hollow or hiding place beneath the plaster? The board was thick enough and sturdy enough for that to be possible. He went all around the edges, stabbing and twisting, fragments of gesso flying off across the room as he became more violent and insistent.

Nothing.

In the gesso frame? He attacked this too with gusto but it was starting to dawn on him that he had been lied to. That little bastard Toby Elden, he'd held out after all.

The knife wasn't effective enough. He took an ice pick from the drinks tray on the sideboard and resumed the attack. The sharp point made more progress against the hard and brittle surface. Again, nothing.

He stepped back and surveyed the mess. It stank, too. He could smell the rabbit skin glue in the fine dust he was creating alongside the sharp, explosive shards. Talcum-powder-fine particles rose up and clogged his nose, drying the membranes.

The eyes of the Madonna seemed to be watching him. She held her son in her lap and the older woman he assumed was St Anne had her gaze fixed on the baby. The Madonna looked out at the viewer. Inviting you to engage with her. Freddie had said it was because she knew herself to be in a state of grace, one she wanted the viewer to share. He had cared about that sort of thing. The intention of the artist, as he'd put it.

'Fuck that!' Harcourt said. He went to work with the ice pick, driving it straight between the eyes, ruining the delicate features, scratching away at the surface until the figures were ruined and then obscured.

Finally he took a poker from the hearth and smashed the image into fragments. The surface of the table on which it had rested scarred and cracked and eventually broke beneath the weight of his blows.

He had been lied to. Toby fucking Elden had dared to lie to him.

No one came to see what the noise was about. He hadn't expected them to. No one dared to come in when he'd dismissed them. Not even Binnie was that stupid.

In the end he picked up the larger fragments and chucked them on to the fire, leaving what remained on the table and the floor. Then, in a fit of pure pique, he swept those remnants to the floor.

He was back to square one.

Twenty-Eight

Sian's interview continued, with regular breaks, until way after midnight. Her parents sat patiently in the reception area.

At twenty past midnight, Vin called them through into an interview room.

'When can we see her?' Tracey demanded.

'Soon. I promise. Now listen, it's been decided that she's going to be released on police bail, because at the moment keeping her safe is more important than locking her away. You understand that. Now, everyone's moved remarkably quickly on this and there's a safe house lined up.' He indicated the young female officer who had followed them through. 'This is Bev, and what we propose is that she takes you, Tracey, back to the house to pack your bags. You'll have another officer with you as well. Or, you give her the keys and tell her where she'll find clothes and anything else you need. You, your husband and daughter will be taken to the safe house, as soon as Sian's interview's finished. And we're going to have to ask you to surrender your mobile phones. And not to make any contact with friends or family. If you think anyone's going to be worried about you, then we'll inform them that you are safe.'

'For how long?' Richard asked. 'I have to get back to work. We have family who will be worried about us.'

'Hopefully only for a few days.'

'A few days? I can't do that.'

'You can and you will,' Tracey told him firmly.

'I want you to remember,' Vin said, 'that there is another young girl out there, still being held. Your daughter may hold the clue to where she is. We've got to use every ounce of information she has.'

'Will she go to prison?' Tracey asked.

'She was under duress, that counts as mitigation. But I really can't say.'

Tracey stood up. 'Right, I'll go and pack, but I've got to admit I'm a bit nervous going back there.'

'If you don't want to go,' Vin told her, 'as I said, I can send my officers. You've just got to tell them where everything is. I can understand you're scared, but we've got no reason to suspect that anyone will go near you tonight. I imagine the fact that we've got Sian will probably slow them down a bit. But we're quite prepared to send an officer to collect your things for you.'

Tracey shook her head. 'No, I can do this. I'll just throw some things in bags and we'll be off.' She turned to her husband. 'You just make sure that Sian is all right.'

She followed Bev, clutching at her handbag as though it was a life raft. Then at the door she stopped, suddenly overwhelmed.

Bev turned and touched her arm. 'Just give me your keys,' she said. 'And a basic list. It's OK, you stay with your family and leave the rest to me.'

Tracey nodded, not really trusting herself to speak.

Binnie had been waiting, sitting on the stile in the field that backed the Price house, his feet resting on a crate. He knew that they'd have to come home at some point and he was ready. When the lights came on, he picked up the crate and carried it across the field and through the gate in the garden fence.

He hadn't been particularly upset to have left Sian behind. He was getting bored with her anyway, but he had made a threat, and he fully intended to carry it out. If people don't carry their threats out, how is anybody supposed to take any notice of them?

A light went on in the annexe, which surprised him as that was Sian's area, and then one in the bedroom upstairs. He guessed that must be her parents' room. He waited. He wanted them to be settled, perhaps even getting ready for bed, and he was good at taking his time.

He gave them another ten minutes and then figured that was long enough. In the crate were a dozen bottles filled with a mixture of petrol and oil and with rags crammed into the necks to use as wicks. Binnie lit the first one and hurled it at the annexe window. The bottle smashed against the glass and broke, bursting into flames, and he heard someone shout within. A man's voice – that surprised him too. The dad, maybe? Whatever.

The windows at the back of the house were double glazed and he knew that he could never hope to break them with a bottle, but half bricks, packed into the base of the crate – that would do it.

The first brick bounced off. Annoying, Binnie thought, but these things happen. Sighing, he picked up his crate and went a little closer to the house, removing from his pocket an automatic centre punch. He pressed the little tool against the corner of the window and it broke instantly with a clatter and a shatter of glass. Most of it fell into the room, but some scattered around Binnie. He shook it off.

There were screams coming from inside the house now, and shouts. Binnie lit another couple of petrol bombs and threw them inside. One landed on the settee and the second, falling just inside the window, lit the curtains. Binnie did a little dance of joy as the flames roared.

The living room door was open and he saw someone run down the hallway so his next petrol bomb flew straight through the door and into the hall after them. He was satisfied to hear another scream and then the front door opening. Moments later a car, engine revving loudly, pulled away.

A pity, Binnie thought. He should have waited until they were asleep. You can't win them all. He had fun disposing of the rest of his missiles and then went back and sat on the stile to watch the place burn.

Bev called for backup while her colleague drove as fast as he could down the lane. There was no telling how many people were involved, and there was nothing they could do about the house. All

226

they could do was call their colleagues in the fire brigade.

'Fuck's sake,' Bev swore. 'It's as well the mother didn't come back with us.'

The main village was at the bottom of the hill and they pulled into the pub yard. By now the whole hilltop seemed to be ablaze. As Bev got out, she glanced at the back seat and the two bags that lay there. Everything the Price family now owned was in those bags.

It took perhaps twenty minutes for the fire brigade to arrive, but it felt like for ever. They didn't need to ask where the fire was; the orange glow at the top of the hill could probably be seen from miles around. Vin had arrived with the other patrol cars and his first concern was to make sure that Bev and her colleague were all right.

'What the hell happened?'

'Craig had gone into the annexe to get the things for the girl. I'd gone upstairs, into the parents' room. All of a sudden there was this crash and a massive orange glow outside the annexe window. I didn't understand what it was at first. Then I saw this man in the garden. He threw something at the patio window – I think he hoped it would break, so I'm assuming it was a brick? Meantime Craig is yelling, comes back into the house shouting about petrol bombs. Fortunately there's a door through to the annexe from the main house, otherwise I don't know how he'd have got out, not with that lunatic in the garden. Anyway, I grabbed the bag and ran down the stairs and then there was a crash like you wouldn't believe, and the window goes. I don't know how he broke it but he did,

227

and then he's chucking petrol bombs inside, into the living room. He sent another one flying in as I ran past the door, and then there's one coming after me in the hall. Craig's already gone through the kitchen into the hallway and is waiting by the door. I'm not kidding, boss, we just took to our heels and ran. There was nothing we could have done. I'm so sorry for the family. But I got the feeling that even if both of us had tackled him we'd have been the ones to come off worse. He didn't bloody care. He wanted to kill someone and I don't think he was bothered who.'

'There was nothing you could have done, either of you. Main thing is you're safe and they're safe. It seems Sian was right about her parents being in danger. He carried out his threat.'

'Doesn't bode well for the other girl, does it?' Craig said. He looked shaken and also angry. It wasn't in his nature to run away but they hadn't been left with much option.

'You've seen the pictures of Kevin Binns; you think you can be definite it was him?'

'No doubt in my mind,' Craig said. 'I got a good look at him as I came back into the house. There was enough light from the fire. It was definitely him.'

Bev nodded her agreement. 'I looked out of the upstairs window. He just looked back up at me. I think he thought I was the mother, but I don't think he was really that bothered. He'd come well equipped, that was for sure. From what I could see he had a crate at his feet, packed with petrol bombs.'

'Get back, make a statement,' Vin told them.

'Put the bags in my car and I'll let the family know what's been going on. There's nothing more you can do here, either of you. And it wasn't your fault. Understand that.'

Twenty-Nine

Naomi had come to sit beside Patrick for an hour or so to give Harry time to go home and shower and change his clothes. He'd barely left the hospital, deserting Patrick's room only when the doctors told him they needed him out of the way. Mari had taken her turn, as had Patrick's mother and stepfather, but Harry had seemed unable to leave his son for more than a short time.

Finally exhaustion had won and Naomi, with Patrick's mother, had persuaded him that he needed to go home for a break. After a lot of convincing, they had managed to take him to a local pizza restaurant. Then they had driven him home so that he could change and, Naomi hoped, get some sleep before he returned. Beth, Patrick's mother, and his stepdad were both suffering severely from jetlag and had said that they needed to get out of the hospital for a while. Mari had promised to come back first thing in the morning, and Naomi told Harry she would stay.

To her surprise she had won that argument and now, at two o'clock in the morning, she was sitting beside Patrick, listening to machines that beat and whirled and whistled and soft footsteps

229

crossing back and forth between beds and desk as the nurses checked vital signs.

She was reminded of her own time in hospital and how it felt at night, cut off from the world, so very quiet.

The nurses had left her alone, just given her a buzzer to press in case she needed to go to the loo or wanted a coffee or anything. No one wanted to risk her stumbling into a bed or some vital bit of equipment if she tried to wander round the ward on her own.

Harry had been reading to Patrick but, obviously, she couldn't do that. Patrick was in a little side room, not completely closed off from the ward but a little bit apart. She could hear others talking to their sick loved ones. A mother talking about a birthday party that her child must get well for. Strictly speaking, the ICU had visiting hours, but as far as Naomi could tell no one enforced these so long as there was only one visitor or, at the most, two, and they didn't get in the way.

Naomi wasn't sure what she should talk about, but she wanted to talk to Patrick about something and so she told him about his painting. 'Someone stole it; they mistook it for one of Freddie's. I guess you'll take that as a compliment because I know how much you admired his work. This was from Bob's studio, and from what I understand, Annie chased them off with a shotgun. You can just imagine that, can't you? Annie with her hair flying all over the place and a shotgun blazing. I wouldn't be surprised if Bob paints that one day.

'There's no news on Bee, yet, but the other girl, Sian Price . . . of course, you wouldn't know about her. She was at Bob's studio, she was with the man who stole your painting. The same person who pushed you off the balcony and who took Bee away, and she says that . . . this Sian says that Bee was all right the last time she saw her. That she's very scared, and terribly upset about what happened to you. But they'll find her. I'm sure they will. They are getting lots of leads now.'

She paused. She wasn't sure this was what she was supposed to be telling a sick person, even one in a coma who probably couldn't hear her, but she knew that if their places were changed, it was the sort of thing she'd want to know about. That progress was being made and everybody was doing their best to put it right, what had happened. 'Bob says, when you get out, and you get back to working for him, he'll help you start again. He said to tell you that the gesso recipe will be better next time. He found a variation that he thinks might be easier to handle. And he's got a whole load of new pigments for you to grind up that will be keeping you busy. I'm not really sure what he was on about, but he said he promised to get you some real lapis lazuli to make real ultramarine. He said that's still the best blue and, in his words, it's a beast to grind. He reckons if you go too far with it, it just goes grey. If you get it right you get that gorgeous blue – but you know all about that, don't you?'

She reached out and fumbled for Patrick's hand. Only the fingers were exposed; the rest was wrapped in tape, holding a cannula in place.

231

'You've not met Alfie yet. He's a private investigator, but not like the Sam Spade kind. Alfie is very sophisticated and I've been doing some research for him. I'm learning all about shell companies and specialist search engines. I'm using all the technology you helped me install and he says I can do some proper, paid work for him. I'm looking forward to that.'

She squeezed Patrick's fingers gently. 'We are all here for you. You better wake up soon. All your friends at uni have been asking after you and want to know when they can visit. You're amazingly popular, you know, for someone as shy as you are.'

One of the nurses came over and asked if she wanted some tea and Naomi told him, yes please, she did. 'You think he can hear me – I mean, really?'

'We think so, and it's best to behave as though people can, don't you think?'

Yes, Naomi thought.

Vin had arrived at the safe house. It was four in the morning but the lights were still on. One look at Vin's face told Tracey something else had happened.

'He was at the house, wasn't he?'

Vin set the bags down in the hall and followed Tracey through to the kitchen. There were two officers in the house, a small detached bungalow at the end of a cul-de-sac on a quiet estate. It was not what most people thought of as a safe house – surrounded by a high hedge and with children playing in the street in the daytime, and

232

people coming and going – but it was surprisingly anonymous. The owners specialized in short-term lets, people between homes who needed something that wasn't a hotel for a few weeks, while their own house sold or their new house was got ready.

And that was exactly what they did, except that this property also served occasionally as a safe house. The owners were ex-police, so it was a good solution all round.

'I've got some really bad news,' Vin said. He sat down heavily. He'd been awake for a full twenty-four hours or more now, and was really feeling the strain.

Slowly and carefully he told them what had happened to their house. That the officers had only just escaped with their lives.

Sian's face was white. 'He said he'd kill you,' she said softly. 'Now do you believe me?'

Her mother took her hand and patted it but she wasn't paying Sian much attention at that point. Instead she was staring in horror at her husband.

'My God,' was all he said.

'But the officers are all right?' Tracey wanted to know.

'Shaken up, but they're fine. Mrs Price, I'm really sorry about this. No one could have predicted—'

'No, of course they couldn't. That boy is mad, always was. I kept telling you to stay away from him, but would you? No. He was always exciting, he was always just a little wild, he was always—'

'Mum, I'm sorry. I didn't know just how . . .

I didn't know just how bad it was. He was. When we were younger he was just fun.'

'Other people didn't see him as fun. You, you were protected for some reason. No one dared to upset Sian because of what Binnie might do to them. What do you think happened to those people that bullied you at school? They were just kids, stupid kids.'

'And I was just a kid being bullied!' Sian bit back.

'And we were doing all we could to sort that out.'

'And it made no difference, Mum. Day after day, day after day, they just went on and on at me. I came home with a black eye and you didn't care.'

Tracey looked horrified. 'You told me you'd fallen over playing hockey.'

'And you didn't ask me any questions. You just accepted that, because it was easier, I suppose.'

'Why wouldn't I have believed you?' Tracey argued.

'Binnie said he'd talk to them, and he did, and they stopped bullying me.'

'Binnie beat one of them up, put him in hospital with a punctured lung. No one knew it had been Binnie for a long time afterwards because the boy was too scared to say. He lied too, said he had fallen, and the girl – who do you think broke her arm?'

'You don't know that! You never said anything about it before.'

'No, I didn't know it at the time. Not for sure anyway. But there were rumours, always rumours.'

'So, if it was just rumours?' Sian broke off. 'Why am I defending him? I know what he can do. I know it now.'

'You always thought of him as some kind of big brother,' her mother said. 'Someone it was fun to hang around with because he looked out for you and because you got up to stupid things with him. And I should have put a stop to it a long time ago.'

'So why didn't you?'

Tracey's mouth tightened into a fixed line and Vin could see that she was close to tears. 'Because sometimes', he said, 'it's easier not to challenge. Especially when you know what happens to those people who do. Bullies continue to be bullies because nobody can stand up to them, and sometimes too they become bullies because somebody *did* stand up to them, someone even more violent.'

'Binnie didn't need anybody else.' Tracey sounded so bleak. 'The thing is, he seemed to care about Sian, to protect her. And she seemed to modify his behaviour too, calm him down. When she went away to university, I thought that would be it. Binnie wasn't around so much any more and I hoped their relationship would just fizzle out naturally. If she hadn't come back home, it probably would have. And Binnic paid no attention to either me or your dad; we were just incidental. I was quite pleased about that. He's not somebody you want to have pay attention to you.

'But I knew what it was doing to his mother. As Binnie got older he got worse and she was terrified of him. I kept telling her, you should go, just leave, and she kept telling me that she couldn't, that she dared not. At first I thought she was just exaggerating. I knew Binnie was bad, but I'd no idea how bad, and then one day she confided in me about his little brother. I knew there were rumours, but he was just a kid, and I thought that was all they were, just rumours. His dad had left, and when he came back for the younger boy's funeral his mum begged, begged him to stay. Or asked him to take Binnie away from her; she thought a man might be able to handle him better. But the dad just walked. He didn't want to know, he knew what his son was.'

'He might just have wanted to start afresh,' Sian's father said. 'I'm afraid a lot of fathers leave the marriage and never see the children again and it's not always the wife's fault.'

Tracey shook her head vehemently. 'She knew Binnie had killed her little boy. She just knew it.'

Vin shifted restlessly. 'Look,' he said, 'this is in the past, and for the moment nothing can be proved. We have to deal with the present. And the most important thing is keeping all of you safe, and finding Beatrix Jones. Sian, can you remember anything else that might help us?'

'I've told you everything I can think of.'

Vin nodded. She looked as exhausted as he felt, and he didn't think anybody could go much further without getting some sleep.

'OK. I'm really sorry to have been the bearer of more bad news and I think the best thing we can all do now is get some rest and I'll come

236

back tomorrow. Sian, you have my number if you think of anything in the meantime.'

She nodded and Vin left them to their arguments and their grief.

Thirty

On the Wednesday morning the warehouse was surrendered back to its owners and the police cordon taken away, apart from the one at the foot of the stairs leading to the studio. That area was still technically a crime scene.

Vin Dattani and Karen Morgan, about to head out to view what was left of the Price house, called in at the warehouse to talk to Mark Brookes and his sons.

Danny, the elder son, was on his own but he expected his dad later. Father and younger brother were off picking up a machine.

'Any news about Bee?' he asked. 'Or the poor lad that was thrown downstairs?'

'Nothing about Bee, as yet. But the boy is still critical.'

'Danny,' Karen said, 'could you spare a minute to take a look at some pictures? See if you recognize anyone?'

'Sure. You want a cup of tea or something?'

Both officers declined. Danny leaned against one of the workbenches and flicked through the photographs. 'Only this one,' he said. 'I ran into him wandering round here one day. Said he was

237

looking for Freddie so I called Freddie down and they both went up to the studio. That was, ooh, probably a month before Freddie died. Then he came round again – about ten days ago, this would be. Said he'd left something in Freddie's studio and wanted to collect it, so I told him no. He was quite insistent, said it was his and that he'd left it with Freddie, but I told him he needed to get in touch with Freddie's solicitor.' Danny frowned. 'You know, I mentioned it to Bee, but he didn't leave a name. Bee just said that if it was something important then he'd probably get in touch again. She said her dad often did work for other people, maybe it was a picture he was restoring or something.'

'Did he happen to mention anything else? What it was he had left in Freddie's studio?'

Danny screwed up his eyes, as though trying to think really hard. 'A picture of the Madonna and child,' he said triumphantly. 'He said it was something he'd commissioned.'

'Thank you,' Vin said. 'That's helpful.'

'There's going to be a patrol car round at the end of the road for the next few days. You see anything suspicious and you dial the nines, OK?' Karen said. She sorted through the photographs, took out one of Binnie and gave it to Danny. 'You see him, you call the police at once. Don't approach him, don't engage with him, and I suggest if you're working here on your own – or even if you're not – you lock the doors.'

Danny looked sceptical but he nodded. 'I hope you find her soon, she's a lovely lass.'

'I hope so too,' Karen said.

'Did you have much reason to go up to Freddie's studio?' asked Vin.

'Umm, most days, I suppose. His post got delivered to the front office here, so one or other of us would take that up. He'd often wander down for a cup of coffee or one of us would go up there to say hello, see what he was up to. He was a bloody genius, that man. Funny too. We all liked him a lot, couldn't believe it when he just dropped down dead like that. But he smoked like a chimney and drank like a fish. My brother smokes, too, so they'd often stand outside and have a fag. He was a nice man.'

'And did you notice a Madonna? A mother and child with an older lady. It might have been sitting on the easel just before he died.'

Danny nodded. 'Yeah, he mixed up this horrible white gloop with rabbit skin glue. Some kind of medieval plaster, apparently. Stank to high heavens and sent dust everywhere. Dried hard as anything. Then he took it out the back and scraped it off with a piece of glass, brought it down, smooth as anything.'

'And you know what happened to it, the painting? Because it seems to have gone missing.'

Danny shook his head. 'Can't help you there,' he said.

'Interesting,' Karen said as they drove away. 'About Toby Elden being at Freddie's studio. So what's so special about some half-finished picture?'

'You think Danny knows more than he's saying?'

'I don't think he's lying about anything he thinks might affect Bee, but who knows what Freddie Jones had lying around in his studio. Even his daughter didn't seem sure so it's not beyond reason that Danny, or his dad or brother, might've helped themselves to odd bits, thinking nobody would miss them. Does an artist have anything valuable in his studio? I mean, something that a casual thief would recognize as valuable? I suppose he might have left some money lying around, something like that. I think there's something Danny is not telling us.'

'He seems to have admired Freddie, but yes, I think you're right. Maybe a little bit of pressure later on?'

'More important business for the moment though, eh?'

Vin was getting to like this colleague of his; it seemed a pity that she'd be going back to her own patch. He liked her ginger hair and blue eyes and her sense of humour. He also liked the way she just got on with the job.

'Off to see what's left of the Prices' house, then,' he said.

The only thing that kept Bee sane was what she now realized was her increasingly ridiculous escape plan. She'd been working on the window with the end of the coat hanger hook, slowly removing the putty and damaged wood. The glass now rattled in the frame and she was genuinely frightened of it falling out, so she worked slowly and carefully, hoping to remove it in one piece, but not until she was actually ready. The cross

240

brace on the window was proving to be much more difficult than she'd thought it was going to be. It separated the two panes and if that came away, together with both panes of glass, she had a chance of squeezing through. Then she'd have to do something crazy like tie the sheets together and lower herself down and hope for the best. She'd tried tearing the sheets into strips, but that too wasn't nearly as easy as she'd thought it was going to be and she was also terrified of doing anything that might be discovered.

Her only visitor was the woman, accompanied by a guard – though never Binnie, not since he had taken Sian away. Just some man who stood partly concealed by the doorway. She was aware of bulk and height, but that was all. She tried engaging the woman in conversation, but the woman just ignored her. She was always well dressed, this woman, in the kind of suit or smart dress people wore for the office, as if she was some kind of secretary. She even wore quite high heels and Sian fantasized about tripping her over and pushing her downstairs. The diet of sandwiches and fruit and orange juice was getting monotonous, but at least she was being fed. And the woman kept bringing painkillers. She wondered who had come up with that idea, doubted it was either Binnie or the man who had told him to break her fingers.

She rationed the painkillers; it was still comforting that she had a final get-out clause.

She was losing track of time; she thought it was Wednesday but she couldn't be sure. And, weirdly, she was bored. She never figured that

241

kidnap victims could get bored but her brain was desperate for something to do other than fantasizing more and more violent conclusions to this whole episode.

She had no doubt that they would kill her in the end but she was obviously being kept alive for something. She had a use, she just couldn't quite figure out what it was. The closest she could get was that maybe they were going to exchange her for something or someone and that made a kind of sense, but she couldn't think what it might be.

And, though she knew it was a selfish thing, she wished she hadn't been left alone. She hoped that Sian was OK, wherever she was. That Binnie hadn't hurt her.

Thirty-One

It was about an hour's drive from the warehouse to Graham Harcourt's hall at Otteringham. It was possible to see the house for quite a while before you actually got to it, long and low and set into the valley. Palladian, Vin thought, but he was never totally sure about his architectural knowledge. He made the suggestion and Karen said she thought it was Georgian, then admitted that she didn't know either.

They both agreed that it was just big.

'Imagine rattling around in a place like that,' Karen said.

'I think I'd rather like it.'

'I wouldn't like the heating bill.'

A long drive led down to the house, but they could get nowhere near that without going through the gates and that meant reporting to the gatehouse. The gates were wrought iron, heavy and black and beautifully made, decorated with ornate curlicues and gilded flowers. A bit over the top, Vin thought.

He sounded his horn at the gatehouse. He remembered what Alfie had told them about the security cameras. They'd spotted a couple as they'd driven round and another on the gate itself. A man dressed in blue shirt and dark trousers came out, pulling on a uniform jacket. Graham Harcourt obviously liked his employees in livery.

Both officers showed identification and said they wanted to talk to Mr Harcourt. They were told that it might not be possible; the man said he would phone to the house and see if Mr Harcourt was free.

'Let's see if we're granted an audience,' Karen said as the man went back inside the gatehouse and closed the door. 'How long do you reckon he'll keep us waiting?'

Vin glanced at his watch. It was nine forty-five. 'At least fifteen minutes,' he said.

'I reckon it'll be the full half hour,' Karen said.

They had intended to visit the burned-out house first, but had changed their minds on the way here. Vin was curious to see how long it would take to get from Otteringham to the Price house.

Naomi and Alfie's research had provided them with a cover: the identification of a number of

243

pieces of artwork that had been sold with seeming legitimacy by Toby Elden to Graham Harcourt. They had arranged to interview or visit (or have colleagues visit) several other customers, to make their cover complete.

Neither of them expected to get much out of this visit. They worried that if they were right and Bee was at the Otteringham house they might be placing her in further danger. It was equally likely that their visit might precipitate further action on Graham Harcourt's part; perhaps he might move Bee or release her.

It was also possible that she was dead already.

Of course, there was a chance that Harcourt was in no way involved – though neither of them really believed that.

In the end, they were kept waiting twenty-five minutes and then given permission to drive down and told that they would be met at the entrance.

'Your boss likes his privacy, then,' Karen said.

The man just nodded and opened the gate.

The drive curved around the shape of the hill. Vin clocked it; it was almost a mile long. 'You wouldn't make a fast getaway from here, would you? Look, you can make out a stable block at the side, and what looks like servants' quarters above. It's possible, isn't it?'

'Most big houses have something similar. But Sian gave quite a good description of the front of the house and the stable block. If we can get some pictures, we may be able to get her to confirm.'

Vin pulled up in front of the house and they got out. A man stood on the steps holding the door open. It was a small door set into much larger and more impressive doors, and it reminded Vin slightly of the warehouse entrance. The man did not introduce himself, simply led them through the hallway and into a room on the left.

Karen looked around, pausing to admire the stained glass. 'Beautiful window,' she said, but their guide merely held the door open for her and beckoned her through.

She and Vin found themselves in a study-cum-library with a big fireplace, an oxblood red chesterfield and two matching chairs. A man stood by the fireplace with a cup of coffee in his hand.

'Take a seat, officers. Would you like some coffee? And what can I do for you?'

'Not for me, thank you,' Karen said. Vin also declined; he'd been up half the night drinking the stuff and couldn't stomach any more.

Karen produced a photograph of Toby Elden and showed it to Graham Harcourt.

Harcourt examined the photograph and then shrugged. 'So?'

'You may or may not know that Mr Elden is in hospital at the moment,' Karen said.

'I didn't. But then, why should I?'

'Probably no reason, but in the course of our investigations into who put Mr Elden there, it's come to our attention that you and a number of other people have bought artworks from him in the last few years. It's also come to our notice that Mr Elden has a reputation for dealing in stolen antiquities and artwork.'

Harcourt studied Karen and then smiled. 'And

245

you're worried I might have bought something in good faith that he sold to me in bad faith,' he said.

'Pretty much.'

Harcourt pursed his lips. 'When you buy art and antiquities, it really is a case of "buyer beware". You have to do your research, and you have to be convinced that what you're buying is the real deal. Of course all collectors will be fooled at some point, that almost goes with the territory. Even the experts don't get it right all the time. I've bought work from Elden, yes. But I've always managed to get it verified. I never made the mistake of buying anything where I couldn't consult with the artists themselves. You see, I only deal in contemporary pieces. Pieces where the artist is either still alive or very recently deceased.'

'So you only deal in modern art?'

'No, my dear. I didn't say that. When people say "modern art" they mean something very specific. I'm assuming you mean abstract and semi-abstract pieces. The Young British Artists and that sort of thing. Frankly I leave that side of the collecting to the likes of Saatchi. Ten years down the road and my feeling is that it will be almost all forgotten. I and a number of other collectors . . . if you're interviewing people who bought works from Elden you'll no doubt be contacting them?'

Karen nodded. 'I'm sure we will. You understand I cannot tell you their names. Neither will I reveal your name to them.'

Harcourt smiled at her and shook his head.

'There are a number of us who like art to be figurative. Who care about the draughtsmanship and the quality of the paint. We may be considered old-fashioned in a way, but we like to buy quality.'

'I believe you own some work by Freddie Jones?'

'If you've done your homework, then you will know that I bought my Freddies from Toby. But with the artist's full authentication. I also own a piece by Bob Taylor, and a David Inshaw. If you have the time, I'd love to show them to you.'

Karen smiled. 'Actually, I'd really like that. Do you mind?'

Her enthusiasm was so obvious that both Vin and Graham Harcourt were taken aback. Harcourt laughed. He sounded delighted. 'Absolutely. Come with me.'

He dumped his coffee cup on the tray and led them through another door into a much larger room. Vin stood in the doorway and watched as Karen accompanied their host inside.

The paintings were displayed like the pictures Karen had seen at the Royal Academy Summer Exhibition. It was a little overwhelming, she thought. She paced slowly along the length of the room, listening as Graham Harcourt expounded.

Vin's mobile rang. 'Sorry to spoil your fun, but we've got to go,' he said.

Karen shrugged. 'Pity. This is amazing.'

Harcourt himself showed them out.

'So, what have we learnt from that?' Vin asked as they drove off. 'You reckon she's there?'

Karen was flicking through some images on her phone.

'You took pictures? How the hell did you manage that?'

'Pictures of the hallway and the study, yes. I managed to grab four, and a couple of the front of the house as we came down the drive. I wasn't sure how good they'd be as I was shooting from the hip.' She grinned at him and he liked the way it made her freckles dance. 'You were standing between us for a few seconds when we came back into the study and then I took a chance in the hall, when I had my back to him.' She studied the pictures critically. 'Not too bad,' she said. 'I'll email them to you for when you go and see Sian.'

She frowned then, the little victory not making up for the rest. 'Yes, I think Bee's there. Still alive, I hope – though what he wants her for . . . information, maybe, in which case, who knows what he might have done?'

'Prepare for the worst, but hope for the best, as my dad always says.'

'This the dad that grows dahlias?'

'Yes. I've only got the one, so far as I know.'

She nodded. 'Dahlias can make you fatalistic,' she said. 'I had an uncle who grew them. He reckoned if it wasn't the slugs it was the earwigs. He used to fill pots with straw and put them on bamboo sticks in amongst the flowers. I think the earwigs were supposed to prefer the straw.' She paused. 'I think he's planning a move.'

'Oh? What did I miss?'

'Just a tiny glimpse of something. You didn't come far enough into the picture room to see. There's, like, a little room off the main one and

248

the door was part open. It was filled with packing cases and bubble wrap. I mean, filled. And all heavy duty, not your "bought it from the local stationers" stuff.'

He nodded. 'Look, we need to get some surveillance on the place. I noticed a farm and a barn; we passed them on the way. I reckon they'll have a view on the house.'

'If they cooperate. He's a big landowner around here, he might even own their farm.'

'If we have to, we'll get a court order. But it has to be done, and we need to apply for a warrant to search the place.'

'There's a lay-by up there – pull in.'

'Why?' But he did so anyway.

'So I can drive, and you can phone. I can't set any of that up, it's not my patch. But no reason we can't be getting on with it.'

There was no arguing with that. Vin stopped the car and they swapped round. It took a couple of minutes to adjust the seat, Karen being quite a lot shorter than he was. Then she unfastened her ponytail and tied it back up again. It was something he'd noticed she did when she was trying to make a decision, or think something through. He rather liked it. And he definitely liked that tangle of curly ginger hair. The one thing stopping him from asking her out was that her rank was higher than his. But was that insurmountable? And it wasn't necessarily going to be a permanent state of affairs.

They took off again and Vin made his phone calls. He wished that Tess was around – she could usually be relied upon to push things through

– but she was still on her course. The DCI listened sympathetically, however. This was a big case – though, as the DCI warned Vin, Harcourt was also an important and prominent businessman. He'd start work on it now but it wasn't going to be easy or quick.

Vin rang off, knowing that surveillance took time to set up, and warrants too.

'Most frustrating part of the job, apart from the paperwork,' Karen said. 'There are times when I get tempted to turn vigilante, you know that?'

'What, full mask and cloak, or more Charles Bronson?' He sobered. 'What are the odds of her being alive?'

Karen didn't even bother to answer that.

Thirty-Two

Bob and Annie slept late and it was almost ten when they finally woke. She was due to teach an evening class at a local college, but had nothing else to do that day. They lay in bed discussing their plans. Bob had some phone calls to make and he had some drawings with him that he would work on later on. They had brought the painting with them and the Bevi Madonna was now in a box, propped up on a chair in a corner of their hotel room. He'd have to let the owner know, he supposed. They were bound to get wind of the break-in at his house, sooner or later.

'I'll go across to the hospital this afternoon,'

250

Annie said, 'see if Harry needs anything.' Not being family they could not take a turn sitting in with Patrick. Naomi seemed to have got an exemption to that rule and it turned out that everyone had assumed that she was Harry's sister. No one had bothered to disabuse the authorities.

Bob announced that he was hungry and that they should order room service, breakfast in the dining room being over by then.

'It's a bit like being on holiday,' Annie said. 'Not that we've done holidays very often. We ought to start.'

While they waited for breakfast Annie took a shower and Bob phoned the painting's owner, Derek Bartholomew, to apprise him of the situation. Bob didn't say a great deal, only that there had been an attempted break-in at the studio and the police were still taking fingerprints and such-like, so they'd moved out for a few days.

'No, in a hotel. But the painting is quite safe, under lock and key,' Bob lied, eyeing the package that sat on the chair opposite him. Somehow he'd felt safer with it in his room, but he supposed he ought to ask the hotel if they could put it into their safe. Maybe later.

Annie came out of the shower just as room service arrived and Bob got off the phone. Before she opened the door he picked up the painting and slipped it into the wardrobe. Then, when the waiter had gone, he put the 'do not disturb' notice on the door. He didn't want housekeeping poking around and seeing what might look like a suspicious package.

251

'We ought to find somewhere with a safe,' Annie said. 'What did Derek say?'

'Not a lot, but then I didn't tell him a lot. He was sympathetic, asked if anything was stolen and I told him no. I didn't want to get into talking about Patrick's painting, especially as it's still part of a police investigation. I don't know, Annie, I feel as if I don't know who to trust at the moment. Is that just paranoia?'

Annie was investigating the breakfast tray. 'No, just good sense,' she said. 'I think the more we keep to ourselves at the moment, the better. Friends aside, of course. You know how I feel about Derek, and most of the rest of them. Out for themselves and I wouldn't trust them an inch. Even if they are good customers.' She smiled at her husband.

'Now, eat. And then, treat today like we've got the day off.'

When he got off the phone to Bob, Derek Bartholomew's next thought was to phone Graham Harcourt. Bob's was not the only odd news he'd had that morning; he'd had an early morning visit from a couple of police officers, and that troubled him immensely.

Graham listened, without comment, as he explained the situation. 'They were asking about any dealings I'd had with Toby Elden. You know, over the years I dealt with him quite a lot, we all have. But have you heard about poor old Toby? Seems somebody beat seven shades out of him; the poor bugger is now in hospital and they don't expect him to survive. Who the hell would want to kill Toby?'

252

Graham laughed softly. 'I think there's quite a list. All of Toby's deals sounded good on the surface, but he always made sure that he came out ahead of everybody else. I suspect you're going to find a few people he pissed off.'

'Pissed off, yes. Not bad enough to want him dead, surely. Have you had a visit?'

'Yes, they left about twenty minutes ago. Two officers. But I reckon they always travel in pairs. Look, don't worry about it. From what I understand this is part of a broader investigation and they're interviewing everybody who's ever had any dealings, or might have had any dealings, with him. They'll be checking everything in Toby's background; the police have to be thorough, after all.'

'You're right, of course. But then just after they'd gone Bob Taylor phoned me. There was a break-in at his place; did you hear about that?'

'Bob Taylor's place? No, heard nothing about that. Was much taken?'

'Bob reckons not. He'd had a new alarm system installed about six months ago and the police were on the scene very quickly. But apparently forensics have been round and it's a bit of a mess, so they've moved out for a day or two.'

'Oh, that's unfortunate for them. Where have they had to move to?'

'Actually, I didn't ask. Didn't think to. A hotel, at any rate. Bob reckons everything will be back to normal in a day or two. Anyway, I'd best get on with the day. Not the start I expected, that's for sure. Let me know if you hear anything about poor Toby, won't you? And I'll do the same.'

Graham Harcourt was smiling as he put the phone down. 'Poor Toby,' he said. 'Oh yes indeed, poor Toby.'

There was a patrol car outside what was left of the Prices' house, though there wasn't much left to guard. There were also two scientific support vans and Karen could see CSIs combing through the garden. The house, one of the officers told her, was still too hot to touch and they were waiting for the fire expert. Not that there was much mystery about how it had been started. Binnie's now empty crate sat neatly in the middle of the lawn.

Vin took some photographs of his own, knowing that Mr and Mrs Price would want to know what had happened to their house. There wasn't much left for them to see. The fire had burned fiercely and it had taken the fire brigade several hours to bring it under control; after that it had more or less collapsed in on itself.

Following directions, they continued on down to the family home of Kevin Binns. Police officers and forensic teams were already there and Karen and Vin were surplus to requirements and basically just being nosy. Karen wanted to get a look at the place, to see what it told her about Kevin Binns, and the crime scene manager took them around, directing them along the common pathway.

'From the look of it,' he said, 'only the kitchen, downstairs bathroom and one of the bedrooms were in use.' He showed them the other rooms, piled high with boxes and junk.

'Any idea what he's storing in here?'

'We're working through it methodically. We've found a dozen petrol cans so far, two empty but the rest with fuel inside. We had those taken out and put at the far end of the field. We found a shotgun and cartridges and we've also discovered stacks of vintage motorcycle magazines, make of that what you will.'

'A hoarder?' Vin asked.

'Maybe, but not in the usual sense. It's going to take us a few days. The only thing we can make any sense of is the usual letters, bills and the odd postcard in the kitchen. And the only thing that is of direct interest to you . . . well, I'll show you, come on down.'

He led them back downstairs and into the kitchen where evidence boxes were stacked on the table. The crime scene manager removed two or three evidence bags and handed them over to Karen and Vin.

'What am I looking at?' Karen asked. 'Polaroid photographs of a room. Whose room, do we know?'

'Well, I'm guessing,' the CSI told her, 'but if you look closely at the bookshelf, there is a photograph of two girls. One of them looks like that Beatrix Jones. I wouldn't have known, but one of the PCs had seen her picture in the briefing room. He thinks it's her.'

'It's hard to make out, but I'm inclined to agree,' Vin said. The Polaroid was small, but one of the girls in the image certainly looked like Bee.

'He broke into her room?' Karen speculated. 'We know he followed her. Anything else like this?'

The crime scene manager indicated the boxes.

255

'Take a look,' he said. 'I figure he's been a busy boy.'

A quick perusal of the boxes backed up the statement. 'I'm guessing this is Sian's place,' Karen said. 'And this,' – suddenly excited, she took out her phone – 'Vin, look at this. This is Graham Harcourt's house, I'm sure of it.'

Vin took the plastic bag from her and shuffled it around so that he could see the photographs inside. He compared the images to the ones Karen had managed to snatch on her phone and also to his own memory of the place.

'That's definitely the window at the top of the stairs. And that looks like the stable block, you remember we caught a glimpse of it as we came down the drive?'

He went and found the crime scene manager again and the evidence bag was signed over to them.

This was the first clear link they had between Bee and Binnie and Graham Harcourt. As they drove away, Vin was back on the phone, adding to the weight of evidence that he hoped would get him a warrant and the surveillance teams he needed.

Thirty-Three

Vin dropped Karen off to make her report to her own team and he carried on to the safe house to see the Price family.

They were understandably subdued and the mood was not lightened when he showed them the photographs of what was left of their home.

He had also brought with him the evidence bag from the Binnses' house and the images Karen had managed to snatch on her phone.

Sian stared at them for so long that Vin thought he must have it all wrong; Graham Harcourt's place was not, after all, the place they were looking for.

'Sian,' he asked, 'anything you recognize? If it's not the place, just say. No one is going to be upset with you.'

She lifted her head and he could see that she was crying, her face red and congested with emotion. 'That's it,' she said. 'I recognize the front of the house, and the window and the staircase look just the way Bee described them to me. She said there was a door she was brought through under the staircase and this, like, maintenance passage to the servants' quarters. Bee said that she read about there being passages in some old houses so the owners didn't have to see the servants. And that' – she jabbed a finger at the picture of the side of the house and the glimpse of what Vin assumed was a stable block – 'that's where they took us. I'm sure of it. I remember the way the walls looked. There's a yard with cobblestones and then a door that leads to the kitchen and another one that goes up some stairs, and that's where they kept us.'

Vin nodded. 'You're sure?'

'Totally.' She looked hopeful now. 'Does that mean you can go and get Bee?'

'I hope so, Sian. I really do.'

He went out to his car and made some more calls. This was it. They could get the warrant, surely?

His boss thought so too. 'Get the girl to put it in writing. Get that to me. I'm working on the rest and we've got a surveillance team heading over to the farm.'

'Already? That was fast.' Vin was exultant. 'Right, I'll get a written statement and head back. Be with you in less than an hour.'

He went back into the house and rustled up some notepaper and a pen.

'I'm going to write a simple statement for you to sign,' he said. 'Just a line or two saying that you recognize the location shown in these pictures as the place you and Bee Jones were held.'

He was writing as he spoke and Sian nodded eagerly.

'Will this help? That she's doing everything she can to help you?' Tracey wanted to know.

'It can't hurt,' Vin said cautiously. He handed the page to Sian.

'I, the undersigned,' she read, 'agree that I have been shown images of a house and the ancillary buildings of that house and that I recognize said building as the location in which I was held prisoner along with Beatrix Jones.'

'It's not very formal,' Vin apologized. 'But it will do the job.'

Sian signed and then printed her full name. He photographed it with his phone and sent it to his boss.

'She's got to be OK,' Sian fretted. 'If anything's happened to Bee, I'm never going to forgive myself.'

Thirty-Four

On the way back to the office, Vin had a thought pop into his head. Something Bob Taylor had mentioned when he and his wife had come to the station to take a look at the items taken from Freddie Jones's studio. The drawings and paperwork that the two young people had been bringing back with them when they had been attacked.

Bob had mentioned a number of blue books in which Freddie recorded his work and commissions. It hadn't registered at the time, but now, especially after the theft of the wrong artwork from Bob Taylor's house and what he'd told them about the painting missing from Freddie's studio, the information about those blue books gained a new imperative.

As he walked through the door, Karen was coming out. 'We've got it,' she said. 'The warrant. Turn yourself about, we're heading out there now.'

'We need to assemble a team.'

'Already done.' She spotted Vin's car parked close by. 'You driving?'

He slid back into the driving seat and they set off following a serial van transporting members of the Tactical Support Group. The door kickers,

Vin thought of them as. And with scientific support following close behind.

'Going mob handed,' Karen said. She sounded satisfied.

'I've been thinking. You remember when Bob and Annie came to look over the stuff from Freddie's studio?'

She nodded and he reminded her what Bob had said about the blue books.

'For all we know it could be just a list of accounts – you know, how much each commission cost in paint and canvas or whatever, but it's worth a look, and I'm thinking we should call Bob in on this. I mean, he knew the man, he's most likely to be able to make head or tail.'

Karen nodded. 'Good idea. Look, after this bit's over, I'm going to be like a spare whatsit at a wedding for a while. I'm not even on secondment, officially. I only came up to review evidence, so—'

'So you take Bob over to the studio and pick up anything he thinks is useful. Good idea.' Vin sighed. 'Mr and Mrs Price are in bits just now. Harry Jones must be frantic about his boy and Bee's aunt is sitting in a hotel room, ready to tear up the town if she thinks it will help. No winners here, are there?'

'Depends whether or not you get out alive,' Karen said quietly. 'I think most people would see that as a win.'

The gatehouse came into view and to Vin's surprise the gates were open.

'That's not right.'

The van had paused briefly and then moved on. Vin stopped the car and got out but the gate-house was unmanned. CCTV cameras showed the house and grounds but nothing moved, no sign of life.

'He's gone, hasn't he?' Karen said as Vin got back into the car.

'Could he have moved that fast?'

'Why not? We did.'

'But what about his collection? You thought he was ready to pack that up.'

Karen shrugged. 'Maybe he just wanted to save his own skin. Like I said, do you get out alive?'

The van was already parked up and the TSG disappeared inside. Vin parked up beside it and they waited on the steps until the commander came and beckoned them forward.

'House is clear,' he said. 'Not a soul inside.'

'The stable block?'

'Next on the list.'

'We think that's where the girl is being held. If she's here.'

The unit commander barked an order and moments later Vin and Karen were jogging along in the wake of three of the TSG officers. They paused in the yard.

'Door to the kitchen.' Vin pointed. 'Door that goes up the stairs. Up there, that's what Sian Price told us. The door is reinforced.' He looked at the 'enforcer', the battering ram that one of the group was holding, and decided that would probably not be an issue.

The officer in question ran up the stairs, his

colleagues following. Vin heard them shout a warning, 'Police, stand clear of the door.' And then a loud bang and a scream.

He followed Karen up the stairs at a run.

Bee crouched against the furthest wall, screaming at the top of her lungs.

Beatrix Jones sat in Vin's car, an old blanket wrapped round her shoulders and a cup of coffee from a flask between her hands, both courtesy of the TSG commander. He had also taken a look at her hand and bandaged it, bracing the broken finger against its neighbour. The paramedics were on their way, even though Bee kept insisting she was fine. Hungry, but fine.

'Is there more coffee?' she asked.

'Sure. A whole flask full. But it might not be a good idea to drink it all.'

That raised a small smile. 'Are you sure Sian is OK? Are you sure Aunt Sophie is all right? She'll be in bits.'

'She's a lot better now she knows you're safe. She'll meet us at the hospital.'

'And Patrick . . . I thought Binnie had killed him. Sian told me all about Kevin Binns. Have you got him yet?'

'Not yet, but we will,' Vin told her. He looked up as Karen opened the door and slid into the passenger seat.

'Looks like he *was* packing to leave. We seem to have pre-empted him. The surveillance team had only just got in position when we got the order to move out. Apparently there was a heli-copter, landed on the lawn at the back about a

262

half hour before we arrived. Or so the people at the farm are saying.'

'He was just going to leave me there, wasn't he? He left me to die.'

'But we found you,' Karen said gently, though she could not deny Bee's logic. 'Just hang on to that. You were found.'

'Bee, can I ask you something about your dad?'

'Sure, what?' Clumsily, she pulled the blanket even more tightly round her shoulders. 'I'm bloody freezing,' she said.

'You're suffering from a bit of shock,' Karen said. 'The medics will be here soon.'

On cue, the sound of a siren echoed down the valley from the road above.

'The blue books your dad kept. What did he write in them?'

She smiled. 'Oh, God, just about everything. Recipes, reminders, orders, copies of receipts. They were like his . . . day books, he called them. Like journals, only not, if you get what I mean.'

She paused and handed the coffee cup back to Vin and then fumbled to open the door. 'Going to be sick,' she said, and threw up on the gravel just as the paramedics arrived.

Thirty-Five

Karen went to fetch Bob Taylor and take him over to the warehouse. Vin was up to his ears in reports and the inquest into the abortive raid on

263

the house. The CSI were overstretched, Kevin Binns's house requiring a team as well as those assisting at the Price house. They'd managed to get a second CSI team from outside the area and, as Vin commented, everyone was just hoping the rest of the criminal fraternity kept their heads down for a day or two.

'At least both girls are safe,' Bob said. 'And Patrick's showing signs of recovery. They're hoping to try and take him off the ventilator tomorrow. Harry's exhausted but at least he's able to share the watch with his ex-wife and her husband now.'

'How's that working out? I imagine it must be difficult.'

'Thankfully, OK. They seem to have an amicable relationship. And I expect Mari is keeping them all in order.'

'Mari. That's the grandmother?'

'Yes. I don't think Patrick has much of a relationship with his mother's family – birth family, that is. I don't know the details. But Beth genuinely likes Mari. She's a nice lady.'

'Do you and Annie have much family? I've got a brother who drives me crazy, but if anything happened to him . . .'

'One brother,' Bob said. 'He's an estate agent, would you believe. I see my parents a couple of times a year. Kenny, my brother, he's got the wife, kids, dog . . . all the predictable stuff. He's the kind of son they understand, I suppose. I was always a bit odd.'

'No other artists in the family?'

'A great-uncle who ran off to Paris, married a

Frenchwoman and eventually bought a bookshop. He was considered something of a black sheep.'

Karen laughed. 'And Annie?'

'No. Annie doesn't have family.'

Karen waited but decided she wasn't going to get any more information. 'Must be tough,' she said.

'Not now, I don't think. Annie has created her own family. She has close friends and is well loved.'

Karen decided that this subject was definitely off limits.

She parked up outside the warehouse and spoke briefly to the officer on duty, telling him that they were going up to the studio. All was quiet, he told her. Danny and his father were working inside; the other brother had just gone off to deliver a machine to a customer.

Karen rang the bell to be let in, glad they had followed advice and locked the doors. Danny welcomed them inside.

'Is it right, what we heard on the news?' he said. 'They found our Bee?'

Our Bee, Karen thought. 'She's all right. Just very shaken up.'

'Thank fuck for that. Sorry, language, but you know . . .'

Karen nodded. 'Good news,' she agreed, and led Bob into the warehouse.

The last time he had been here Patrick, bloody and only half alive, had lain at the bottom of the steps. The blood had soaked into the concrete leaving an iron brown stain.

'You OK?' Karen asked him.

Bob nodded and preceded her up the stairs. 'Just a shock,' he said. 'Seeing him there like that. And the blood still there.'

He shook his head as though to clear it and then took a look around the studio. Karen watched him, wondering what he was noticing. 'Everything as you remember?'

'Hard to say. Bee and Patrick have moved things round, of course. But I think so. If I remember right, Freddie kept his files in here.' He crouched down next to the layout table, reached underneath and pulled a small, two-drawer filing cabinet from beneath. He paused. 'Do we need to put things in evidence bags or anything?'

'No, we just need to log everything. If it becomes evidence later, then we re-log it as such.'

'Right.' He pulled the file cabinet all the way out and then opened the drawers to reveal stacks of small blue exercise books.

'Look like the ones I used at school,' Karen said.

'They're cheap.' Bob smiled. 'They'd get chucked around the studio, splattered with paint, carried in his pocket or the car. He bought them by the dozen.'

'That's a lot of stuff to go through,' Karen said. 'You're going to need a hand, maybe?'

'You offering? Annie will be working until late so I gave Naomi a call when you asked me to come over here. She and Alfie are going to help me out. You too, if you like. There's a good Chinese takeaway near Naomi's flat. That's if it's not against regulations or anything?'

Karen pondered. It was hard to know, in a setup like Freddie's, what would prove useful. She took one of the books from the file cabinet and flicked through. 'I don't even understand the words,' she said, 'never mind the context. OK, I'll join you all for Chinese and fact finding.' She laughed. 'We'll just have to log you as an expert witness.'

'Don't need to. I'm already on the list,' Bob told her. 'Mind you, so was Graham Harcourt, so I'm not sure what that tells you.'

Thirty-Six

'Harry, there's someone wants a word with you,' one of the nurses told him. 'She's waiting in the corridor.'

'Thanks, Gena. I'll come out.'

Wearily, Harry hoisted himself out of his chair and smiled at his ex-wife, who was sitting across the bed from him. They'd been taking it in turns to read aloud to their son. It was probably the most time they had spent together since she had left.

'I'm guessing you must be Harry Jones.' The lady waiting in the corridor was tall, black and looked as tired as he felt.

'I am. I'm sorry, I—'

'Sophie O'Dowd,' she said. 'I'm Bee's aunt. I don't know if the police have told you, but she's been found. She's here at the hospital, and she's all right. But she insisted I come up and talk to you.'

Harry smiled. 'DS Dattani let me know. I'm so very pleased.' He leaned back against the wall, exhaustion suddenly hitting him. 'Sorry, just very tired.'

'I'm sure you are. I don't think any of us have slept since Sunday. And how is Patrick doing?'

She had a slight accent, Harry thought, almost but not quite American. Transatlantic, he supposed they called it. Like a Brit who'd lived abroad for quite some time. 'Improving, just a little. The swelling in the brain has gone down and they're talking about taking him off his ventilator tomorrow. If he breathes on his own, then we're on the way.'

'That's good, that's very good. I'll let Bee know.' She took a slip of paper from her cardigan pocket and handed it to him. 'I wrote my number down for you, just in case you wanted to get in touch.'

'Thank you,' Harry said. He felt oddly pleased by that. Sophie had the most beautiful eyes, he thought, and a really nice smile. 'I don't have anything to write on.'

'That's OK. You text me when you get a minute.'

'Thank you,' Harry said again. 'I'd best be getting back. Give my love to Bee; I know Patrick likes her a lot.'

'Well then, we'll have to make sure they get together, won't we?'

Harry went back to the ward with something of a spring in his step. He sat down and looked at his son, knowing that nothing had really changed and yet, somehow, everything had changed. The world was full of possibilities.

Bob emptied the boxes on to the table and then stood back.

'OK,' Alfie said. 'It looks like we've got quite a job ahead of us. How far do these go back?'

'These, only about two or three years. I expect he's got more in his home studio, but I don't think we need those. Freddie used to archive things in a big box at home. Lord alone knows what's in it.'

'So what are we looking for?'

'I think we need to look for names, dates, titles of paintings,' Karen said. 'But I really don't know. Anything that might be useful, though I'm not sure I'll know it's useful until Bob says so. We're looking for links, I suppose, between Freddie and Graham Harcourt and Toby Elden. Maybe even Scotts, I don't know.'

'OK,' Naomi said. 'Give me a couple and I'll see if my scanner can cope with it. It's not that good with handwriting, but who knows?'

'These seem to be from last year,' Bob said. 'See what you can come up with. I think it's going to be boring,' he predicted.

Naomi took the books and settled herself in the corner of the room where her computer and other equipment were set up. She had a reading machine that she used for books that weren't available as audio and also a scanner, hooked up to read back on her computer.

Freddie's handwriting must have been

reasonably clear because the reader could cope with some of it at least. She plugged in a headset and one earbud and listened to the attempts her technology made; she also half listened to what was going on at the table across the room.

Bob was right, Freddie recorded everything. It would have made a fascinating archive had they not been in such a hurry.

At six thirty Naomi went with Napoleon and Alfie to the Chinese restaurant down the road to pick up the order that they had phoned through, taking a bit of a detour so that they could give Napoleon a walk. So far the search had been pretty fruitless.

When they got back they discovered that Karen, in their absence, had found the first reference that might be of use. It was about Toby Elden.

Karen read aloud. "'I'm afraid I had to lie to poor Toby. I told him that I had hidden the documents he was looking for behind the backing board of the Madonna I was working on. It was all I could think of at the time. I feel sorry for him. I know this is going to lead to more trouble for him but what can I do? I can't risk that bastard getting hold of Bee.'"

'So someone was threatening his daughter. I don't think we have to guess who,' Karen said.

'So, what documents?' Alfie wanted to know. 'We've been looking through all the most recent stuff, and there's nothing. The earlier books are full of lists, reference material, stuff he was working on, who he was selling it to and how much for. He even made little notes about where he'd eaten lunch, but all he seems to have in the

270

last eighteen months or so is stuff like pigment lists. Recipes.'

They cleared space on the table and Alfie distributed plates and then laid out the food.

'Recipes, pigment lists.' Bob was thoughtful. 'Alfie, pass me that last book you were looking at.'

He read silently while they all chatted and ate. 'You got something?' Naomi asked.

'I think I have,' Bob said. 'I noticed that this book isn't as thick as the rest. Look, he may have ripped out the odd page, but they're mostly about the same thickness. This has maybe three or four pages missing from the middle. And you'd have to know what you were looking for to realize that the information that starts on this left-hand page doesn't carry on to this right-hand page. I noticed the same thing in one of the other books. I thought it was just – well, these things happen when you're writing stuff down, he may have ripped a page out without thinking, but now I'm thinking it's deliberate. Freddie was hiding something. And whatever it was, Toby Elden had been told to get it back.'

Thirty-Seven

The decision was made to release the CCTV footage of Binnie snatching Bee from the warehouse. It was the clearest image of him that the police had, apart from some photographs that Sian had taken on her camera. These stills were shown alongside the video with the warning that the man must not be approached. That he was extremely dangerous.

And then of course the calls started coming, sightings of him everywhere.

Karen had reported back to Vin about the blue books. They'd carried on until just after midnight and found references to Graham Harcourt and to the Scotts' gallery but also to other dealers and collectors and, as Bob said, it was the kind of record you would find in the paperwork of just about any artist who was selling regularly and working to commission. On its own it proved nothing.

Freddie had indeed been meticulous about recording details of paintings: the customer's name and address, the materials used in the production, and here and there were records about provenance relating to similar paintings in the artist's *oeuvre*. From this they made a guess that sometimes he was producing missing works.

Again, Bob suggested, there could be innocent explanations a lot of the time. Freddie made a living copying quite legitimately for customers who needed to keep up appearances of wealth, or who wanted the original to be safely in a bank vault. Occasionally Freddie marked something as a 'pastiche' and that too was open to interpretation.

But there were almost no clients' names for the past eighteen months and yet Freddie's bank balance seemed to have remained relatively healthy. No large sums deposited, nothing unusual, but it hadn't fallen off either.

272

'He's earning money,' Vin said. 'But exactly where from?'

Alfie felt that given time he could probably find out; it was what he did, after all.

At midday on the Friday, Harry texted Naomi. Patrick was off the ventilator, he was breathing on his own. Later that afternoon Alec arrived home and Naomi felt oddly inclined just to settle down for the weekend. There was nothing more to be done and it had been one hell of a week.

They found themselves watching the rolling news avidly, but there was nothing about Kevin Binns, only a rehash of the kidnap and the murders, and now there was speculation about Freddie Jones and whether he had in fact died of natural causes.

The only additional information was that Toby Elden had died. Poor Toby, as Freddie had called him, seemed to have paid the ultimate price as a consequence of Freddie having to lie to him.

The search of Binnie's home had revealed a stash of stolen goods. Money, jewellery, antiques, though whether Binnie had been stealing on behalf of his employer or on his own account was moot and likely to remain so.

Graham Harcourt had gone to ground.

By rights, Karen thought, she should be off back home. She had her own investigation to pick up – though at least they now knew who had killed Antonia Scott. What they didn't know was who had ordered the killing or the theft of the portfolio

273

– but the assumption was that it was Graham Harcourt.

She was sitting in the main office with Vin, logging in the blue books and trying to put them into some kind of order – they'd not even looked at some of them, she realized – when a call came in. It stood out from the background noise of sightings because it included footage captured on CCTV. Binnie was in a shopping centre on the outskirts of town, eating a burger as though all was right with the world and it was just an ordinary Saturday.

Armed police were mobilized, but instructed to wait until Binnie was outside. The restaurant was crowded, so was the shopping centre, and from the way Binnie swaggered as he left the restaurant and wandered into another shop looking at T-shirts, it was almost as though he knew they were there and didn't care.

He was followed into the car park, challenged as he got to his car. Binnie turned slowly, looking mildly amused. He raised his hands without question but he seemed totally unperturbed to be surrounded by armed officers and told to get down on the ground. It was almost as though he'd been told to smile for the cameras.

Thirty-Eight

'Nothing to say,' Binnie told them. 'I told you I got nothing to say.' This had been his refrain ever since he was brought in and three hours had passed and nothing had happened. Vin thought he was just amusing himself; it was as though Binnie was the one in control and they were rushing around trying to do his bidding. The only response he'd made was when he was asked if he wanted a cup of tea or told that he'd be having a food break in another half hour. He told them that he didn't care what he had in his sandwiches as long as it wasn't chicken.

'Chicken stinks, it's just cat food,' he said.

Vin was tempted to tell whoever arranged the sandwiches that they *had* to be chicken.

Just before Binnie's meal break was due, Vin was called out of the interview room. He was a little annoyed, but the look on Karen's face told him that this was important. 'What?'

He followed her back through to the main control room, where officers were still working their way through the evidence bags that had been brought from Freddie's studio. 'He was a clever old sod,' Karen said. 'Talk about hiding stuff in plain sight.'

'What do you mean?'

'The missing pages from the blue books. He must've had to hide them in a hurry, so do you know what he did?'

She pointed towards a young officer who was sitting at a desk with envelopes next to him. Vin recognized the letters that had been brought along with the stuff in the portfolio. 'Junk mail, so—'

'Craig here noticed there was something wrong with the seal on one of the envelopes. It was ever so slightly misaligned. It looks like a letter from the credit card company – you know, one of those "you have been pre-selected to apply" things. Everybody gets them. Most of us just chuck them in the bin or they get put down on the side and forgotten about.'

'You've lost me.'

'So Craig opened the envelope.'

'So Craig can now apply for a credit card?' He looked more closely at the paperwork laid out on the desk. 'Bloody hell.'

'Exactly.'

Vin donned a pair of latex gloves and picked the pages up, studying them closely. On two pages were lists of paintings, customers and the provenance that had been used, created by Freddie. On another was a list of payments which had obviously never made it into Freddie's bank account and must have been stashed away somewhere else.

Last of all was a confession, of sorts. In it Freddie admitted to creating about a dozen works for which he also created the provenance. He gave names and dates, buyers and sellers, and implicated Toby Elden and Graham Harcourt, amongst others. One of the others was Antonia Scott's brother.

'This is what Toby Elden must have been after. Graham Harcourt must've discovered that he kept a record. He must've threatened Freddie's daughter if he didn't give it up but Freddie died first, before he could do anything.'

'So chances are he wasn't murdered.'

Karen shrugged. 'Well, unless Binnie confesses to that one as well, we're not going to know.

Not for sure. But now we don't need Binnie's evidence. We have enough to pull the others in. We can piece the rest together. You tell him that, I don't think he's going to be best pleased. My guess is that Binnie is a typical narcissist; he wants to be the centre of attention, no matter what it's for.'

Thirty-Nine

There was a strange little coda to all of this. Danny and his father turned up at the police station on the Sunday morning, along with a Catholic priest. He had a package under his arm, brown paper tied up with string, and they asked to see either Vin or Karen.

'Danny tells me you've been looking for this,' Mark Brookes said. 'I never meant to cause any trouble. It was just after that bloke had been hanging round, and it was obvious this was what he was after, so I got worried. Freddie'd made me promise I'd keep an eye on things if anything happened, look after his girl's inheritance. I thought at the time he was just being dramatic, like he could be sometimes. Then he was dead and this bloke was claiming the picture was his. So I moved it, gave it into safe keeping, like. Danny didn't know what I'd done. I thought the fewer people that knew the better.'

'Oh, Dad,' Danny said. 'I had a feeling you might have done something when I noticed the painting had gone. You could have told me, you know.'

Mark untied the string and opened the paper, disclosing a small painting, half finished, of the Madonna with the Christ child and St Anne. 'I thought one Madonna would be much like another in a church, so I asked my friend here to look after it for me. I didn't know anybody with a big enough safe, apart from Father Bennett. And I knew he had someplace to lock up the church silver so I thought he might as well lock this up as well.'

'And you never thought to tell anyone.'

'Well, I was going to tell Bee, but then all that happened and, to be honest, I felt a bit embarrassed about it. I didn't want anyone to think I'd pinched it. That's why I brought Father Bennett along today, so he can tell you what I told him when he took the painting for me.'

Gently, Karen turned it over. 'There's no backing board,' she said.

'Well, no, there wouldn't be. He'd not finished it. Anyway, he probably wouldn't need one on a work like this. Freddie sometimes put something on just to cover up the gesso on the back. So he could stick his picture labels on to it. His attributions, he called them.'

Karen must have been staring at him because the man shifted uncomfortably under her gaze.

'We just thought we were helping out,' Father Bennett said. 'It was part of that young woman's legacy – no harm meant.'

Vin thanked them, and told them that they were

going to have to make a formal statement about it. But no, tomorrow would do.

'Attributions,' Karen said. 'Attributions, so that it had provenance. I think we've been talking to the wrong people.'

Epilogue

'Binnie confessed,' Naomi said thoughtfully as she sat back down beside her husband, who was watching the late film. 'Karen says he seems to be enjoying himself, telling everyone just what he did and how. He killed Toby Elden and Antonia Scott, said it was all at the instigation of Graham Harcourt but that he did the actual work.'

'Work?'

'That's what he called it, Karen said.'

Alec leaned back against the sofa cushions. 'You think he's mad, bad or just . . . I don't know, what are the other options? Evil?'

Naomi shrugged. 'I think that's open to interpretation,' she said. 'Evil acts, evil man? Somehow that takes away the responsibility, don't you think?'

'Maybe so. And any news on Harcourt?'

'As yet, no. But the man has money and resources and could be anywhere by now. Private plane or boat, he could have crossed the Channel from any number of locations. The alert was out pretty fast but it would have taken a couple of hours to reach isolated airfields, and we both know there are any number of marinas or even little coves up and down the coast that a small boat could leave from. No one to notice.'

'True,' Alec said. Even a tiny motor launch would be enough; it could rendezvous with a larger vessel a mile or so out to sea and even if the coastguard noticed it, chances were it would not be thought of as remarkable.

'Alfie is already looking at his business dealings. Reckons I can help out with the research,' Naomi said.

'And you're looking forward to that, I can tell.'

'I might well be.' She smiled. 'Karen reckons they can swing it so Alfie gets brought in as a consultant. Informally, but, well . . . we make a good team, don't you think?'

She settled beside him, enjoying the feel of his arm around her shoulders. 'And Bee is going to be all right, I think. She's moving back with her aunt for a while. Patrick is showing signs of improvement, and all will be as right with the world as it can be.'

'Except for the dead, the damaged and the lost,' Alec said.

'Except for those,' Naomi agreed.